T0351421

KILLING HAPPINESS

THE GERMAN LIST

KILLING HAPPINESS

FRIEDRICH ANI

TRANSLATED BY ALEXANDER BOOTH

LONDON NEW YORK CALCUTTA

GOETHE INSTITUT

This publication has been supported by a grant from the Goethe-Institut India

Seagull Books, 2022

First published in German as *Ermordung des Glücks* by Friedrich Ani.
© Suhrkamp Verlag, Berlin, 2017

First published in English by Seagull Books, 2022
English translation © Alexander Booth, 2022

ISBN   978 0 8574 2 895 0

British Library Cataloguing-in-Publication Data
A catalogue record for this book is available from the British Library.

Typeset by Seagull Books, Calcutta, India
Printed and bound in the USA by Integrated Books International

CONTENTS

Foreword

My reading passion is translated crime novels. By becoming immersed in another culture's popular fiction, we have a sense of its preoccupations, both political and domestic. There's no pretension. The story carries the reader along, but as we untangle the plot, we learn about a different country's prevailing morality, the trivial details of everyday life, the family values. There's a delicious voyeurism in the process. It's like walking down a suburban street at dusk, just as the lights inside are switched on. We glimpse the interactions inside, food being eaten, couples laughing or fighting, children playing, or sitting morosely and quietly in a corner. We begin to understand what matters in this different world and where the priorities lie.

Killing Happiness is, above all things, about family, so family, we realize, is the priority here in this German town. It matters more than the wider community. From the first scene, when a mother is waiting, longing for news of a missing son, so anxious, so wrapped up in grief that she has lost grip on reality, we understand that these relationships will be at the heart of the novel. As the story unfolds, we learn about the ties that bind the mother, Tania Grabbe, to her brother and her husband. We see immediately her overwhelming, unbalanced love for Lenny, the dead son. The book explores the nature of family secrets, those kept, and those known and shared but never spoken about.

This is, however, a murder mystery and it follows the convention with a twisting plot and multiple suspects. Fans of traditional crime fiction will find it immensely satisfying. Who killed Lenny Grabbe as he walked home from school in a storm? Why was he not riding his bicycle as he usually did? How did his body end up in a playground? We read on, because we want to know. We want to solve the puzzle—or perhaps we don't, at least not until the solution is revealed by a skilful writer, because there is nothing fans of the detective novel like better than the cheap thrill of the surprise ending.

In the way of these books, we have a brilliant central character in retired detective Jakob Franck. Franck has always been idiosyncratic; he appeared first in *The Nameless Day*, also by Friedrich Ani, which, like *Killing Happiness*, was beautifully translated by Alexander Booth. In the earlier book, Franck was still working for the police force. He was an investigator, but he always took on the task of informing relatives of a violent death. Even in retirement, in this later novel, he has volunteered to maintain the same role. He, not the investigating detective, is the person who knocks on the door of the cafe run by Tania and her husband in order to tell her that Lenny has been killed.

We see Franck first through Tania Grabbe's eyes, a solid presence, despite the fact that his image is blurred by snow and the glass of the front door. He provides immediate reassurance, although he's bringing such terrible news. There's nothing flash about Franck. He's stolid, still, almost nondescript and he invites confidences and confessions *because* he's so ordinary. He's persistent. The killer is uncovered because Franck follows up on the small, tedious details missed by other officers. Perhaps this tells us something about the culture's values too. The crime is solved by a patient man who puts aside his own needs and desires to get things done. He *thinks* his way to a solution.

This book, however, is more than a clever police procedural with an interesting European background and an intelligent sleuth. The writing makes us feel Tania's confusion, her descent into a deep depression. Truth shimmers and shifts. Often, there are a number of different points of view within the same chapter. A wonderful flashback narrative describing a scene on a beach after a fog has suddenly descended, sums up Ani's style for me. In narrative and in descriptive terms, I felt as if I was stepping into an Impressionist painting. Reality was there, but it was blurred, hard to grasp. There are no firm lines and no certainties. Franck isn't a police officer and yet he's not quite a civilian. He's separated from his wife yet not quite apart from her.

This a subtle novel and all the more interesting because of it. I celebrate Seagull Books' initiative to bring it to a wider audience.

Ann Cleeves
2021

When there is no more
You cut to the core
Quicker than anyone I knew
When I'm all alone
In the great unknown
I'll remember you

Bob Dylan, 'I'll Remember You'

CHAPTER ONE

In Striking Distance of the Sea

I

From the reflection of the front door, a disintegrating woman gazed back at her.

The longer she looked, the more surprised she was at still being there after so many days of total absence. Today marked exactly thirty-four days.

She was standing close to the pane, as if it would be the easiest thing in the world to just grab the handle and open the door. Passers-by stared, but they were cowards who would not raise a finger; they simply stood there disturbing the snow that belonged to her alone.

It had been like that since she was little: as soon as the first snow fell, it was all for her. She would collect the snowflakes in her apron and bring them home, saying, *Look, Mom, I've brought you star thalers, they're still real fresh.*

It crossed her mind almost every year. She never told a soul, not even Lennard.

The thought of him infuriated her. She inhaled the cold but could not taste the snow. Something's off, she tried to call out, but her voice did not pay attention.

She tilted her head and listened. The snowflakes knocked silently at the door. One by one, the faces disappeared. Eventually, not a single person was coming down the street any longer, not even a car. In the honeycombing darkness, the snow whirled up the building sides. To her, the silence was like an unearned blessing.

For a few seconds, she forgot the pain and turned back to the little girl with her apron full of melted snow thalers.

Then the man appeared, dispelling her reflection and any fleeting sense of comfort.

She automatically took a step back towards the cake counter. On the street, the man's face looked old and grey and threatening. His black shawl welled up out of the collar of his brown leather jacket; the black strap of his shoulder bag ran across it like a scar.

After taking everything in, she shut her eyes and clenched her fists. Then, as soon as she noticed, she quickly reopened her eyes. For a moment she panicked and thought that in the meantime the stranger had walked into the cafe. Then she remembered that the door was locked, the key in the cylinder. She looked over. That was when the man knocked.

She flinched again, but this time did not move. In the adjoining room with the tables, the newspaper sticks and the roofed wicker beach chair a light was still on, casting a milky glow across the counter. The woman trembled and felt exposed.

The man knocked again, not loudly, almost delicately and without changing his expressionless face or suggesting any hint of impatience. He simultaneously gave the impression of absolute resolve, the woman thought, and she risked a step forward.

His hair and cheeks collecting snowflakes, the man immediately straightened up and folded his hands before his stomach. His gesture confused her.

She hesitated. With a business-like impulse, she wondered how late it could be and whether she would normally have opened at that time. Absurd. The cafe had been closed for a week.

If it had been up to her, they would have closed that Friday more than a month ago. Stephan had been against it, and Claire, her employee, had promised to work every day from morning to night.

She had almost reached the door before she got spooked a third time. Her eyes clawed into the face behind the glass. She knew that kind of man, the way he looked at her, the way he stood there, upright, confident, determined; his well-kept appearance, his perfectly shaven face, the close-cropped hair, the leather jacket.

Over the last few weeks she had frequently encountered those kinds of leather jackets, that kind of body language, those quiet and yet sly eyes, and back at the beginning, daily. Most of the time they appeared in twos, and she always felt cornered. Though she tried to appear friendly, that was when her anxiety really erupted.

The man outside was a criminal investigator.

She had never seen him before. He probably did not belong to the department that was looking for her missing son, otherwise the lead investigator, whose name she could not remember at the moment, would have pre-announced his colleague by phone.

Which meant, she thought as she stretched her hand towards the key, the man was not directly responsible for the search for Lennard but had other questions—like the inspector who had been interested in how Lennard was doing at school.

With a sigh of nearly forgotten relief, she opened the door.

Snowflakes blew into her eyes. She blinked and smiled and quickly rubbed a hand across her face, like the curious people she had observed from inside. She wanted to greet and invite the police officer in with unexpected verve. But he beat her to it.

'Are you Tania Grabbe?'

His voice had nothing of the cheerfulness of the snow.

'Yes, of course I am *Frau* Grabbe, and you're a police officer?'

'My name is Jakob Franck. I'm a former investigator. Shall we go inside and sit down? I have terrible news for you and your husband.'

That was when the world around her disappeared.

When the world came back, Tania Grabbe was no longer a part of it. Stephan was sitting next to her, holding her hand. She did not understand why. He had laid his arm on the table and was looking at her as if she were a stranger; she almost told him her name.

This man, she thought, probably isn't Stephan, just some-one who looks like him, someone who's got the same curly, silvery-black hair which was once again too long, right down to the collar of his white shirt. (For years she'd had to warn him regularly to get his hair cut and to make sure that it did not turn into just another hangout session but a proper haircut; a pastry chef had to look neat, God forbid a hair land in the glaze or the dough or anywhere else). He hadn't shaved either.

Who was this man next to her, continuing to hold her hand?

Alarmed, she turned her eyes away from his face and towards the table; a colourless hand stretched out of the arm of her blue dress and was encircled by fingers with very short nails; her hand; Stephan's hand. She could not believe what she saw. She raised her head and came into the line of sight of a man she had seen once before. But when? She did not know.

That was when she realized that they were the only guests. They were sitting at the first table by the passageway to the half-dark sales room, and no one was coming in. Something about the silence wasn't right, it belonged there as little as she did, Tania Grabbe thought, and looked at her hand again, which was enclosed in the fingers with the little dark hairs, as if the man had every right to do so.

Little by little, time came back to her.

She remembered how they had stood there, more or less in the middle of the room, between the cake counter and the door, while people out in the swirling snow had stopped to stare as if she were an animal in the zoo. She had not reacted at all, she knew that much, and the thought caused her a few seconds of satisfaction. Then the onlookers had disappeared, and the snowflakes had danced for her alone, just the way she liked it.

The man with the leather shoulder bag had disturbed the magical show before her eyes, and everything was dead.

'It's your fault.'

'Shouldn't we notify a doctor?' the man across from her asked. She could not manage to look at him. Being in the strange hand's grasp triggered a stiffness that went all the way to her neck.

She grew dizzy. Strangely, she was not afraid of blacking out, as she used to do in disorienting situations and that, afterwards, always made her feel incredibly ashamed.

Instead, a surprising quiet spread through her body, as if she had taken some of Dr Horn's medicine or two glasses of the heavy red wine they would drink on their anniversary.

Even if she was afraid of making a shameful impression, as deeply as she sat there, in her worn dress, with her brittle hair, the sudden soundlessness of her thoughts just about reconciled her to the presence of the two uninvited guests.

Only the silence, outside as in, continued to bother her; she did not trust it, it felt false.

'*Frau* Grabbe,' the man in the leather jacket said. He was speaking into her left ear; she looked at him from the corners of her eyes. 'Have you understood what I have told you and your husband?'

'My son is dead.'

Tania Grabbe heard her own voice but was convinced it had nothing to do with her. All of a sudden, she looked at the man beside her and wanted to hug him, sitting there as if frozen, his hands in his pockets, his dark gaze. In the ceiling light's yellow glow, his face looked as if it had been covered in wax, she would have scraped it off if she had only known how.

'Say something.' She carefully ran a hand through his hair. She bent down and gave him a butterfly kiss on his cheek with the lashes of her right eye. She inhaled the familiar scent of his aftershave, sniffed and leaned back.

A moment later her memories took over.

She gasped for air, cast the man on the other side of the table an incredulous glance; even his name came back to her and what he had told her after she had confused him with an innocent inspector.

As if a demon had ruined the sleep she had finally been able to enjoy for a blink of an eye, she jolted.

She looked around, recognized the world again and began to emit sounds from her torn mouth that sounded to Franck like the wheezing of some kind of animal. He knew that they were the echoes of his own words which only now, an hour after his arrival, were beginning to reverberate inside her with untameable force.

As in the instant of sudden understanding she had taken leave of her husband, Franck reached for her hands; she flinched, as she had already many times, and hid her hands in her lap.

'Shall we speak with one another?' Franck felt Stephan Grabbe's eyes on him, but he concentrated on the woman.

'Haven't we been all along?' she asked absently, wheezing again.

'No, you wanted to remain quiet.'

She only managed to close her mouth on the fourth or fifth try. As soon as she noticed the sound she had been making—lips pressed together, she was snorting through her nose—she sank her head in embarrassment.

Until then, Franck had only told the couple that the body of their missing eleven-year-old son had been found, nothing else, none of the details surrounding the circumstances or the place. A friend from the homicide division had begged him to do so.

Back when he was still on the force, Franck had already made it his job to deliver the news of death to those left behind, regardless of whether he was directly involved with the case. One day—driven by a crime that was the same as all the others—he had taken the decision; after that, whenever he was asked, he took the responsibility upon himself. His being retired had not changed a thing.

He had already expressed his condolences and those of his former colleagues and repeated the words when her husband arrived. Grabbe had explained that he had no longer been able to take the closeness, and for the last two hours had been wandering along the Isar, 'away from all the horrible Christmas to-do,' he had added.

With a decisive movement, Grabbe took his hands out of his pockets and laid them on the table. 'Thank you for taking so much time, *Herr* . . .' he said.

'Franck.'

'So, our Lennard didn't simply die but was . . .'

'Weren't you listening? Lennard is dead.' Without having raised her voice, once again Tania stopped speaking. Both Franck and her husband stared at her; she had lowered her head and was chewing on her lips.

'Your son,' Franck said, 'will be examined at the forensic institute, only then will we know what happened to him.'

'He was murdered,' Grabbe said.

'That is not yet certain.'

That wasn't a lie, Franck thought. Denying it would have been a lie.

Having said that, his colleague in charge of the investigations was fairly certain that the boy had not been the victim of an accident but a violent crime. At first glance it appeared as if the perpetrator had struck the boy in the face with brute force, causing the back of his head to slam against some kind of object. The exact cause of death would be determined in the next couple of hours or over the course of the following day. As to whether where the body was found was also the scene of the crime Franck had received no clear answer, the investigators had their doubts.

'And the woods,' Stephan Grabbe said, 'where he was found, where are they?'

He had already told them. 'To the south, at the edge of the city.'

'Where, Inspector?'

'Simply Franck, please. You will receive all the important information as soon as the initial examinations have been completed. Trust me. Would you like to tell me something about your son? Would you like for us to pray together?'

Tania Grabbe raised her head.

In her eyes Franck saw something he called the eternal light—a flickering that fed upon the unceasing love between the dead and their neighbours, a rearing up against the all-encompassing darkness.

'I would like to see him,' she said. 'And you will take me to him, right now.'

As so often in similar situations Franck adopted the glance of the person across from him to be his own. For a moment, he was silent and paid attention to his tone of voice. 'I will go with you, if you like, but we still have to wait. If you like, I will wait with you.'

'How long?' Her voice scurried out of her mouth, which immediately closed again.

Franck said: 'I don't know.'

A minute went by, maybe two. Suddenly Grabbe reached out her hand, waiting for Franck to take it, and stood up. 'Then come with me, you promised.'

Franck walked around the table, hand in hand with the woman. They walked behind Stephan Grabbe, who took a while before he grasped the situation and turned around. By that time his wife had already reached the blue-and-white-striped roofed wicker beach chair on the back wall. She let go of Franck's hand and sank onto her knees; she pressed her hands together as if in prayer and looked into the shadowy piece of furniture whose bamboo wickerwork and foam cushions looked new and unused.

After a while, during which no one spoke a word, Tania slipped off her white, fluffy house shoes—they made a curious contrast to the wrinkled, though fine, fabric of her ultramarine-coloured dress.

Franck noticed that Stephan was rocking back and forth in his chair; he took a step to the side so that he would no longer be in his field of vision.

An aura of devotion enveloped the silent, kneeling woman with the blonde hair. Her mouth touched the ends of her fingers as she gazed into the empty, covered seating area.

Franck thought of the name of the cafe they were in—Café Beach House—and his glance fell onto the framed photographs on the wall across from the beach chair: an enlarged shot of a white beach and dunes in the wind, a bit out of focus, blurry. Franck put himself in the photographer's place and imagined he could hear the rush of the sea behind him.

And as if there were a connection to the absence of people in the image Franck returned to the one question which Tania and Stephan Grabbe had not yet asked and whose answer was not in his power to give, as much as he would have liked to.

When, on what day, at what time after disappearing on the evening of November eighteenth, did eleven-year-old Lennard Grabbe die?

Tania Grabbe was not thinking about anything else either, kneeling before the wicker beach chair, appearing to pray. She saw him sitting there, her boy, shirtless and in shorts; his legs did not make it over the cushions, he was so happy his parents had put a real beach chair in the cafe. He wanted them to flop onto the chair next to him, but there was not enough room; so his mother put him on her lap, while his father sat beside them, and Lennard stretched out his arm and pointed to the sea, which was the wall, and the sun shone in from outside.

Those moments were like summer on the North Sea; like a time that never passed away.

That is what Tania Grabbe was thinking about and the question she had not trusted herself to ask. Secretly, she had expected Stephan to take the question away from her. Where was he anyway?

She turned away from the beach chair and got spooked again. She had forgotten the man who was standing next to her, who was guilty of everything, who refused to give her the answer to a question that he had to know raged inside of her.

Stephan continued to sit at the table, far away.

Her knees hurt from the stone floor.

Snow fell outside the window.

Thirty-four days ago Lennard had disappeared, and today he had reappeared.

So where was he?

'I would like to see him,' she said a second time.

'What are you thinking about?' And don't tell me you're not thinking about anything.'

'I'm thinking about you.'

'Here I am.'

'I'm thinking about what you might have been like as a little girl.'

'Don't get started with your age again. And don't even think about starting with mine, got it?' Marion Siedler pushed the glass of beer closer towards him. 'Finish it already, then I'll get you a fresh one. What's with you? I thought we were going to watch the film.' She was about to stand up. 'You're thinking about the boy. About his mother, who spent the whole night in the beach chair after you got there. Have you been in contact with her at all over the last few days?'

Franck finished his beer and put the empty glass on the table but did not let go.

Eight days had passed since his visit to the Café Beach House. Without requesting his assistance, a day after his visit, the parents had identified their son's body. The cause of Lennard's death was to a large extent resolved.

Due to a massive blow to the head, he had suffered a skull fracture and internal bleeding. The perpetrator had dropped the corpse off in the woods near Höllriegelskreuth by the Isar canal, hidden it beneath branches and wood debris until it was found by a walker's dog. After the preliminary conclusion of his examinations, the forensic pathologist had felt it likely that Lennard had been killed on the evening of his disappearance. Clues as to the scene of the crime, as well as the perpetrator, were still absent. The boy would be buried the following Saturday, on New Year's Eve, at the East Cemetery. Franck would be there.

He did not want to talk about it.

'What was it like growing up in Germering?' He did not ask as a diversion, he had other reasons.

From the very first conversation he had in connection with the Lennard Grabbe case, another crime had become just as present to him, one he thought had been solved.

'What do you mean Germering?'

'That's where you grew up.'

'I didn't grow up in Germering,' his ex-wife said. 'Are you drunk?'

'No.'

'Would it cost you too much to drop your police-like stare?'

'Since when did you not grow up in Germering?'

'Look, I'll send you home if you keep talking like this.'

'I just asked you a question.'

'Who ever said I grew up in Germering?'

'You did.'

'I did not.'

'Of course you did.'

'You never listen to me.'

'I'm listening to you now.'

'You listen to your suspects, your culprits, your witnesses, and let's not forget: the family members. But clearly not to me. Otherwise you would know that I wasn't born nor did I grow up in Germering, but . . . ?'

'But?'

'But in Unterpfaffenhofen. How long have you known me?'

'Unterpfaffenhofen, Germering, it's the same thing.'

'It's not the same. Back in my time, Germering and Unterpfaffenhofen were separate places, and you know it.'

'I forgot.'

'How much did you have to drink before you came over here? Be honest.'

'Nothing.'

'You're lying.'

'I'm not lying. I'm asking you because . . . because . . . let's watch the film.'

Marion put the red wine glass she had been holding in her hand the whole time onto the table and reached out her hand. 'You're not thinking about me at all,' she said. He looked back at the wall, as if caught. 'You're thinking about your sister. The young boy's fate reminded you of her. Look at me.'

He did. 'I really was thinking about you.'

'How so, Hannes?'

'Well . . . well . . .' He felt like a stuttering boy trying to justify himself and not seeing how. Again, he avoided her glance.

In his mind, Marion was the girl he could see outside the window in the back courtyard, in a brown coat and a pink hat, with a pom-pom as white as a snowball. For an hour he had been staring out the misted pane into the snowstorm, as if he might recognize a pattern there, a message, a clue about the monster that had beset his family and then disappeared without a trace.

The more time passed, the more he felt obliged to act, to grant his parents release, but he had no idea how.

Standing at the window, hands in the frayed pockets of his favourite jeans, staring at the girl in the courtyard and the uniformed police officer talking with her, he forgot his football training, his physics and history homework, his upcoming English exercises and everything his mother had said to him before she had asked him to go to his room and wait.

I shouldn't have listened to her, he thought. I should've gone down to the courtyard and forced the police officer into telling the truth.

He had never seen his father cry before. His father simply did not cry; like his mother, he had spluttered and sobbed, the tears seeming to spray out of his eyes, and the sounds he emitted were the most unsettling sounds his son had ever heard.

His father's tears also filled the child's room. Jakob did not dare to turn around in the fear of finding his father standing in the doorway, swollen with pain, his hands twitching with impotent fury.

As if spellbound, he looked down at the girl in the winter coat. When she raised her head and turned her pale, snow-wet face towards him, he was incredibly frightened and his heart pounded.

'It was you,' Franck said. 'You alone.'

His glance, his voice, his silence revealed to Marion Siedler that he did not expect any response. He nodded, as if thanking her for her understanding. 'I saw you before my eyes the whole time. I bet you wore that kind of hat in the winter. Like the little girl in the courtyard. I don't know her name any more. She was a neighbour, she happened to walk by and see the squad car. You looked up at me, I almost passed out.'

'We didn't know each other back then. And I know you didn't go to Unterpfaffenhofen even once in your whole childhood.'

'No, probably not.'

'No,' she said and did not mean to go silent.

He had told her about that winter day as a child back when they were still continuously forging their intimacy. Later on, he locked up the accident in his memories, and she did not push him. Now, however, it seemed as if he was asking her to help make speaking easier.

She said: 'I would've liked to get to know you both. After everything I've learnt, the two of you, you and your little sister, were a real team.'

'She was taller than I was. But two years younger. Sometimes she'd kiss me on the head.'

'Lina.'

'You haven't forgotten her name,' Franck said.

'You liked that, when she kissed you on the head. I used to do that now and again too, by the way, when you were asleep, most of the time it stopped you from snoring.'

Something in his memory got scared; he did not want to know a thing about it. 'I had to think of her all week long,' he said quickly. 'Every single day. Like I haven't in a long time.'

'What happened?'

He fell silent, which surprised Marion. From back when they had been married, she knew him to be a closed person thanks to his career. Over the course of time—he had begun to travel back and forth from the land of the dead, for whom he was responsible as the head of homicide division, and therefore gradually forgot how to love—she had grown to accept his behaviour as an eerie as well as serious idiosyncrasy, unsuitable, however, for marriage.

At the same time, she had never known him to be someone who kept secrets from her or who ever spoke out of pure self-interest. Hannes—the name she had used for him ever since the days they started going to the movies together, just as he called her Gisa—physically refused any kind of conscious, manipulative silence. He considered people who acted that way to be liars, and liars already used up all his patience at work.

'Why do you look like that?'

'Now it's my turn to have been thinking about you.'

'And?'

She stood up, smiled briefly, took his beer glass and walked into the kitchen. She leant against the refrigerator and forbid her thoughts from getting any closer to her heart.

CHAPTER TWO

Can You Hear How Silent They Are?

The year disappeared behind a white wall.

Tania Grabbe, the woman in the black dress with the blue stone on her necklace, laid her hand against the windowpane and wanted the snow to take her where her son was now, in a roofed wicker beach chair by the sea.

The clattering of silverware continued to echo within her.

Since having sat down—someone had pressured her to, most likely the police officer or her husband, she did not know any more—she had been rubbing the knuckles of her fists together, tortured by questions: Why do people make so much noise? Why are they so loud? Why is the coffee machine running the whole time? Why do I have to be here? Why is everything the way it is?

Through the curtains of the pub windows, she could see the heavy snow. When she shut her eyes, she could feel the hard wood of the sled beneath her and Lennard's weight and the wind blowing into their faces. When she opened them back up, a man in a black suit was sitting next to her, staring at her hands.

For a few seconds, she found the sound of her almost mechanically rubbing knuckles annoying. Then, once again, she noticed the throbbing that had begun back at the cemetery in that place in her body where, twelve years earlier, she had first felt his presence.

From then on, she had explained to Dr Horn while reminding him of his professional confidentiality, her life would be complete. Up to that point she had been nothing but the shadow of a woman. She trusted Dr Horn enough to speak freely.

Now she saw the doctor sitting at a table by the bar. The grey-haired woman next to him did not allow him to get in a word. He simply listened, as he always had, just like he had always let Lenny speak, whose flow of words at times seemed endless.

Nothing but the throb inside her. Her body, she thought, could remember.

For a while she could not stop wondering who had forced the doctor to sit at another table. He had no doubt wanted to sit next to her, and someone had got in the way. Just like someone had stopped her from sitting at the top end of the coffin in the cemetery chapel.

'Wouldn't you like to eat something?' the man next to her asked. She turned her head, observed his face with the strangely familiar eyes, his far too dark, almost as if dyed, hair, which she had remembered differently, longer, curlier.

Stephan, she wondered, what do you get up to when no one takes care of you?

In front of her was a salad plate with a slice of tomato on top. Just the sight of it made her feel ill. She quickly reached for her husband's hand, dug her nails into his skin and only stopped when, as if inspired, she looked back into his face. He was biting his lips and was clearly holding his breath. She immediately let go. He opened his eyes, rapidly breathed in and out then, like a hurt child, blew into the palm of his hand. The embarrassing gesture upset Tania Grabbe so much that she began to sob loudly.

The conversations stopped. The doctor cast them a worried glance. A man with a full beard sitting at the same table got up and edged himself onto the bench next to her. He put his arm around her, and she nestled her head into his shoulder. He caressed her face and nodded to the other guests. The conversations picked up again in a quiet tone.

Her brother's proximity helped Tania a little with being alone. It had been that way back when they were ten or eleven. Whenever Max would take her into his arms or pick her up—for no reason, out of high spirits—she would feel all her weight fall away, all her shyness and fear.

Everyone in the pub knew Maximilian Hofmeister. Most of them knew about the trusting relationship the siblings had, which clearly had not been affected by the marriage. Over the years, however, one or other of their friends had to have wondered how the boy's father, Stephan Grabbe, felt about it and whether it depressed him or even hurt his feelings.

Though as a business owner Grabbe had to be present every day—together with his wife he ran a cafe near Münchner Freiheit square—people considered him reserved, bordering on arrogant. Every weekend, no matter the weather, he would accompany his son to play football. Every summer, the three of them would drive to the North Sea. After his holidays, Lennard, in his well-known, talkative way, would tell everyone he knew how strongly he and his father had swum and how many hundreds of mussels and stones they had collected and how they had played football on the dog beach until all the dogs were completely worn out from chasing the ball back and forth. Lennard had never uttered a bad word about his father.

'I would like to say something.'

Tania took her fork and tapped it against a water glass. Conversation ceased. 'I would like to say something,' she repeated. 'I can't stand up.' She closed her eyes for a moment. Not a single sound, not even came from the kitchen.

Almost silently, accompanied by only a dull buzzing, a tram passed by on the snow-covered tracks.

Surprised by his sister's unexpected decision, Maximilian Hofmeister slid away from her and rubbed his beard in puzzlement, until he noticed the sound and stopped.

To Father Olbrich, the black-clad woman with the silk veil in her blonde, almost unruly hair had an aura of tragic youthfulness and aged desires. At that moment he was unsure if she had ever felt fulfilled. As to the psychological catastrophe that the death of a child triggers in every mother, she had not uttered a word in the discussions that Olbrich had with her and her husband. Instead, she had asked him, both at church as well as in the cemetery chapel, to be allowed to sit alone at the head of the coffin which was decorated with white roses. As he could not think of any convincing counter argument, Olbrich had agreed. Nevertheless, Stephan had refused his wife's request, which she seemed to accept without question.

When Lennard's mother began to speak, Arthur Olbrich folded his hands before his chest and noticed that, two tables away, another funeral guest had done the same. When the man raised his head, the priest remembered that the boy's father had told him that the man had delivered the message of Lennard's death two days before Christmas and stayed until midnight.

Then something happened which almost wiped the smile off the experienced priest's face. After folding his hands, he thought of a psalm that he wanted to go over in his thoughts; at the same time, a passage of the Quran he had recently read occurred to him: All of us belong to God; all of our roads lead to him; O serene soul, return to your Lord; you were a benefactor to others, come back to your Lord well-pleased; enter among my servants, and enter into my garden.

While Olbrich continued to wonder what God hoped to achieve with this leap of thought after the burial of a Catholic boy, retired inspector Jakob Franck recited the psalm which he had often heard at encounters with those who were left behind and which the priest had originally had in mind: Before the mountains were born or you brought forth the whole world, from everlasting to everlasting you are God. You turn people back to dust saying 'Return to dust, you mortals'. A thousand years in your sight are like a day that has just gone by, or like a watch in the night.

'My son did not die,' Tania Grabbe said. 'He is sitting at this table and watching us because we are all guilty.'

She did not look at anyone, only the framed photo with the black band in front of her on the table, next to the vase with the white roses.

'Which elephant has bigger ears?' she said. 'The African or the Asian one? It always tripped him up, my Lennard, he was so sure that the right answer was the Asian. Things like that. I'm certainly not any smarter than he was. I don't know a thing about football. He's unbeatable there, better than any of his classmates.

'He's a striker. You all know that. He's already had fifty-seven goals this year and thirty-three assists, or whatever you call it when you help someone else score a goal. He made me write the number down, I had to remember because he'd asked me. Fifty-seven goals, that's a school record, and he received a special certificate for it.'

She reached out towards the photo, without touching it. 'Then a man came from out of the snow and knocked on the door.'

She made a fist and knocked on the table four times. 'I knew right away who it was. A police officer. How do you recognize a police officer? By the uniform, Lennard says, and he's right. But a uniform doesn't just have to do with the clothes, a uniform also has to do with the eyes and how one acts and says things like: Your child is dead. No one but a police officer says something like that.

'I recognized him right away and made a mistake. I'm so stupid. Why didn't you understand that right off the bat? Lennard asked, sitting in his beach chair, as he always does. I'm so stupid, so very, very stupid, he's right.

'Everything full of snow. People rushing past the cafe, thank God they weren't coming inside. That's when the man came down from heaven, a leather bag hanging off his shoulder, and I thought: A police officer, he wants more information, something about school, or the director sent him to return the football certificate. The fifty-seven goals. It was the last day before the Christmas holidays.

'That's what I was thinking when I unlocked the door and let the man in. He was completely white and the tip of his nose was red. He said something to me at the door. I didn't listen. I didn't listen later on either. Well, no, later on I did, but I can't remember. Then Stephan came, too, I don't know where he had been, maybe he'd been making a snowman. You often don't have any idea what Stephan's up to when he's not cooking or baking. Most of the time he's cooking or baking, as everyone knows.

'I've never been that wrong about someone. I was right about the police bit but I put together the rest on my own. Lennard will never forgive me.'

'Not a word of what the police officer is saying is true. We both know that. I thought: We can hang the certificate in the living room, if you're OK with that, on the wall next to the TV, then we'll always be able to see it. You can think about it.

'Not that I want you all to think Lennard's a TV addict. He likes to watch football, sometimes late into the night, but only when he doesn't have school the next day. We pay attention to that, Stephan and I. This is my husband, here, next to me, and this is my brother, also next to me, he runs the Hofmeister Hair Salon on Fraunhoferstraße, our family business. That's my mother, Hi, Mom, hope I'm not embarrassing you, talking like this, telling people things about our private lives. It's got to be this way, or else no one will understand what's happened.

'The police officer from the snow is guilty. If he hadn't come, we all could have lived a tad longer, you, Mom, and you, Max, you too, Stephan, and me as well. Now only our Lennard is alive.

'There he is, on the Isar after winning the match against the team from Pullach, four to one, and he got two goals. Look how soaked his white jersey is. He looks exhausted. He keeps on running when all the others are on the ground. Where does he get the stamina? Definitely not from me, probably from his father. I took photos of him during the match, afterwards too, they were all standing in a circle and celebrating because they had beat their worst enemy. Look at him laughing. He never liked people to take photos of him, but I got one, how about that. King of the Goals, Lennard Grabbe.

'You didn't make it home, no one knows why, not even the ever-so-clever police officer. He knows a thing or two about being dead, a little less about being alive. If he really knew a thing, he could tell me which way Lennard took after school and where exactly it happened. But wait, that can't be true at all. It can't have happened because there isn't any evidence, and what can't be proved, doesn't exist anywhere in the world.'

After that, she stopped speaking.

No one made a sound. The cook—the pub-owner's husband—and his Ethiopian help had silently come out of the kitchen to lean up against the wall behind the bar and follow the woman's constantly breaking, faltering but insistent sentences, her right hand yet again balled into a fist. Each of her still-inconspicuous movements caused her dress to rustle in a peculiar way—as if the fabric was trying to rub against the silence. To the young man standing behind his boss, hands hidden beneath his cook's apron, her talk was like a bad omen.

For a long time she stared into Father Olbrich's face. As he did not lower his eyes, which she would have found appropriate, she turned away. When she saw the man whose presence she had forgotten, she started. Her reaction to Jakob Franck was no secret to anyone, so he had no other choice but to imperturbably endure her stare.

Franck was there because Stephan Grabbe had invited him, and he would—not for the first time in such cases—say a few words if any of the relatives asked. Police words. Pre-coordinated statements from his colleagues as to the state of investigations. Words of comfort fashioned out of long experience as the dispenser of words in those nights of unceasing speechlessness.

'I would like to know the truth,' Tania said, in Franck's direction.

She was not counting on a response. Her attention was once more directed at the photo, the roses, the world within her alone. 'I would like to know who Lennard drove to Höllriegels-kreuth with. What did he want to do there? What's there to see?

Was there some kind of ogre he wanted to meet? I'll never believe it. Someone forced him to come, but who? The investigators are covering it up, they just ask questions and maintain things I don't understand. When you say something that no one understands, everyone thinks it's got to be important. What a lie! And what a way to insult someone! Who picked Lennard up from school and took him to Höllriegelskreuth? He's disappeared into thin air, or buried himself, or taken off for America. This person supposedly killed my son. But how?

'The paper says that Lennard was beaten to death. By whom? By an invisible person. Or did one of you see him? No. No one saw him, not even the police.

'I am Lennard's mother, what gives you the right to lie to me? The paper says that someone stole his bicycle and that that's why he had to walk home, that's why everything turned out the way it did, everything. If he had ridden his bicycle I wouldn't have had to throw away his toast. That wasn't so bad. In general, though, you shouldn't throw food away. We don't do that either, do we, Stephan?

'Toast Hawaii, with pineapple and ham. He likes that just as much as fish fingers and noodles with ketchup. They were in the oven, the slices of bread. He was supposed to be back at seven-thirty. I waited. No, that's not true at all. What would I have been waiting for? I knew that he would be coming any minute.

'I don't know what I did instead, probably started straightening things, took the laundry out of the dryer. I cursed the rain, the wind, the godawful November. Maybe I turned on the TV to see if the weather was supposed to get any better or whether it'd just rain up through the end of the year. No umbrella. Lennard hates umbrellas. He likes the rain. When the rain hits his head, he laughs, like in the photo after the match. Look how happy he is.

'No one's looking at him. He's looking at me alone. Because he knows me and knows I would never lie. Honesty, I taught him, is the daily bread we share with one another, and that's why he became an upright boy. Without honesty, we would all go hungry.

'You haven't told me what happened to my son on his way home, Inspector, you promised me you'd solve the puzzle. We're still waiting for release, my son and I, we're sitting here waiting, and I don't know how much longer I can be patient.

'It was dark, it just kept on raining and the rain and its accomplice, the wind, washed away all the clues, is that right? For two hours I listened to your colleague. He explained that the police had searched the area with all their super technological devices, for hours, days. It sounded impressive. But the rain kept on going, and the wind kept on going, and the sun had already gone down, and not a witness far and wide. No one saw a thing.

'Can you believe that, Lennard? That no one was out when you left school and looked for your bike in the pouring rain? The whole part of town empty? I asked the inspector if any trams had passed. Yesyes, he said, and what about taxis, cars in general? Yesyes. I guess they were all full of blind people or inmates with fogged-over glasses.'

'We go our way alone, Father, trusting in God, the Lord, they say. What can God, the Lord, do about a storm? Nothing apparently. Helpless up there in Heaven, poor sight, a lousy day. I passed a supermarket. That's where you buy yourself a cola sometimes, or something sweet, you've never told me what exactly. You don't have to. That's not included under honesty, it's just a game. When I find out, though, you'll have to fess up about what you bought and admit that I'm smarter than you, at least now and again. The checkout woman knows you, I showed her a photo, she says you're a polite boy, even a bit shy. She sees you often, though not often enough. On the evening of November eighteenth she was at the register until eight, you didn't show up. She didn't go out to smoke like she usually did, she said, because it was coming down in buckets, and she wanted to stay where it was dry, it's understandable.

'I walked on alone, down Eintrachtstraße, past the pub where we are now, and I considered going inside and warming up, having a tea with rum or a fruit schnapps. I didn't. I didn't have any time. I held on to my umbrella with both hands so it wouldn't fly away. Don't cry, I said to myself, why are you crying? Then I understood that I wasn't crying at all, but that the rain was constantly throwing its tears into my face. If I say so, you've got to believe me.

'I walked along the cemetery wall, turned onto Regerstraße and followed it all the way home. On the way I asked everyone I ran into: Have you seen my son? Have you seen my son? Have you seen my son? And they all said: Nono; they all said: Nono. They lied to me, am I right, Lennard?

'And the kid who stole your bike says he wouldn't recognize you if he saw you. The police let him go, he's a thief, they say, but he brought the bike back on his own. Could be. Might well be. He brought the bike back, but without you on it.

'What good is the bike to me if you're not on it, pedalling? What's the point? Can you explain that to me, Inspector? Father? Is there anyone here who can be honest with me?

'Can you hear how silent they are, Lennard?'

The boy was named Hendrik Zeil, he was fourteen and playing dumb. That was a real test of Franck's patience. He had received permission from the Chief Inspector of the special division, his old friend and colleague André Block, to ask the boy a few questions.

Hendrik had called the police after the eleven-year-old Lennard, who had been missing for weeks and went to the same school, was found dead.

He had, Hendrik explained during Chief Inspector Block's questioning, simply taken the bike that evening 'because it was raining so hard, and I wanted to get home quicker'.

It became clear that bicycles were regularly stolen from the Asam Gymnasium without anyone ever being caught.

'It's normal,' Hendrik said, 'it's just something you've got to live with.' On that particular evening, he had 'palmed' one of the bicycles still out in the schoolyard. When asked whether he had picked the lock, he answered: 'Wasn't necessary, there wasn't any.' He did not know the missing Sixth Grade boy.

After that evening, he did not use the bicycle to go even a single metre; he left it at a friend's house and then never thought about it again. It was only when his mother mentioned the missing boy at some point and how tragic it was that he still had not turned up, 'and, in the meantime, could be dead, which turned out to be true' that he 'somehow ended up with a bad conscience'. For a while he had 'thought back and forth' but then decided to call the police and report the theft.

'That's it,' the boy said to Chief Inspector Block. 'The thing's in one piece, I swear, not a scratch, the rear rack was bent already.' Block asked him whether he had ever stolen a bicycle before. Hendrik opened up his arms and turned his head back and forth. 'No, I swear, I don't do that kind of thing, I never steal, had never done it before. That evening the weather was so shitty and the whole day had just been stressful. If it'd been locked up, I would've left it alone, a bunch of bad things just came together; it's not my fault. I'm really sorry the boy ended up dead.'

After a strong warning to Hendrik Zeil to not let even the smallest thing happen throughout the rest of the school year—otherwise he would experience 'bad things' in connection with being arrested—Block decided not to charge him and sent the fourteen-year-old home.

Franck had gone to find Hendrik a day later at, according to the boy, a 'super bad time'; the boy was in the process of collecting his legions—or whatever it was that Franck had no interest in knowing—in order to decimate his opponent. Franck forgot the name of the computer game as soon as he heard it.

'On November eighteenth, you left the school building around six o'clock,' Franck said. 'You took the bicycle and left the schoolyard immediately.'

Hendrik drummed his knees with his hands and twisted back and forth on his red swopper. Now and then he cast a glance at his screen. 'This a rerun? I already told the sharpshooter at the station everything.'

'Which sharpshooter?'

'The dude with the 'stache.'

'Chief Inspector André Block.'

'Exactly.'

'Do you think he's a sharpshooter?'

'He had his piece on him the whole time.'

'Did you see anyone, Hendrik? In the schoolyard? On the pavement? Someone just standing around? That looked like he might be waiting for someone?'

'No. It's all in the report.'

'I know that,' said Franck. 'It also says that you only used the stolen bicycle once, that evening, and never again.'

'And?'

Franck was standing in the doorway of the child's room, whose chaotic impression made him think of a room which only existed in his mind and that of his ex-wife.

For a while he watched the boy with interest as he swung back and forth ever-more restlessly. The show that Hendrik was offering his visitor—in the middle of a mess of clothing, shoes, boxes, cables, speakers, discarded electronic parts and yellowed stuffed animals leftover from some distant childhood—demanded a certain amount of professional respect from the former inspector. He did not think the boy was a malicious liar; just someone who liked to play, whether with computers or with people.

'And then you simply forgot the bicycle,' Franck said.

'It happens.'

'And you didn't know the boy.'

'No.'

'And that evening there was no one else in the schoolyard, just you.'

'You're slowly starting to get on my nerves. The others are waiting for me.' He pointed to the screen. 'What do you want from me? You're not even real police, you said so yourself.'

'I brought the family the news of their son's death . . .'

'I know. Respect.'

'Will you be coming to the funeral?'

'No idea. When is it?'

'In three days. On New Year's Eve.'

'That'll be a bit tough,' Hendrik said.

'Do you have meetings?'

'And if I do?'

Franck stepped into the room, careful not to crush anything underfoot. 'You should go.'

'We'll see . . .'

'You should tell the parents that you knew their son and that you are very sorry that you stole his bicycle and that you want to ask for forgiveness.'

'What? Are you nuts?'

'I'll accompany you, if you like.'

Hendrik threw his arms into the air and waved them about. Franck was not sure what he wanted to express.

'Hey . . .' Hendrik began before falling silent. 'Let's be honest now . . . honest . . . yeah?'

'Be honest, Hendrik.' Franck came another step closer; standing straight, his hands folded behind his back, eyes directed towards the boy across from him, he gave off an air of authority which did not tolerate any disagreement; anyone who tried, he knew that much from his decades of work on homicide, would not be a lay person anywhere near the crime but in the end someone who would end up standing before the court.

'Honest.' Hendrik slid off the twirling stool and pathetically avoided his visitor's glance.

'No one is accusing you of being involved in the boy's disappearance or of having anything to do with his murder,' Franck said.

Hendrik needed a while before he had his thoughts even partially under control. 'He really was murdered, or what?'

'Yes.'

'Jesus, what a mess.'

'Did you talk to Lennard that November day?'

'No. Maybe. No idea. He always wanted to play on our team, the midget. Sorry. Super striker, of course. No one's denying it. A day earlier we'd had a match, he got two goals, the dude. With his left foot, man. Right on. He never locked up his bike or, if he did, in a way that any git could break the lock. The thing is black with green stripes, looks great, totally. He would've lent it to me if I'd asked, hundred per cent. I don't have anything against him, I respect him as a striker, really, everyone does. What happened to him really sucks.'

'Naturally, you were out and about with the super bicycle in the days following the theft.'

'Yeah. I wanted to bring it back, I swear, but then it was all like, Lenny's gone, disappeared without a trace. What am I supposed to do? What'll I look like? Like an asshole. I didn't say a thing, I waited. My boy, Tom, said the thing had to go into his garage, in the courtyard, it'd be safe. I ditched it. Really, I know I did, I took the bike on a Friday. No?'

'Yes.'

'Exactly. Friday. So I rode it on Saturday and on Sunday, at most an hour, I swear. Then I put it in the garage and left it there, it's full of stuff, Tom's, Tom's dad, he's a bus driver, actually he's a hoarder, collects all kinds of crap that no one needs. Fuck it. On Monday, all of a sudden they were saying, Lenny's away, and then he didn't show back up. I didn't ride his bike through town, I'm not nuts. Time went by, not a fucking trace of Lenny. Then it's Christmas, my Mom reading out loud from the paper all that stuff about Lenny and that he's dead, that kind of thing. What do you mean dead, I wondered. I didn't feel good, I felt real bad. Thought, I've got to explain this. Wanted to talk with Tom about it, he was off at his grandparents' in Husum, I thought, fuck it, I have to take care of this myself. And I did. Called the cops. Bad stuff, all of it. Your colleague didn't ask any other questions, and I apologized, and he said, In the future you need to get a grip on yourself, I said, I will, for sure, I swear. But I won't go to his parents, you can forget about that. I've told you everything now, that's got to be enough.'

'It's not enough,' said Franck.

'It is.'

'It's not.'

'I'm not going to do that, no way, get it? No, I'm not going to do that. You can forget it.'

'That was stupid, the thing with the bicycle, I didn't mean to do it, that was really stupid of me. Please forgive me, *Frau* Grabbe and *Herr* Grabbe. And my condolences, really. Lenny was a great striker . . .'

Tania Grabbe did not seem to have heard him. Held up by her husband and her brother, who was also holding the umbrella, she scurried past Hendrik and Franck in the direction of the exit, hunched over, wrapped up in her black coat, eyes hidden behind the veil. Franck estimated the number of students among the mourners to be at least a hundred.

The snow around the open grave was strewn with flowers in all colours, wreaths and garlands, the coffin down in the ground almost completely covered with white roses.

'And now?' Hendrik asked. The snowflakes sunk into his black wool hat.

Franck said: 'Don't forget to visit the grave every so often.'

'I won't.'

Franck gave him his hand; the boy hurried over to the group of his classmates who had been looking at him bewilderedly.

Church bells rang. The wind swept snow into the open aisles of the cemetery chapel.

Before Franck left the cemetery to go through the chapel and onto the street where the pub was located, he turned around once more. He saw Hendrik embrace his mother. He seemed to be clinging to her.

CHAPTER THREE

A World with No People

I

Back from the centre city, in his study, which at one time was supposed to become a child's room, Franck made a two-hour long call to André Block. He told him about the mother's speech and that Hendrik had actually managed to be brave enough to apologize to Tania and Stephan Grabbe. They had already discussed Hendrik's admission that he had indeed known Lennard and had thus not been honest with the head of special investigations.

Block was angry at both his sloppiness and the boy for having so nonchalantly and arrogantly lied to him, even if the statement was not of great importance. The fact that the two students had run into each other every now and then and even played football together once did not cast any useful light onto the investigations.

Where was the boy's book bag? If the perpetrator got rid of it the night of the murder, there was hardly any chance they would find it or secure any fingerprints or traces of DNA. Even the football that Lennard had received on his tenth birthday and that he brought to school every time he wanted to play with his own ball during an important match had disappeared without a trace. The perpetrator must have taken it along with the blue book bag with the reflective stripes. The ball was black with an orange pattern and a yellow spot with a puma jumping over it.

When Lennard left the gym around seven o'clock that November evening, according to witnesses, he had the ball under his arm, as always; he normally stuck it on his rear rack while keeping his bag on his back. In all probability, Block and his colleagues from the special commission believed, Lennard, after realizing that his bike had been stolen, had not carried the ball but kicked it ahead of himself and even against a few house-walls out of anger.

The fact that, according to the investigations thus far, not a single person—no house owner, no car, tram or taxi driver— had noticed the boy dribbling his ball on the almost-one-kilometre-long stretch between the gym and Welfenstraße on the other side of the cemetery led André Block's team to conclude that the student must have been killed, or at least assaulted, immediately after leaving the school building.

But the circumstances had hindered the search for the murderer in a dramatic, and for the investigators devastating, way. Thanks to the driving rain and the muck of leaves, broken branches and rubbish that the gusts of wind had blown across the pavements and green spaces, the police's search for relevant clues had been in vain.

One point in particular bothered Block and his colleagues up to the day of the boy's funeral: if someone had picked the boy up in their car and—according to the forensic pathologist— killed him the same night, then Lennard must have known and trusted them. His parents unanimously agreed that he would never have got into the car of a stranger.

The doctor excluded sexual abuse. His findings supported a violent, most likely spontaneous, blow to the head that led to the fracture. Despite the rain and the relatively long period of time they spent in the soggy, dirty ground, tiny particles of bark suggested that the boy's skull had smacked against the trunk of a tree. Lennard died within minutes. According to the doctor, a premeditated act was extremely unlikely.

Still, Block thought over and over again, the perpetrator had remained level-headed, he was able to think quickly and managed to remove the body from the scene of the crime and hide it outside the city in a stretch of woods.

Not far from where the body was found was a pub which had been open on the night of November eighteenth. The questioning of the guests and the employees brought nothing, they had not seen or heard anything or, more than a month later, could not remember.

The perpetrator, Block thought, must have been very sure; even if the area had been familiar to them, there was always the risk of running into someone from the pub. All the traces that the murderer had likely left behind on the narrow, unsurfaced road along the canal and on the path through the woods had been destroyed by the rain.

Block and his people had returned empty-handed.

Even the questioning of the family's circle of friends and acquaintances, around the school and the owners of the mobile phones that were logged that evening around the gym and the area of the East Cemetery had delivered no clues. The evaluation of the mobile data was ongoing, but Block's optimism remained muted. So far there had been no matches at all with any numbers from Höllriegelskreuth.

Lennard had not had a mobile with him. As so often, he had left it at home. Forgotten, his father said; Lennard was afraid of the radiation, his mother said, that's why he used it so seldom. Apparently Tania Grabbe shared her son's concerns, Block almost never reached her on her mobile, only on the landline at their flat or in the cafe.

As to the things the boy had taken with him in the morning—bag excluded—nothing was missing. In his pockets were a 5-euro bill, his house keys, a Swiss Army knife, a package of tissues, five Panini-football pictures with the images of Spanish players and an in-the-meantime melted bar of chocolate. The analysts at the state textile laboratory verified a large number of traces of which not a single one matched any saved material in the police computers or any registered offender.

When the papers came out on Monday with the photos of the funeral, the entire special unit would be standing there like a waste of a whole mountain of taxpayer money.

'We're at a dead loss.'

Franck could hear Block lighting a cigarette. 'Did they lift the smoking ban in the office?' he asked, as if wanting to distract him.

'Just now,' Block said.

Franck cast a glance through the window. In the late afternoon's grey light, only a few single snowflakes continued to fall. From the distance he could hear fireworks, pre-echoes of New Year's Eve. In the glass holder in front of the balcony door, a green candle burned.

'Your investigations aren't over by a long shot.' On Franck's desk were pieces of paper with the notes of his discussions; next to them, in a clear plastic folder, the files that Block had copied and put together for him, with a photo of the boy on top, beaming—the same one as at the funeral.

'If the mobile data don't deliver,' Block said, 'we'll need a miracle.'

'Where are you with the cameras?'

Block took a drag and blew the smoke out heavily; the soft sound made it to Franck's ear. 'There aren't any cameras, or, in any event, none that are pointed to the street, not in Pullach or in Grünwald, in the case that he went that way, which, from the school, would be the closest. You can see him in the images from the school cameras, but as soon as he leaves the entrance he's invisible, it's like the little kid is made of mist, like he disappeared into a parallel dimension. Why Höllriegelskreuth? A few hundred metres away from the Brückenwirt pub. Why didn't anyone notice anything?'

'No clues among their acquaintances?' Franck asked, not for the first time.

Block was silent.

'Are you alone?'

'I'm on the john,' Block said.

'You want me to call you back?'

'No. I don't have to go, I'm just sitting here.'

'Why there, of all places?'

'So that no one will see me if I start to cry,' Block said.

They had known each other for more than twenty years; Franck had never heard his colleague say anything like that before. 'Do you want to come by, we can drink a beer and go over everything again?'

'As far as I know, you're retired,' Block said. Not the slightest hint of irony, simply sad exhaustion. 'On top of it, I'm on duty, together with four colleagues, the others are with their families.' He stopped speaking, then asked: 'And you? Why aren't you with Marion?'

'She's gone out for some Thai food with a friend,' Franck said. 'I'm invited, but I'm not going.'

'That's a mistake.'

Franck looked into the darkness; once again he could hear the reproachful voice of Lennard's mother, her invocation of a world that no longer existed. He would have liked to speak with her, but when saying goodbye at the pub she had just shaken her head. On the way to the tram, an icy wind had smacked his face, as if heaven had wanted to slap him for the failure of the police. 'Someone's lying,' he said. 'You've got to subpoena the mobile users one more time.'

Block lit another cigarette, picked up the ashtray he had brought from his office and balanced it on his thigh. 'And if they didn't have a mobile with them?'

'Unlikely,' Franck said.

'Unlikely but possible. Did you notice anything in particular at the cemetery?'

'Too many people, the weather was too poor,' Franck said. 'I noticed your photographer, he was really professional.'

'Rufus, a real *paparazzo*, a chameleon. He's from Weimar, studied photography, broke off his studies and went to the paper, then the police, was temporarily undercover. A year ago he married a girl from Munich and that's why he moved here. You don't need to explain a whole lot to him, he's very dependable. I haven't seen his photos yet. What about the press?'

'The students agreed on a kind of action,' Franck said. 'They organized themselves around the parents and the family the whole time and were all carrying colourful umbrellas they had opened. They press didn't stand a chance. As far as I was able to ascertain, not a single student gave an interview, nor did any of the parents or teachers. A group of older students kept the reporters from pressing forward—the boys formed a phalanx, as if they were at a demonstration, no way of getting through. They only ended their action once all the mourners were inside the pub. I don't think there will be any usable photos of the parents by the grave.'

'They won't be easy on us,' Block said. 'You're right, we'll check out all the people who were there that night again, on the street, at home, everywhere.' He took another drag, stubbed out his cigarette, put the ashtray back on the ground and nudged it away with his foot.

He had given up smoking a year ago and started back up one month earlier. He took a deep breath as he began to speak again. 'There are two groups of people we haven't screened yet. The teacher and the students—three teachers were signed in that night and an eighteen-year- old student who lives right around the corner. Naturally, we checked the four of them out. Our inquiries are continuing.'

'Did Lennard have any trouble with any particular teachers or students?' Franck asked.

'Not that we know of.'

They were silent.

Block stood up, stretched, sniffed and bent down for the ashtray. Franck had also stood up, undecided whether he should get a beer from the refrigerator or not; he was incredibly thirsty.

Block unlocked the stall door. 'Go see Marion, go eat with her and her friend and think about something else, about the new year, for example.'

'No,' said Franck, on his way to the kitchen. 'I'm going to read and call Marion later.'

'Bad idea. Thai food is supposed to be really healthy.'

Franck smiled. His friend's eating habits were about the same as those of a teenager who had grown into his computer. 'I'll give Marion your regards,' he said.

The other end of the line was silent; Franck stopped in the hall and waited. After a while he said, 'André?'

The silence continued, then Block said, 'I know where Lennard's mother is right now.'

They both did.

Tania Grabbe was standing in the child's room that was a child's room no longer.

She had closed the door behind her and locked everyone else out. How they all whispered and her mother cried; because of her; because she would not speak; because back at the pub she had gone silent after speaking so much. About what? I was wrong, she thought; that's why she'd gone outside with Lennard; someone had followed her and put a coat over her shoulders and talked to her; and because she had recognized his voice, she had gone back inside with her brother; it seemed to her as if the people all looked at her as if she had come back from the dead.

She lowered her head and noticed that she was holding a framed photograph in her hand. That's you, she said, looking at the sunny face. She was speaking to him alone, not about him, not to the others, just to him, her son; whenever he was around, she did not need anyone else. When he came to the world, he brought her with him. Stephan had never understood that.

Who is Stephan?

Then she was ashamed of her thoughts; she had not gone insane; she had just forgotten her husband's name for a moment.

There had been so many people around her today that it was impossible for her to keep every name straight; Stephan; she recognized him in her son's face, the dark, narrow eyes, the round cheeks, the curly hair she liked to run her fingers through.

She wanted to turn around and yell into the hall: Those are just appearances!

She was incapable of moving. As back at the pub, which she no longer remembered, she pressed the photo to her stomach and, feeling the cold glass, pushed harder in order to warm it up; to protect him from the snow, that careless boy who didn't pay attention to any kind of weather, running around in the pouring rain as if he were just having a walk along the beach like a playful little dog.

Tania listened to the rushing of the sea flooding through her body. An unexpected warmth spread throughout her, she was so taken by the thought that she was sitting in a wicker beach chair, side by side with her little one who was eating an ice cream, kicking his legs with joy and scaring off the greedy seagulls.

She looked around and was surprised by how straight everything was; the blue wool blanket taut across the bed; the books and binders stacked perfectly on the desk; his toys, arts and crafts materials, novels and comics in order along the wall shelves; a white rose in a glass vase on the windowsill, next to it a white candle. Not a speck of dust on the piano; the wall-to-wall carpet freshly vacuumed; the window clean. In the air, a hint of vanilla.

Someone, she thought, had to have regularly cleaned the room. Someone was taking care of its tenant. Someone showed the angel the way.

Carefully, so as not to leave a scratch, Tania placed the framed photograph on the piano, right in the middle, facing the bed. Bending over the instrument, she could smell the polish. It occurred to her that Lennard did not like the smell; in the future, she would use a different kind.

She tilted her head above the piano and concentrated on the lovely melody which he could already play two-handed. With his back straight and his hands level like his teacher had showed him, he would sit on the leather-covered stool and his eyes would dart back and forth between the sheet music and the keyboard. After the last note, he would let his arms sink and let out a soft groan. His mother would clap.

Tania confusedly looked at her hands and listened again. The flat did not make a single sound. That's what I was, she thought, and nodded and folded her hands.

Her eyes fell onto the boots that she continued to wear; the tips were edged in white. That she had walked into the clean room in dirty shoes bothered her. Tears came to her eyes, and her body began to tremble. She was afraid she might faint, just like she did when she was young and thought she would fall out of the world from pure confusion.

She balled her fists with all her might and breathed through her open mouth until her heart rate returned to normal. She had been paying attention to her heartbeat since the time she first grew aware of her body.

When she was five or six, she found it unsettling that there was something inside her that she could feel, even hear, but over which she had no influence at all. She almost began to mistrust the individual life of her heart; at night, the sound scared her awake. She spent hours listening to it and pressing around the place in her chest in the hopes that the beating would cease. In tears, she begged her mother to make it stop. Only through the patient support of the family doctor was Mathilda Hofmeister able to convince her daughter of the organ's necessity and secret power, and make her familiar with the independent existence of the human body.

Nevertheless, Tania still reacted with small blackouts now and again to incidents and sensations that overwhelmed her capacity for integration and her senses in puzzling ways. Afterwards, she could no longer remember what had caused them.

She sat down on the edge of the bed, pulled off one boot, then the other, and put them both on the parquet between the carpet and the door. Then she stood up. She palmed the bedspread smooth again, and looked around another time—carefully, like someone looking for something in particular or imprinting every single object in their memory. She decided upon the round piano stool.

While she spun back and forth for a while on the rotating chair, she hummed a melody that she had made up, but which she was convinced her son had once played.

She forgot time.

Someone knocked on the door.

Tania did not react. More knocking. She looked to the window and began to hum louder. On the third knock, she turned her head to the door and thought that she must have misheard—a heart could not beat in a wooden door.

A voice called out her name. She stopped humming and pressed her lips together. The door handle moved. Tania held her breath. Her brother cracked the door and stuck his head into the room.

'Max,' she said softly.

He pushed the door open more widely. 'We're worried about you.'

She imagined finding crumbs in his beard. 'I don't want any cake.' Her voice could barely be heard.

'We're not eating cake,' Hofmeister said. 'We're sitting in the living room, waiting for you.'

'But I'm here.'

'Please come sit with us. Mom has been crying the whole time.'

Tania closed her eyes; as a child, she was convinced that every time her mother cried, the tears flowed automatically out of her eyes, which she found unjust and unkind; it was never that way with her brother.

'Come on, Tania,' he said.

Gulls were crying in her head. She looked at the ceiling, there they were, in a fish net, five white birds with yellow beaks, always in the same place, motionless and alert. The net was stretched from the door to the window, the gulls were grabbing fish, starfish and mussels out of the air. There was even a red lobster lying dormant among all the sea creatures Lennard had collected.

'The lobster was his favourite stuffed animal once, do you remember?' she said.

Maximilian looked upwards. 'He brought it back from his holidays.'

'From the island.'

'Let's drink a cognac together,' Hofmeister said.

'He just put it in the net last year. The stuffed animal days are over.' She looked towards the shelves that one day Lennard had emptied: the animals disappeared into the wardrobe and he did not say another word about it. Since then his shelves had been full of old notebooks and the box with the old recorder he no longer played.

Tania turned to the window and wondered why the candle was not burning. 'Someone blew it out,' she said.

Exhausted, her brother cast a glance to the end of the hallway where the door to the living room was ajar. He made an effort, stepped into the child's room and grabbed Tania by the arm. 'We're all in the same boat,' he said. 'None of us know how to move forward. The only thing we've got is our shared memory and the fact that we will stick together and be there for one another. Are you listening to me? Lennard was not only your son, he was my nephew and mother's grandchild and the kid we loved the most. We're a family, you can't shut yourself off, every one of us needs the others.'

'That hurts,' she said and shook her arm; her brother did not let go.

'Get up.'

'Only when you let go.'

He did, waited, and felt the anger rising up in him, like an unjust pain. 'Good God, get yourself together.'

He had not wanted to say that, or in any event, not in that tone of voice; he wanted to add something, a familiar sentence of brotherly reconciliation.

His sister stood up silently, walked to the bed, pulled back the cover and the sheets, crawled inside, tucked her legs up against her body, covered herself, buried her head in the pillow and turned to the wall.

For the first time in his life, in the presence of his five-year-older sister, Maximilian Hofmeister felt like a little child who did not belong to anyone, as no one else existed; everyone had simply forgotten him.

'Happy New Year.' Franck stood in front of the closed balcony door, mobile up to his ear, and looked out into the exploding New Year's Eve, studded with dazzling stars.

'We missed you,' Marion said.

Five minutes after the new year had begun, their conversation ended. Franck's ex-wife and her friend Elke polished off their second bottle of wine; Franck got another beer from the refrigerator and went back to the picture of the dead boy on his desk.

Eleven-year-old Lennard Grabbe's silent laugh defied the fireworks going off throughout the suburban streets.

CHAPTER FOUR

A Glimmer of Hope

Franck found out about the thing with the ball on his New Year's walk through the centre city. As every year, on the first of January he left his house around nine. From Aubing, where he had already lived with Marion, he took the suburban rail to the main station. From there, he wandered around to observe the people, buildings, streets, spaces and architectural changes in the light of the new year on his own terms and to grow happy in a way he did not know how to name—if possible, just by seeing his reflection in a shop window, with the idea that January would be the beginning of a wonderful friendship between him and yet another year of life.

When he was still with Marion, they would walk together, at the beginning a concession of hers as she would have preferred sleeping in till noon and then greet the new year with a lavish breakfast. Over the course of their marriage, however, she had begun to enjoy his ritual and so she would go along with him on his unplanned route which—the second time already—inevitably ended up in a pub, often the Weiße Bräuhaus im Tal or in one around the cathedral, where they would almost always run in to one or two other police officers on their lunch break from the nearby station.

Marion almost found it touching how Franck would assiduously maintain that their encounters were completely random. Even in his free time, she realized that much right away,

Franck's thoughts revolved around current cases or the fate of those who had been left behind. Sometimes his absence hurt her feelings; sometimes his official as well as considerate dedication earned her respect. At the end of their marriage, however, she had felt shut out and superfluous.

As Franck was crossing the snow-covered and abandoned Viktualienmarkt, grumbling about the distance he still had to go and feeling hungry and cold, his mobile rang.

Even though he made an effort to perceive the city's stillness; the leftover paper, wood and bottles from the previous night's fireworks; the stores' gloomy displays; the shuttered wine stands; the hustle and bustle of children and their parents at the skating rink; the hooded faces of young men in front of a fast-food restaurant, exchanging dubious little packages at a quicker pace than the burgers were being flipped inside, he could not shake Tania Grabbe's distant voice evoking a life that had gone out like a magical flame.

'We just got unbelievably lucky,' André Block said. 'We might know where the crime scene is now.'

Franck stopped. He noticed the red carnations on the Karl Valentin fountain, which looked as if someone had just brought them to the bronze actor and comedian that morning. 'Where?' he asked, instantaneously determined to go inspect it.

Block hesitated. 'Nothing's certain yet, but we think that the boy might have died very close to his school.'

'What happened?'

'The ball showed up, Lennard's football, the one he'd been playing with that evening.'

'What does the ball have to do with the crime scene?'

'Well, everything or nothing,' Block said. 'An eight-year-old boy from the neighbourhood found the ball and took it home.

Today he was playing with it and his mother asked him where he got it and he had to admit it wasn't his, that he'd found it under a bench on the playground. That's right in front of the house where the boy lives, and the school is just three minutes away.'

'Spitzingplatz,' Franck said. 'I was there, I questioned the checkout woman at the supermarket.'

'We questioned her too . . .' Block interrupted the conversation to have a quick exchange with his colleague. 'Elena is going through all the neighbours' interviews again. Of course we looked around everywhere in the area. The rain, the storms washed away the traces, you know that, we didn't find any clues. And now there's the snow.'

'When did the boy find the ball?'

'He's not all that certain now,' Block said. 'We'll get it out of him. He'd hidden it in the bicycle room, behind a box full of stuff. His mother recognized the ball from the paper. Good news for us.'

'Hopefully.'

Thirty-four days lay between Lennard's disappearance and the discovery of his body. In the meantime, ten more days had passed, and the state of the evidence had grown increasingly poor.

In Franck's experience, the possibility of discovering any useable blood or traces of DNA after such a long time and the miserable external circumstances was around zero. Luck—or, as Franck used to say when he was still on the force, the Mephistopheles of luck—was still on the unknown murderer's side.

'Does your colleague have enough experience with eye-witness testimonies?' Franck had already made his way to the next tram stop to travel to the crime scene.

'She's our best,' Block said. 'You met her at one of our colleagues' funerals.'

After a trip to the pub, the police officer had been walking along the side of the road drunk and was hit by a car; he died at the scene. Franck had gone to the funeral because, when time allowed it and the funeral was close by, he went to all the funerals of his colleagues, in his eyes it was a given. To Marion, however, his behaviour had more to do with a kind of manic professional zeal, which—not forgetting his function as the one who delivered news of people's deaths—little by little drove her out of the house. It was very likely, she thought sometimes, that the horrors and residue of death filled Franck with more life than the close needs of his loved ones.

Franck had forgotten the woman's surname. If he was not mistaken, she had been related to the unfortunate policeman or had been a good friend. He asked Block.

'Holland, like Belgium,' the Chief Inspector said. 'We're going to have the playground cordoned off, that won't change anything, but you know . . .'

'Send your photographer,' Franck said. 'Have him take pictures of everyone who shows up. The fact that the playground is being searched will quickly make its way through the neighbourhood. Maybe the perpetrator is, in fact, from around there.'

'Straws in the snow,' Block said.

'I'm out and about.'

'How did it go at dinner yesterday with Marion?'

Franck stuck his phone into his pocket, pulled his shawl tighter around his throat and felt the cold on his head. Thanks to his whirling thoughts, when he left the flat he had forgotten to grab his hat.

People were huddling up on the pavement in front of the building, wondering what the three men and the woman in the white protective suits were hoping to find on the snowy playground. Like the other curious onlookers, a man in a grey winter coat was taking pictures with his smartphone of himself and anyone who happened to walk through the frame; he seemed pretty busy. And he was doing so, Franck discovered a short time later, not out of any disrespectful curiosity but because he was a police photographer.

Rufus John, the 'chameleon' as Block had called him, did not even need ten minutes to register every single face that appeared anywhere on the playground and save it to his phone. Quick and inconspicuous, wool hat pulled down into his face, he darted about like one of those volunteer citizen reporters working for a tabloid that, in the service of so-called truth, was not allowed to miss a thing, however private or unofficial the occasion might be. Whenever someone noticed him, John would approach them and get them caught up in a discussion about the non-transparent methods of the police.

His reservations about the potential success of the spontaneously organized search for clues increasing, Franck—he had positioned himself away from the action, in front of the supermarket on the main road—had to think of an old, tragic case whose shadow had once more come to find him decades later.

Just a few hundred metres from where he was standing, a schoolgirl had hung herself. As Franck was to find out, the circumstances surrounding her death only partially fit the results of the investigations. The real reasons came to light only twenty years after the familial catastrophe, of which the girl's mother had also become a victim, thanks to his informal reopening of the case. Nonetheless, he doubted whether he had been able to free the husband and father from all that pain.

To Franck, the fact that the girl and the dead Lennard Grabbe had gone to the same school was simply a coincidence. And yet, it was not the first time that certain details in two completely different crimes coincided. He wondered whether there was a hidden meaning somewhere, one that contained a secret clue to solving the case that he had failed to recognize before.

Four, he thought and saw André Block stepping away from his group of colleagues and walking over towards him—he had left behind four unsolved murder cases when he retired from the force, and no one believed they would ever be solved.

The idea that Lennard's murderer could also fall through the cracks to simply end up an eternal question mark made Franck shudder and transformed the rising, horrible east wind into a claw, scraping at his skull. He would not just look on. He would do something.

And yet he knew he did not have any authority at all.

'You doing all right?' Block asked.

Franck looked at him confusedly. 'I was just thinking . . . What's the boy got to say?'

'Is the snow wearing you down? You look really grim. You want to go sit in the car? You need something to drink?'

'Everything's fine. What's the boy got to say?'

André Block could not remember ever having seen his former colleague and boss so distracted and distraught.

'Talk to me,' Franck said.

Block flipped up the collar of his leather jacket and stuffed his hands into his pockets. Then he shook himself and cast a dark glance towards the intersection, as if trying to intimidate the wind. 'We can assume that the boy discovered the ball and took it with him one or two days after Lennard's disappearance. His mother has gone through her calendar ten times and tried to reconstruct all of her appointments and routines, she was extremely helpful. Since that day the ball has been in the cellar, today the boy took it out for the first time because he wanted to play football with a friend, despite the weather. In the meantime we've sent the ball to the lab, you never know.'

Franck surveyed the playground, the intersection with the school on the other side. 'Somewhere around here Lennard encountered his murderer. He had a car or a van or some kind of estate car. And the two of them did not run into each other on the open street, but somewhere less visible.'

'And that would be?' Block too took a look around, nodded in the direction of the playground. 'If the ball was under the bench, it can't have rolled a long way.'

'The murderer and his victim were together on the playground,' Franck said.

'Why would Lennard choose to go through the playground? That's out of the way. He always takes the road, his friends confirmed it, his mother too. He never goes round the block here, that takes far too long. He wanted to get home quickly, it was raining and he was angry that his bike had been stolen. So how does the goddamn ball end up under the wooden bench? Someone's got to have seen something!'

Franck asked what chief inspector Holland had discovered. 'She isn't done with the interviews yet,' Block said. 'Up to now no changes, no one can remember, no one saw anything. Assuming that the crime took place on November eighteenth, the doctor is pretty certain and now we have the clue with the ball, we can hardly hope for a late epiphany from one of the neighbours.'

'People often need a point of reference to help them remember.'

'That's obvious. Elena and I are going to make a second round of the houses tomorrow morning, and we're bringing the ball with us.' Block sighed and looked at his friend once more. 'To be honest, you look like you're going to fall over any minute. What's wrong with you?'

'I'm thinking,' Franck said.

'You're thinking about something that's overwhelming you and for which you are not responsible, my friend.'

'An unpremeditated crime.' Franck looked like he was speaking to himself, somewhere he was alone. Block let him continue. 'A spontaneous argument. The boy isn't paying attention, he runs out in front of a car, the driver manages to brake at the last moment, visibility is bad, the rain's pouring down, not a soul around. The driver gets out, just as angry as the boy, words are exchanged, the man strikes, the boy falls down and is hurt, the man pulls the boy into the car, takes off, he overlooked the ball, it rolled away, he takes the book bag with him. The boy dies. The driver brings the body to Höllriegelskreuth, keeps a low profile, no one suspects him, his mobile wasn't logged in.'

The wind whirled the snow, tore at the red-and-white barrier tape encircling a patch of earth that seemed to have been haphazardly trampled here and there and was bare. The investigators—standing together in a circle like a secret society, talking with their colleagues from homicide—had not uncovered any new leads. Tirelessly, talking privately with various neighbours, Rufus John made his way through the rows of people, taking photos.

In the meanwhile, two more squad cars with eight officers had shown up; they were there to keep the growing number of reporters and photographers at a distance. From the surrounding windows, locals were following the unexpected Sunday entertainment with binoculars and cameras. Children's shouts made their way down to the street and now and again the sound of Middle Eastern music.

Block shrugged his shoulders. 'A lot's possible,' he said to Franck. 'The boy could also have run into an acquaintance with paedophiliac tendencies, he takes him, wants to take advantage of him, the boy defends himself, the perpetrator hits him. We still don't know where exactly Lennard was killed. It could well be that the perpetrator and victim ran into each other here. In any event, it's a start. We don't have anything else at the moment.'

Hands behind his back, Franck stepped off the pavement and into the narrow street that ran between the building and the playground and was blocked at the other end by a squad car. He turned towards the intersection. 'The boy,' he said, 'never came this way, far too visible for a violent encounter; for whatever reason, he went across the playground, we don't know why, and the perpetrator . . .'

Franck turned back in the other direction, towards the spinning blue light in the distance splitting the growing dusk. '. . . Either came from the direction of the cemetery or one of the two side streets that branch off from the playground here. The perpetrator and victim met at the northern end of the playground, any other variation is inconceivable.'

'Not so,' Block said. 'The perpetrator placed the ball here to lead us down the wrong path. He knew that we would make a particularly intensive search of the school area, so he put an obvious clue in the way. He couldn't have counted on the fact that another boy would steal it, however. The perpetrator assumed that we would focus our search for him on one of the houses around here. A cunning plan.'

'If so, we're dealing with a professional,' Franck said.

'Why should we exclude that possibility?'

Franck was silent. He did not believe in a pre-meditated crime.

In his estimation—and, if he was being honest, Block did not disagree—the investigators had to assume it was a chance encounter. Otherwise they would have already discovered concrete evidence in the victim's personal life a long time ago and would not have to be shovelling snow on a piece of land swept clean by the weather, trying to convince the media and the neighbours—in the absurd hope that curiosity would drive the perpetrator back to the scene of the crime.

Things like that, Franck knew from thirty-two years of service in homicide, rarely happened, and when they did, it was thanks to plainclothes cops being on the scene, ready to arrest the suspicious person.

Until now, in the Lennard Grabbe case, there were no suspects, no voyeurs, no stalkers, no previously convicted paedophiles, no suspicious relatives, acquaintances, teachers or fellow students.

On a rainy, cold November evening, Lennard Grabbe had left his school and disappeared. He disappeared, just like five other boys and three girls before him had over the course of forty years in that city, boys and girls whose bodies were never found, their fates forever black holes, a maelstrom that had destroyed the happiness of marriages and families.

Which is precisely what gave Franck a glimmer of hope on that first day of the new year: the fact that Lennard had not been lost, but that his body had been found and been buried.

In addition to his death—of that much he was suddenly convinced—it would be possible to reconstruct the surrounding events and, despite all evidence to the contrary, the murderer could also be caught.

'Let's start at the end,' he said.

'What are you thinking about?' Block asked. 'You don't look like someone who's about to pass out any more but like someone who's been shot full of adrenaline. Your eyes are like saucers. Did you take some pills or something?'

'No.' Franck raised his head. 'I just have a wider perspective at the moment.'

Block understood that his former boss had not been retired long enough yet, not by a long shot.

CHAPTER FIVE

Buster Keaton Gets an Idea

Franck's perspective slowly faded, from day to day, from week to week. The snow began to melt.

The twenty-one members of special unit 'Lennard' were busy following up hundreds of leads. They were working on matching mobile data, intensifying their questioning of students and teachers, digging up every inch around the place where the body had been found. They accepted help from state crime-scene analysts, evaluated all the surviving state CCTV recordings (even those that had only captured the way the boy took to a small degree), and every night had no idea what their boss, André Block, would say to the journalists the following day. For the moment, Block hesitated to mention that, following a month of fruitless searching, the unit would be reduced to fifteen people.

When Franck learnt about the special unit's reduction, he felt like the sixteenth man in a faceless city.

On a bright day he saw nothing but shadows. He could not understand how, with every step, a crew of experienced investigators only increased the darkness.

Franck found his own failure worst of all, his wandering between halfway fixed coordinates and his imagination's presumed points of reference.

In the meantime, he had grown ashamed of his outburst that busy January afternoon, a day that now seemed incredibly far away. Today, his previous belief in a quick solution to the case seemed inexplicable.

Every time he woke from restless sleep at five in the morning and shuffled barefoot to the bathroom, he was shocked by what he saw: the exact same thing as the day before.

A blind man trying to use his eyes.

More than nine thousand cameras were distributed throughout the area, the majority of them belonging to transportation companies and the German railway. Three hundred of them oversaw the flow of traffic down in the tunnels, another hundred what was going on aboveground on the streets and at the intersections. In the police operation centre, day and night an officer conducted 'virtual patrol', as they called it, watching the thirty-two monitors and notifying their colleagues on the scene if anything stuck out.

In places considered potential trouble spots, the police had six stationary cameras with high-resolution zoom capabilities in use. In addition, hundreds of private citizens and businesses had their properties monitored, often far beyond what was permitted by law.

How often had Franck discussed with his colleagues whether there really was a chance of observing a crime thanks to one of the countless recordings? And then how much of a chance there would be to quickly identify the perpetrator or even hinder the crime? They all said there was, but it was a rather helpless response, and one dependent on theory; for none of them had ever experienced the real thing. And as to whether people really felt safer thanks to the almost ten thousand more or less visible eyes was also written in the stars.

Nevertheless, the cameras were there, Franck thought, imploringly, and they worked, even on that calamitous eighteenth of November.

And yet no camera, no virtual patrol officer had noticed a thing. Only one thing seemed to be one hundred per cent certain: the unknown person had assaulted Lennard on the playground, with fatal consequences, there, where the boy from the neighbourhood had found the black ball with the puma.

In the bark of a tree close to the wooden bench, one of the investigators found hair, the DNA of which matched that of the victim. Whether Lennard died there or first on the way to Höllriegelskreuth would likely remain unknown. Up till then, the forensic pathologist had not been able to establish an exact time of death. All the same, he remained convinced that the eleven-year-old had lost his life the night of his disappearance; the entomological examinations of the body, which with great probability had been lying in the woods since that very night, would leave no doubt, the doctor wrote in his final report.

Thus far Franck was as familiar with the report as he was with the majority of the files. His hope—three weeks after the boy's funeral—was based on old investigative experience: no attentive investigator was ever immune from overseeing something, from failing to understand a connection, evaluating a detail poorly, from at times even having the definitive piece of the puzzle before their eyes but not recognizing it. Franck called it the 'fossil'—that very material or immaterial link that placed the act's past in an unassailable connection to the crime's present and held the genome of the truth to solving the case.

In a daze from reading for hours, Franck stood up from the desk. For a while, he paced back and forth in his room. He cast an eye at his desktop calendar—it was the third Sunday in

January—and then did something he had shied away from over the last number of days.

'This is Jakob Franck,' he said into his mobile. 'I'd like to meet you.'

An hour later, he was sitting with Maximilian Hofmeister at the back of Fraunhofer Gaststätte, just a few metres away from where Hofmeister had his salon and next door to where he lived.

By then most of the visitors to the morning music session had gone home, those who had stayed behind were talking with the musicians or reading the paper. No one paid any attention to the two men deep in conversation at a small table by the wall, barely touching their beer, a conversation that, according to the help, was halting.

'Sorry,' Hofmeister said. 'I'm happy you called, you're the only person I trust myself to talk to, but looking at you now . . . Good Lord!' He ran both of his hands across his head with its bun. 'Sorry,' he said again. 'As much I'd hoped you'd call at some point, I was really afraid because . . . well, you can see what's wrong with me.'

He leant back. The way he put his hands in his lap and balled them into fists reminded Franck of Tania Grabbe. It seemed as if her brother had lost weight, and he was a bit dishevelled.

Hofmeister had shaved quickly and exuded the smell of musty rooms and clothes worn too many times. Beneath his checked shirt, he wore a greying t-shirt; his winter coat, which he unzipped only after half an hour, had dark spots, as if from dried-out liquids. And though the pavements were wet and covered in dirty snow, he had opted for worn sneakers;

his jeans scuffed the floor. Franck thought Hofmeister had probably forgotten to put on socks. He decided to invite the hairdresser to eat.

'You're very worried about your sister.'

Hofmeister bent over the table, hands pressed between his
knees. 'She's changing. She doesn't talk. When she does say
something, her voice is so soft that we have to ask her what
she said, but she refuses to repeat herself. How's that supposed
to go on? I'm her brother, she even treats *me* like someone
annoying or who she doesn't even register though I'm standing
right in front of her.' He quickly grabbed his beer, took a gulp,
smacked his lips and seemed about to excuse himself again.
A sad smile crossed his lips.

'I could recommend a psychologist to your sister, your family, if you like,' said Franck.

'Your colleague made us the same offer. Tania refused, of
course. I don't know. . . Sometimes I get angry when I think
about her, can you believe that? I can see her right in front of
me and then . . . then . . . '

'What do you mean, *Herr* Hofmeister?'

'I think . . . Sometimes what my sister's doing just seems so
over-the-top. It's awful. You're not supposed to say stuff like
that. I don't really mean it. Really, believe me, I don't really
know what I'm saying, how I'm reacting, how I should help her,
how I . . . '

He stopped. Franck waited. He did not want to interrupt
the man's silence, his repeated gasping.

'Do you know what she's started doing? At night she
doesn't sleep with Stephan any more, she goes into the boy's
room and gets in to his bed. Every night. Stephan called me and
asked what he was supposed to do. What *should* he do? I told

him to leave her alone, it'll change again, I said. But up till now it hasn't.

'She gets up in the mornings and locks herself in the bathroom—for a whole hour. Stephan just hears the water running constantly. At the beginning he asked her what she was doing in there for so long, and she answered, taking a bath. That was it. In the meantime, she does the same thing every morning.

'Eventually she goes into the study and does her work, writes invoices, places orders, takes care of the things that have to be done when you've got a business. She's a trained saleswoman, she can do it. She works till noon, then she makes a soup and eats, alone.

'Stephan's at the cafe, he keeps the whole thing going, together with Claire. If it wasn't for her, he'd have to close up shop. A week ago, he hired someone else, a young Afghan woman, they say she's really engaged and understands the guests real well. I haven't got to know her yet. My sister says she hasn't met her yet either.'

He reached for his glass, paused and shook his head. 'What a family. I don't even want to imagine what our father would say about it all. He's not alive any more, you know that.'

'Yes,' Franck said. 'Is your mother taking care of Tania?'

'She's trying. Every day she comes over to Welfenstraße, cleans, straightens up, if there's anything to straighten up. Nothing goes on there any more, who could make any kind of mess . . . now that Lenny . . .

'Yeah, well, my mother hardly does anything else any longer, she goes shopping, she talks with Tania, asks her to go with her on walks. Two or three times she was successful in getting Tania out of the house. They went through the neighbourhood, towards East Station, over to Haidhausen, away from the cemetery, as my mother said. They didn't talk much. As my mother told me on the phone, she wasn't able to get Tania to think about anything else. To think about anything else . . . Easy to say. I don't think about anything else either . . . '

Franck almost said: Me neither.

'All of a sudden there's nothing but emptiness.' Hofmeister looked past Franck to the window where the dark was already coming down again, cut only by the timid lights of the trams. 'People give you their hands, express their condolences and then disappear, one after the other. At work, everyone looks at me with that insecure glance: Are you allowed to talk to him about it? How is he doing in general? Was it the right thing to go to a hairdresser whose nephew was murdered? He surely can't be counted on to do a good job . . .

'How are you supposed to react? I couldn't afford to keep the shop closed any more, times are tough for people like us. In our line of business, the low-cost guys are taking over, just like with the bakers, in the restaurants, in retail in general, nothing's allowed to cost a dime any more. Quality? Doesn't matter. Technical skills? Overrated.

'Today, you can get your hair cut for 5 euros, highlights and dyed for 10, there's a place on every corner. Or people want something stylish, you know, cool music in the background, dudes with scissors on their belts who can talk about the latest trends, who'll give them an espresso, a glass of water, a *prosecco*, wellness for your scalp. I don't do any of that.

'We never have. Our parents were serious business people who gauged their clients perfectly, above all the women, recommendations were made, things were discussed, one respected their desires. Then it was down to work, with dedication, without any unnecessary chatter or posturing.

'That's how I grew up. People loved our parents, people knew who they were, not just in the neighbourhood but all the way to Schwabing and Perlach. I still remember how sometimes clients had to wait two weeks to get an appointment, and they would because they didn't want to go anywhere else, just to Hofmeister Hair Salon, and . . . '

Once again he suddenly stopped speaking, as if he dreaded going on or was ashamed by what he had already said. He took a quick drink of his beer and cast the inspector an embarrassed glance.

'Sorry,' Hofmeister said. 'What are you supposed to do with my stories? But I'm . . . ' He looked down at himself. 'I apologize for showing up like this, I didn't think about it. After hanging up, I felt relieved in such a crazy way, the fact that you wanted to see me and I had a reason to leave the house, you can't imagine.

'I had a schnapps out of pure anticipation, embarrassing as it is to admit. Then I brushed my teeth and got ready to go, threw on my jacket and left. Don't laugh: I forgot to put on my socks, can you believe it? Can a grown man forget to do something like that?

'On a Sunday like this, I simply don't know what to do with myself, I don't think about a thing and I think about everything. I hole myself up inside and hate myself for it. This afternoon I was supposed to go see Tania and Stephan, like every Sunday . . . since Christmas. We wanted to eat together, mother made her famous "Mathilda" macaroni casserole, it's fantastic, it's got bacon and hot dogs and a lot of Gouda cheese. Tania and I loved it when we were kids. We used to argue about who would get to scrape out the dish. Our mother's name is Mathilda, but surely you know that already.

'I wasn't up to it today. I called and cancelled. My mother was disappointed, of course. I don't know about Tania, maybe she didn't even notice that I wasn't at the table. Please don't think I'm talking trash about my sister, I'm not, I just want to . . . I want to . . . I would . . . Should we get another beer?'

He had finished his drink and was looking at the empty glass in surprise. He looked at Franck and clearly wanted to continue talking. But he simply opened his mouth and then stopped speaking again, which lasted until the waiter took away their glasses and brought new ones. Hofmeister immediately seized his glass but did not drink; he looked as if he wanted to hold himself down with it.

'I'd like my sister to start living right again some day,' he said. 'And I'd like to be the one to help her do so. Sadly our father's not alive any more, otherwise we could've asked him for advice. He died far too early, thanks to an aneurysm the doctors diagnosed far too late. He was dizzy, had to vomit, went to the hospital and before the examinations were truly begun he was dead. We were all standing around his bed, Tania was in her fifth month, none of us seemed to grasp what had happened.

'I looked at my father, he was lying there, his face soft and slightly tanned, the white sheet went all the way up to his chin. It looked like he was sleeping and would open his eyes any second. Tania cried without stopping, not out loud, mind you, the tears just ran down her face, and her whole body shook. Not a single sound. She held our mother's hand, stared at our father, like all of us. Stephan was there too.

'That was that. Now he's no longer here, our father. Who should I ask?' Hofmeister waved his hand through the air as if trying to scare off every answer. Then he raised his glass, nodded at Franck, drank, put the glass back down and held on to it with both his hands, his head lowered and his eyes closed.

Franck delayed his question. 'Did your sister and your father have a good relationship?'

'No,' Hofmeister answered immediately. He let go of the glass and stretched his back. 'You couldn't say so. Back when we were kids, there weren't any problems. I think. Or when we were teenagers, as far as I can tell. Tania's five years older than me. The misery began when we started to talk about who would take over the business.'

'What misery do you mean, *Herr* Hofmeister?'

'The misery of not being able to speak. They stopped speaking to each other, my father and her. For a long time I didn't understand what was going on. I was still living at home, Tania was already doing her training, she was sharing a flat with her friend Leslie in Neuhausen and only came home, at most, every two weeks to eat. I'm really slow with certain things, things that have to do with interpersonal relationships for example. No wonder I'm still single . . . sorry, that's a stupid observation.

'My father wanted Tania to learn the same trade he had so that she'd come to the salon as soon as possible. He was a passionate motocross fan, he hardly missed a single big race, and I think his hobby became more important to him than his career. He never would have admitted that, but mother accused him of as much. They began to argue more than before. Everything changed. Tania started to rebel. She didn't want to come to work there—she had her own plans. You want to know what they were? Being completely honest? No idea. I can only guess. My sister never told me a thing, not even me. At the beginning I thought, "So what, it's got nothing to do with me, she's older, she doesn't have to explain anything to me . . . " But then . . . '

He placed his hands on the table, looked at them—Franck noticed the small wounds and scars on the fingers, the extremely short fingernails—and stood up. At first, it looked as if he felt sick and had to vomit. Hofmeister pressed his hands to his stomach, closed his eyes, bit his lower lip, took a deep breath. With a jerky movement he turned to the side, nodded absently to Franck and made his way across the pub.

Franck watched him go and wondered if he should follow. The waitress cast him a questioning look. He stayed put and tried to arrange the image of the Hofmeister family into some kind of frame.

In front of the door to the pub, Hofmeister leant against the wall and looked up into the darkening sky. He inhaled the cold air through his open mouth; he did not feel the cold coming through his shoes and onto his naked feet. His mind was a mess: in the middle of it, was his father's face. It had been a long time since he had thought about him as intensely as he had in his talk with the inspector, the inspector whose patient presence confused him as much as it encouraged him to take new leaps.

Hofmeister wondered what all he had told the stranger. He was afraid of having gone too far, of having placed his sister in the wrong light, his parents, little Lennard.

It occurred to him that they had not spoken about the boy at all. Or had they? What did the inspector want from him? Hofmeister wondered, and looked distraughtly at his worn sneakers and frayed jeans. He had gone out like that! He remembered his father's words: A businessman must look put together even outside his business.

From the roof of the building across the street, the one with the pharmacy on the ground floor, a chunk of snow slid over the gutter and clapped onto the pavement. Hofmeister flinched and looked upwards; above him too he could see frozen snow. He instinctively took a step forward before asking himself whether he might not be safer standing against the building.

He could not leave the man sitting alone in the pub for so long, it was rude. Rudeness is the death of business, his father had always said. He did not want to think about his father any more. He wanted to go back home, close the door behind him and do what he had been doing for days when he was alone: leaf through his book of Buster Keaton photos.

Just thinking about the actor he had admired since he was young made him relax for a moment. He imagined Keaton standing on the other side of the pavement, waiting for the snow to fall with that famous Stoic look of his. And as if protected by some kind of magic, he would remain completely unscathed. Seeing the snow pile up and block the way, he would start to make snowballs, throwing them back onto the roof, constantly, faster and faster, one after the other, hundreds, thousands. Eventually the pavement would be clear, and all the snow back up top. But hardly would he have turned to go and the house would collapse under all the weight. In a fright, Keaton would glance around and, panicking, take off into the black night.

Hofmeister let out a guttural laugh. He moved back and forth in place and, without realizing it, began to wave his arms around in an odd way. Having come outside to smoke, the waitress looked at him askance. Noticing her, he stopped and for a few seconds put his hands in front of his face, as if trying to make the world disappear.

Then, ignoring her eyes, he walked back inside. He found the warmth of the heated room unimaginably pleasant.

'Sorry about the disappearing act.' Hofmeister sat back down. Franck did not seem to have moved a centimetre.

'Shall we order something to eat?' the retired inspector asked. 'I'd like to invite you.'

As discreetly as possible, Hofmeister rubbed his ankles together under the table. 'That's really nice of you, but I've already eaten.'

'What did you eat?'

'Chicken soup.'

'You cook?'

'I have to, or I'll starve,' Hofmeister said, feeling no need to keep on drinking his by now flat beer.

'You learnt how to cook from your mother.'

'A bit.'

'Does your sister also like to cook?'

Hofmeister nodded. Then he bent forward and lowered his voice. 'Do you think that the police still have a chance of catching Lennard's murderer?'

Franck had been expecting the question and did not hesitate to respond. 'No one will be able to give you a straight answer, but my colleagues are working night and day, and I'm helping them a little.'

'How?'

'I'm checking leads and asking questions, listening to you and other people who were close to Lennard.'

'What's that supposed to do?'

'I will hopefully get to know your nephew better and learn something about his behaviour, the way he was with others, his dreams.'

For close to five minutes Hofmeister just stared silently into the distance. He stopped rubbing his feet together and once again balled his fists in his lap. He looked at the grain in the table or at a table in the next room, into a different time. The silence he radiated kept the waitress from coming to see if they wanted to order anything else.

Franck sat completely still, just like when he had been the chief investigator and during questioning a new door opened to shed light onto what he believed might be the buzzing of a new confession.

'As far as my nephew's dreams are concerned,' Hofmeister said thinly, 'all that's left are scraps of paper. Two handfuls of Panini pictures, that's it. Lennard's underground and never coming back. He was still a kid and turned into a body without a childhood. I wish I were in his place instead . . .'

CHAPTER SIX

Care at the End of the Road

'I wish I'd picked him up from school that goddamn evening. I couldn't make it. I couldn't get away. We'd had some water damage from construction next door. Thanks to the storms and a flooded basement, the power went out. Short circuit. For two hours *nada*. By the time the fire department finally showed up, it was almost evening, and I hadn't been able to get hold of him. How could I have? Once again Lennard didn't have his mobile with him—he almost never did. I don't want to get radiated, he'd say. Don't give me that kind of look, I know that mobiles are full of electromagnetic rays and can be dangerous, but not if you just hold them to your ear on saints' days or whatever. Right? I'd like another beer.

'I wish everything could've been different that day, above all the weather; and that the fire department had been quicker in reaching us, they're right around the corner. They'd been going around town all day long, sure, it had been raining for days, the creeks were overflowing all over the place, in all the old buildings the basements were underwater. You can understand why we had to wait.

'But explain this to me: the world's coming apart and my sister lets her son come home from school alone, and in the evening of all things, in the pouring rain, during a storm? And me? Just standing around, I couldn't even serve my clients because there wasn't any power. *Frau* Haberland was sitting

there and wouldn't leave, *Frau* Behrend too. What was I supposed to do?

'Jana, my employee, was on the phone nonstop with her
thirteen-year-old son who was alone at home. That was in the
afternoon.

'In-between, of course, I hadn't thought about Lenny, I had
to talk with my clients. We were all standing by the window,
looking outside. Traffic was backed up, chaos everywhere, you
remember? And the day before the storm, I thought it would
knock out my panes, all the old masonry. When I was a kid,
things didn't look any different around here. Having said that,
the building where I live was renovated in the '80s, but the windows still aren't worth a damn, they're poorly insulated and the
sound travels upwards, like we learnt at school. When the trams
rumble past, my silverware clatters.

'Why didn't I just go? What was wrong with me? At six, I
started to wash *Frau* Haberland's hair, I knew she wouldn't be
leaving the salon before eight. Why did I do that? I should've
gone and picked Lennard up in the car. Then we would've
driven over to his house and eaten Toast Hawaii. His favourite,
an extra piece of pineapple, since forever.'

'Lennard would've become a great musician. Over the last
six months he'd taught himself to play guitar. He started off
with piano, he'd already mastered a couple of songs, you know,
he hears a song on the radio and can play it half an hour later.
You don't believe me? I was there, I'm a witness. His ear's
extraordinary.

'His father thought Lenny should concentrate on school
instead, but the boy wouldn't let himself be distracted. I'm
proud of him. Did he fail his first year at *Gymnasium* like so
many others, have to go back to middle school or switch to the
Realschule? No, he managed, and made it to his second year

and even told me how happy he was to learn Latin. Latin, *Herr* Franck. How'd that happen? Why's he happy? Why? I asked him and he said: Because it's a dead language and we're making it come back to life. He's eleven. Was. Eleven. Lenny.

'He doesn't like when people call him Lenny. He wants to be called Lennard. The name was my sister's idea, by the way. Stephan thinks she actually wanted a girl, she would've been called Eleonora, that was our grandmother's first name, and we were both really close to her.

'Eleonora was also a hairdresser, a lot of parents brought their children to her 'cause she managed to calm them down and make a game out of the whole thing. Eleonora was sixty-three when all of a sudden she died, her heart just stopped, no one knew why, not even our family doctor. Dr Jessner used to see all of us and had always been there, day and night. But he was powerless against our grandmother's sudden death. Afterwards our father would say that his mother had sometimes complained of dizziness and chest pain, but she didn't worry about little things like that, she had a business to run, a family to feed.

'I can't tell you if it's really true or not, Tania wanting a girl, she never said anything to me about it. The baby came, a boy, and she convinced Stephan to baptize him Lennard. The fact that she had to convince him first was something he told me later. If it'd been up to him, he'd have called the boy Emil, like his father. He thought that old names were back in, the boy wouldn't have to be ashamed of anything. Tania won. No other Lennards in his class, in the whole school he's the only one. There are two Emils, though.

'Lennard, my friend, my nephew, he was fearless. He came to the world and cast his own shadow. No one gave him any outlines to follow. He knew his own way all along.

'Whenever someone wanted to teach him something he'd listen, and if he thought they were right, he'd pay attention, if not, not. You know, I watched that boy from the time he learnt to walk. I followed his steps, observed him. Can you believe it? Me, the old grownup, and he the little boy. I wanted to be close to him, like he was some kind of Buddha that wanted to teach me the right way to walk, the right way to think, the way to walk the earth without being afraid.

'Sorry. What I'm telling you's got nothing to do with anyone, especially not the police. But you're here. You're the only one who's here. Tomorrow's Monday, we're closed, that's why I'm going to order another beer. Can I invite you to a schnapps? An *Obstler*? A real vitamin-bomb.

'Frankly, I still do that because of my parents. The day off, I mean. Mondays. Most hairdressers in town don't follow that tradition any more, haven't in ages, business above all, what else?

'Madness closing one day a week in this day and age, like all the pubs used to do too. Today, you'll be hard pressed to find a single owner who trusts themselves to. Competition everywhere you look. Just not by the police, right? The police are competition-free, like the fire department. The rest of us aren't. Even public schools are competing for students, today parents look for the best place for their kids, Waldorf schools, other private schools. Naturally, just those parents that have a little bit of money left over, but who doesn't in this boomtown? It's been booming here for decades, and the fun just never stops. We've got to make it through somehow, and Lennard, I know, had a plan, and no one would have challenged it, not his teachers, not his father, no know-it-all adult, no one. Music would have been his world.

'I don't understand a whole lot about music, but I understand what happened to Lennard when he came into contact with it: he trusted it. You get what I mean? The six-year-old boy who takes a recorder into his hands for the first time and starts to play at the end of the lesson is no longer the same boy as before. Inside him, a new life has begun, and he understands that it's his own, his raison d'être, ultimate freedom. And he took it up and started to make his way along the path, in the process vicariously representing someone like myself.'

'No, I wanted to say to my father when one night he called me into his study to tell me that, due to his health, he couldn't run the business any more and that my mother would be overwhelmed by herself. That I was supposed to take his place, just like he'd always envisioned. He grabbed my hand. His eyes were full of tears, I didn't recognize him. He was quiet for so long that I started to feel bad about not saying anything either.

'No, I wanted to say, I don't want to become a hairdresser, as little as my sister did, who had decided to do something else and couldn't be forced into being his successor.

'No, I wanted to say. I wanted to get up and walk out of the room. I wanted to take my heart in two hands and listen to the voice inside me saying: You don't have to, you've got a choice, you can choose to do something else. But then I stood up . . .'

'I stood up and looked down at my father, who looked lost in thought and old, a lot older than he was, and my voice trembled when I said: Yes, I'll do it, if that's what you and Mom want, yes, yes. Tears started to run down his face again and he pressed my hand even more strongly, and I stood there and knew that everything was decided.

'Something like that, *Herr* Franck, would never have happened to my nephew. Lennard sensed that he was safe, no matter what he decided to do with his life, and that he wouldn't get lost, not even in the darkest night.

'And yet, he got lost.

'And we're all guilty, just like my sister said after the funeral, no one will ever be able to free us from this responsibility, no priest, no police officer, not even you, *Herr* Franck, who was brave enough to tell my sister the truth and go along with Lennard on his final path.

'I should've picked him up and I didn't. Why are you even listening to someone like me, nothing but a miserable excuse of a man? To cut an old woman's hair at a ridiculous moment just to earn a couple more euros instead of paying attention to a kid! What do you expect someone like that to do? Throw himself off a roof out of shame? Would that bring our Lennard back?

'There's no coming back. I'd decided once and for all: I'm not going out into the rain and the storm, I'm going to cut *Frau* Haberland's hair, I'm going to pay attention to the highlights and make sure I do everything just like the last time I did her hair, I'll talk to her about the trees in the neighbourhood which cover her yard in leaves. I'll listen to her and agree with her about how rude her neighbours and their dogs are and think: it's not all that bad, Lennard's super cool, he'll just jump on his bike and pedal home, nothing will happen. What's the big deal? Nothing'll go wrong.

'Sorry, I'm a tad drunk and gravity's dragging me down. Don't worry, I'm not going to climb up on the roof or anything. Should we get another round?'

Hofmeister looked about one more time before going through the passageway to his front door. The inspector, who had accompanied him from the pub to his building, had disappeared; he probably would have come to his front door if Hofmeister had not stopped him with what most likely was an inappropriate gesture. He had put his hand on Franck's shoulder and almost pushed him against the wall.

Hofmeister braced himself against the railing. Although Franck had invited him to eat numerous times, he had declined. He just wanted to drink and straighten a few things out; at the moment, he did not really remember what exactly, but he was happy to have done so.

People did not understand his nephew at all. The police were useless. He wondered whether he had told the inspector as much. Bent forward, his hands grasping the metal rail, he tried to remember how many beers he had had. Six, seven? The cold bothered him, scratched his throat, made seeing difficult. He closed his eyes and breathed through his mouth.

He felt a gurgling in his stomach. If he made the five steps to his door, he would only need to fish the keys out of his jacket and the day would be saved. He straightened up, swayed and stretched out his arms.

'This life,' he said up into the dark sky, 'doesn't mean a thing any more when a child is cut out of your heart, you understand that? Every child that comes into the world has the right to live and you're taking that right away. Why? Who gives you the right? Then keep the child to yourself. Why are we toys? I don't want to be a toy. My sister Tania doesn't either.

'Do you know my sister Tania? She was a lovely woman. Can I tell you something?

'I'm going to tell you something because today's Sunday and the bells are ringing and people are crossing themselves and acting holy. Listen: I haven't believed in you in a long time, it's not just since you killed Lenny. Back when my school friend Jockel died, I stopped believing in you. Maybe you remember? Run over by a motorcycle. Jockel was riding his bicycle, on his way home, the biker was racing down Lindwurmstraße and swept him right off the asphalt, throwing him against a tree. Died immediately, the doctor said. No one knows if that's true. And when Evelyn died of leukaemia, I knew the priest had lied to us. No one's sitting around the tabernacle and watching out for us, or wherever it is the saviour supposedly hangs out. Evelyn was eight, and that's all she got? Really?

'And when our father suddenly fell over and didn't wake back up. Is that how your system works? No. You haven't got a system. It's all random.

'But no one gets any answers from you, do they? That's always been the case. When a mother cries her eyes out of her head, do you give her new ones?

'Today's Sunday and I didn't cross myself. I got drunk and, on top of it, on someone else's tab. I talked about Lenny, Lennard's his name actually, you knew him, you killed him. That's why no one can find the murderer. If you had the guts to come down here and introduce yourself to me, I'd grab the straight razor I inherited from my grandfather, the one with the mother-of-pearl handle, and take your scalp off. After that, I'd take off the top of your skull to see what's inside.'

Then Hofmeister yelled: 'But you don't trust yourself!'

Just as out in front of the pub Hofmeister began to wave his arms in a strange motion. He bent his upper body to the side and took a few steps away from the stairs; then he slid across the frozen snow, regained his balance and stared at the old woman who was standing in the passageway to the street.

'What are you yelling about, *Herr* Hofmeister?' She was wearing a brown coat and boots with synthetic fur and holding a black shopping bag in her hand. 'You look a real mess, come on, I'll open up for you.'

'No,' Hofmeister said. 'I still have got someone to visit.'

'You're dressed far too lightly. And you've had a bit to drink too.'

'That's true, *Frau* Henning.'

'You must've had a lot to drink, you always call me Christa.'

'Sorry.'

'Come on.' She already had the keys in her hand and was walking up the stairs. In front of the door she turned around. 'Where are you? Should I help you?'

'Did you go shopping? Today, Sunday?'

'Today I was in the mood for a pizza, so I picked up a frozen one down at the corner shop, with spinach, and a glass of plums. It's great that they're open every day. Come on, *Herr* Hofmeister, you're going to meet your death out here.'

For some reason he tilted forward, took a breath, tried to pull up the zipper of his leather jacket, which was halfway closed and had got stuck, and ran his hands across his head. 'I've got to go, enjoy your meal, Christa.'

Before she could say another word, her neighbour staggered out onto the street.

At the intersection with the 24-hour corner shop at the southern end, in front of which, as usual, a line of young and old regulars had formed, Hofmeister leant against the traffic light. Water found its way into his tattered shoes, and he suddenly felt the icy cold numbing his calves.

The light turned yellow. He crossed Erhardtstraße. Cars honked, someone cursed at him. He attempted to quicken his step, which with the slippery ground was difficult. Skidding with his sneakers, it was tough for him to keep his balance.

Wrapped up in thick coats and anoraks, the few pedestrians coming his way avoided him. Propelled by the drink and his spinning thoughts, he took the space between the pavement and the bridge railing as his own.

Impatient with the red pedestrian light at the next crossing, he crossed the street and walked on towards Nockherberg. Now and then gasped for air. Steam exited his mouth. On top of everything, for a long time he had had to pee.

He stopped in front of a pub. Inside, the lights were on. The illuminated sign next to the door said 'Raven's Head'. Hofmeister swayed his head and coughed. The movement almost caused him to soil his trousers.

He tore open the door and slammed it behind him. Three minutes later, he was back outside. He fought for a round with the door, scraped by, slipped on the step and fell onto the pavement.

He did not feel a thing. New snowflakes fell from the darkness, melted on his eyelashes; he blinked. Lying there on the ground, no one came to help him up.

For a while he held his hands in front of his face. Then he forced himself to move, crawled to the side of the building and leant back against it. He sniffed the air and wondered what was going on with him. He had lost a shoe. He painstakingly stood up and looked around.

His eyes rested on the glass case with the menu; in the bottom right-hand corner was the photo of a man. Hofmeister bent down and looked more closely, recognizing it to be an image of the deceased one handed out at funerals and similar to the one he had of his nephew. Probably the owner, he thought. The cold in his naked left foot ripped him back out of his thoughts.

Balancing his sole on the somewhat warm jeans of his right leg and against the side of the building, Hofmeister looked for his other shoe. He saw it in a heap of snow at the side of the road. The sight of it stumped him; how it had ended up there was a mystery.

After standing in place for a while and swaying, he finally managed to get on his shoe and tie the laces, before going back to tugging at his jacket's zipper. Then he angrily stuck his hands into his pockets and started off again, uphill along the winding street with the tramlines, until he reached the wall of the East Cemetery.

Once there he turned left and, after almost an hour, interrupted by multiple pauses when he thought he could no longer feel his legs, reached his sister's building.

Staggering and exhausted, he put one foot in front of the other. He had almost fallen over a second time; he could still manage to take hold of a street sign.

Hofmeister made his way along the facade metre by metre until he reached the front door. Raising his arm and pushing the buzzer cost him an unbelievable amount of strength. When he heard a voice, his head tipped forward and he bumped his forehead against the brass nameplate.

'It's me,' he said cheerlessly. 'Me, Max, alone.'

Afterwards he had no idea how he had managed to get up the stairs to the second floor. Stephan Grabbe made his brother-in-law some black tea, gave him a pair of thick wool socks and a blanket which Hofmeister wrapped around his legs. Then he sat down on the sofa, drank a cup of tea and did not say a word.

Twice within half an hour, Grabbe went into the hall and knocked on the door behind which his wife had been since the moment her mother left.

Hofmeister declined a serving of leftover macaroni casserole; though his stomach was growling, he did not feel hungry. He sat with the teacup in his hands, disappointed with his state. 'I've got to talk with her,' he said, putting the cup on the table next to the plate with the cheese sandwich Grabbe had brought him and he had ignored.

'She won't open the door.'

'Let me try.'

'Go to sleep,' Grabbe said. 'You're totally out of it. You can speak to each other in the morning.'

'Now.' Hofmeister threw the blanket onto the couch and took his socked feet to his brother-in-law in the hallway. He listened to the door, gave two long knocks and two short ones. After a minute or so, shuffling steps could be heard, the key turned in the lock. Tania Grabbe cracked open the door.

Hofmeister softly pushed Grabbe to the side and darted into the room. Tania immediately locked the door again. She casually ran her hand across her brother's cheek. She was wearing nothing but a long blue nightshirt; her hair was unkempt. She silently crawled back under the blanket, with her face to the wall.

Hofmeister stood still in the faint light of the candle burning in the window of the child's room; next to it Lennard's mother had placed a vase with a fresh white rose. The room smelt of furniture polish.

He did not move.

Cars passed by at irregular intervals; beyond that, there was no sound at all.

When Tania opened the blanket, he went to the bed, hesitated a moment then crawled inside. He put his arm around her. She quickly grabbed his hand and put her fingers in his. She held on to it tightly, as in the past when they took care of each other before they would be separated by their dreams.

That Sunday night, however, neither one of them slept.

CHAPTER SEVEN

Thirteen Years Ago

I

Suddenly the fog was there. They were facedown on their beach towels, asleep. As if being rescued from a nightmare, Maximilian was the first to wake, his face and naked upper body damp with sweat. He raised his head, turned in fright, then lay back down. He touched his sister on the shoulder; she did not react. Then, remembering their childhoods, he tapped her head with the knuckle of his index finger. She shot up, gave him a slap and let out a scream, but was unable to close her mouth. She could not believe what she had just done.

Maximilian shook his head and smiled. Whenever he had the impression that his sister, in a moment of total surprise, had catapulted herself out of the usual quiet reserve that had been there ever since she was a kid, he grew happy in an inexplicable way. He probably thought that there was a second, high-spirited girl living undiscovered somewhere inside her.

Crouching next to each other, silent, her hands in her lap, Tania needed a moment longer than her brother to understand why he was nervous.

The land and sea had disappeared behind a billowing and impenetrable grey-white, damply cool wall. It was as if the world had dematerialized in a matter of seconds and been transformed into silence.

Both Maximilian Hofmeister and Tania Grabbe sat on their towels without saying a word; they did not even trust themselves to stand—afraid that even the slightest movement would cause them to be lost.

Their eyes bored into the nothingness. It was as if someone had hidden the beach in a massive, seaweed-smelling sack that set loose an unsettling tingling sensation and covered their bodies with goose flesh. And something else triggered a previously unfamiliar anxiety in the two. While the houses, the excursion boat in the harbour nearby and the horizon seemed to have been erased and a single, snow-coloured expanse opened up before their eyes, the light—just like the sea at low tide—appeared to retreat and leave them alone in an utter absence of shadows.

Tania instinctively reached for her brother's hand; her heart beat in her throat. Maximilian was worried she would black out, as in the past, when he was around four and they were on the carousel at the Auer Dult fair—he on his mother's lap, Tania next to them—and she suddenly let out a scream, her eyes growing wide, and then fell over on her side. The operator, a friend of their parents, stopped the machine immediately. Tania woke up not even a minute later and wondered why everyone around her looked so frightened. The doctor said that there was no reason to be concerned, the girl had just had a quick shock. From then on, Maximilian worried about his sister—often when he did not even have any particular reason to.

On the fog-bathed beach, he slid behind her so that she could lean back, put his arm around her shoulder and ran his other hand through her hair.

As if relieved by the contact with her brother's lanky and familiar body, Tania began to hum, and the two of them looked out to where they thought that the North Sea was. But they could not endure what they saw through the strange, wavering curtain of a million tiny drops of water, and closed their eyes.

Tania and her brother both hoped for the same thing: that when they opened their eyes, the sea would be back in its old splendour, with gulls circling above it, greedy for forgotten crumbs.

'Keep going,' she said softly. She could feel his fingers on her scalp and hummed a vague tune.

'Do you see anything?'

'No, you?'

'I can only smell something, your hair, it smells like oranges.'

After a pause Tania said: 'We're childish.'

Maximilian fondled her hair. 'Let us be childish.' Then he added: 'And, in any event, no one's looking.'

She giggled and almost opened her eyes; she did not trust herself enough yet. 'I'm cold,' she said.

He put both of his arms around her and pulled her to himself. At that moment, a thought smashed the feeling of safety she felt in her brother's presence, and she grew incredibly scared.

She would never have expected that, in the five days she wrestled away from her everyday life upon Maximilian's urging, she would be reminded of that old wound which had been a secret pain ever since she left home and began a life that, in terms of material security, seemed incomplete and at times even miserable.

She freed herself from his embrace, bent forward and hugged her legs. With her head on her knees, she sank into herself, as she had far too often, in a whirlwind of self-loathing.

At first her brother did not consider the change important. His eyes closed, he thought Tania would just stretch her back and change her position in order to sit more comfortably. He listened in to the dull silence and wondered whether, when they were here with their parents, she had gone through something similar; he could not remember.

The last time he had been on the island had been with Yella, exactly one year ago. They had been staying with the Fehrmanns, a family he had known since he was young, and there had not been even the slightest hint of how everything would end after their return.

Overwhelmed by despair, he put his hands in front of his face, a gesture that immediately struck him as ridiculous. He knew that the images would not disappear into thin air like the village had in the fog.

He reached for his sister's shoulder but caught only air. Consumed by the strange thought of having lost his sense of orientation, he quickly opened his eyes. There she was, cowering before him, contorted and motionless, her tanned skin unnaturally pale. He could not match the tired wheezing he heard to his sister's voice.

'Tanny?' he said quietly. 'Tanny? Tanny?'

He turned his head to the right and left as if expecting to find a face that was making the disquieting sounds, or at least an indication. Feeling tense, he held his breath; he managed almost a full minute. When he exhaled he was no longer sure if he had really heard a thing. He listened. Then he understood that his sister had gone silent.

'Tanny?' he asked again. Not receiving any answer he yelled: 'Tania, good Lord!'

As if not having heard she sank even more deeply into her underworld of self-accusations and the eternal evocation of an authority for which she had no name; she did not particularly believe in God. She did not blame anyone but herself and her body for her doubt.

'What is it?' Maximilian propped himself up on his hands on the large towel and slid closer until he was touching her again. He nestled his head against hers.

'Don't be afraid.' His voice almost a breath, just like when he was a boy and would lay next to her at night to whisper that he had conquered and killed all the ghosts, that she could go to sleep and there would be funny rabbits in her dreams. Sometimes she giggled; sometimes she pressed his hand so strongly that it hurt; she begged him to come into her dreams to protect her if anything went wrong.

He had once asked his mother what his older sister was so afraid of; she did not know. And so he crawled into bed with Tania again when she asked him and swore he would not leave her the whole night long.

'Tell me,' he said. Her hair tickled his chin. 'What's wrong with you?'

At last she spoke again. 'It doesn't matter,' she said, relieved by his urgent tone of voice. 'We need to talk about you. We've been here for two days and you haven't said a thing. You've got to let it out or you'll suffocate, you know that.'

'And you? You don't let *any* thing out.'

'Don't change the subject.' Her eyes were still closed. He saw her red-painted toenails popping up out of the dull grey sand like crafty eyes. 'What happened that night when Yella left you from one minute to the next? We came here to talk.'

He bent forward and looked into her face. 'Where are you?' he asked.

'Here. And you?'

'Where you are.'

They were silent.

Then she opened her eyes. 'Should we get away from here? Simply keep on walking until we reach the sea or the harbour or the next street? What could happen?'

'I'd rather stay here,' he said.

'Why?'

'I'm tired.'

Another number of minutes passed in silence.

In-between, they believed they had noticed a change in the temperature and the light, but they were not sure. No one said a word.

The wind grew stronger, blowing bits of sand onto their naked skin, into their eyes; they rubbed them with their fingers, and listened to the whistling breeze. From the distance came a buzzing that was impossible to place.

Although they had barely moved, they hesitated to fix their eyes in any particular direction; the North Sea was to the north of the island, the mud flats to the south, Hammersee Lake to the west. This much was obvious: the coast was only about 8 kilometres away and, on a normal day, you could see it clearly, just like the more than 20-metre-high dunes with the water tower.

'Where are we?' Tania Grabbe inhaled the cold, sandy air and began to wheeze again, at first in quick jolts, then ever-more sharply, as if she would suffocate at any moment. She waved her arms and seemed to lose control. Maximilian crouched down, avoided her punches and was about to grab her when she jumped up.

She pounced forward, spun around in a circle and staggered, her arms whirling in the same circles over and over, as if she were in a cage, emitting dark, gurgling sounds. Then she went weak in the knees, swung back around, stumbled into a hole, doubled back and, out of breath, fell facedown onto the sand.

For a few seconds Maximilian imagined the fog was getting heavier and swallowing up his sister. Her silhouette began to dissolve; the yellow of her bikini grew pale and seemed to melt into her skin. The wind continued to blow sand across their bodies. She lay on the ground, arms and legs sticking out, her tousled and knotted hair studded with sand that looked dirty and like tiny little animals.

He haltingly freed himself from his torpor. He stood up and then went and kneeled by his sister, touched her carefully at the back of her head; she whimpered softly.

'Did you hurt yourself?' he asked, as he had done so often when they were kids and she had fallen off her bicycle again, but no one knew how.

She raised her head; sand trickled down her forehead. 'Lay down next to me, and tell me everything.' When he saw how she was smiling, he was overcome by a sadness that reminded him of that horrible night Yella wanted to disappear.

He would have preferred to lie back down on his towel, but he knew that his sister would not leave her spot. He had barely lain down next to her when she grabbed his hand and turned her pale face with its bits of sand to him. Her voice calmed him down.

'We don't have to go anywhere,' she said. 'Here is just as good as anywhere else.'

'Yes.'

'Are you crying?'

'No, it's just sand.'

'What did Yella do, Max?'

'That's not important any more.'

'But that's why we're here. The trip was your idea.'

'I regret it now.'

'Why?'

'Because I can see you're not doing well, and I've got to help you.'

'You don't have to help me.'

'I do.'

She smiled again. Then she cocked her head and squinted; the eyelashes of her left eye tickled the tip of his nose. When he was a boy, she had woken him up almost every day with a butterfly kiss; sometimes he was already awake and waiting.

'No one's listening.' She gripped his hand more tightly.

'You've got so much to take care of at the cafe and I tore you away from it all.'

'I'm happy that we're here. Did she cheat on you and you catch her?'

'I'm too dumb for that.'

'She admitted it to you.'

'I wanted to marry her,' Maximilian said. He had spoken so forcefully that sand sprayed into Tania's face. She wiped her cheeks quickly, like shooing away a fly.

'I know,' she said.

'The wedding rings cost 2,000 euros.'

'You showed them to me.'

'She said yes.' He could feel her breath on his face and closed his eyes for a moment. 'I'm a twat, I am blind, deaf and dumb.'

'You're my brother, I know that you're blind, deaf and dumb. You needed a whole day to figure out that the cockatiel on the curtain rod wasn't real but made out of fabric.'

'Mom told me I wasn't allowed to climb up on the chair and pet him because he'd fly away and never come back.'

'He only had one eye and didn't make a sound for hours,' Tania said.

'I was three.'

'You were four and got on Mom and my nerves by wanting to know what his name was.'

'His name was Mr Clean.'

'That was his name because Mom couldn't think of anything else and was cleaning.'

'That was mean. Where'd that bird even come from?'

'A friend of our father's brought it from Dult, he thought it'd make us happy. Mom thought it was awful and wanted to throw it away, but I said we could attach it to the window and wait to see how you would react.'

'You all took the piss out of me.'

Tania gave him a peck on the lips. 'As compensation, you were allowed to eat two *Kinder* eggs and keep the figurines.'

'I really thought the bird was real and would start singing at any moment.'

'Cockatiels don't sing.'

'How do you know?'

'Our neighbours had one,' Tania said. 'The Linners, they had two daughters, Franziska and Clara, and a cockatiel named Hansi, of course. If he made any noise at all it was a shrill chirping you could hear all the way over on Prinzregenten-straße. Don't you remember?'

'No.'

'Clara disappeared without a trace when she was around thirteen.'

'I can't remember.' He was silent until his sister pressed his hand again. 'Yella lied to me and cheated on me and I believed everything she said. Just like you guys with the bird. I'm just as gullible as I was back then.'

'No, you're not.'

'She's pregnant. Not from me. In the third month. I didn't check. She said, I've gained weight, and I believed her; she's really slim, as you know. We'd been together a year, fourteen months to be precise, and saw each other twice a week, she always spent the night at my place. I was only in her flat in Pasing once, the one she was sharing with a friend, two rooms and a nice bathroom, not enough space for the two of us if I was going to spend the night. We were a couple, we talked about the future. We'd spent Christmas together, you were there too, and Stephan, our parents. They didn't like her that much, you didn't like her at all, neither did Stephan, I don't think. I didn't care.'

'I couldn't figure her out. And our parents are always sceptical, they were that way with Stephan too.'

'That was a nice evening, Yella was happy, she told me later.'

'Keep going, Max.'

'Pregnant. In the third month. Not from me, that's obvious.'

'Who's the guy?'

'Some dude or other.'

'Where'd she get to know him?'

'I didn't ask, I wanted to know how long she'd been sleeping with him.'

'Yeah?'

'For half a year. Deaf, blind and dumb, you're right, you don't run into idiots like me every day. Six months, and I didn't notice a thing.'

'But why . . . why . . . '

'Why was she still together with me? Why didn't she tell me anything? Why the whole show? Why wasn't one guy enough for her? Why was she sleeping with two guys at the same time, or who knows how many? Why is she that kind of person? Why is she such a coward? Why is she a goddamn whore? And why and why? And why?'

He let go of his sister's hand and sat up, crossed his legs and folded his hands in his lap. Tania turned to the side and looked at him.

'No one knows why,' he said, his head lowered. He spoke haltingly, had to make an effort to finish his sentences. 'During the night, I almost vomited in front of her feet. I . . . I got a grip of myself. That evening was . . . it was different than usual, she noticed how . . . how I was looking at her. She'd got undressed . . . I didn't want to sleep with her. Tears . . . were running down her face. That's when I hit her. A reflex. Can you . . . can you understand that? Blood ran out of her nose. I hit her with . . . my fist. Why'd I hit her with . . . my fist? I don't know. She was kneeling on the bed and . . . didn't even tip over. Maybe it wasn't that strong a punch . . . I asked her what was going on . . . She got up and . . . walked into the bathroom . . . she wasn't bleeding any more when . . . when she came back. She got dressed . . . underwear, jeans, blouse . . . her shoes too, leant back her head, dabbed at her nose and . . . I was in bed, in my underwear, and . . . and I listened to her. I can listen, you know that. Right?'

'Yes.' With a slow, hesitant movement, as if she did not want to make her brother insecure, Tania sat up as well. He cast her a timid glance and then looked back at his hands.

'She didn't say she was sorry . . . or not in any way that I would have believed her. Then . . . I told her . . . I told her to fuck off.'

'You didn't ask her any questions? Why she . . . '

'No.'

'But she cheated on you and . . . '

' . . . lied to me and screwed me over; she did. And now she's dead.'

'Sorry?'

'I jumped up, she got scared . . . she went right out the door. You know how narrow the stairwell is. Yella tripped . . . I wasn't really looking . . . no light. She fell three floors . . . head over heels . . . I think she broke her neck.'

'What are you saying, Max?'

'She wasn't alive by the time I got downstairs . . . I felt for her pulse, there wasn't any . . . her head was turned . . . little blood.'

'Good God.'

'I waited for someone to open the door. No one came, everything was quiet. Three in the morning. The other tenants were sleeping the sleep of the righteous. I kept on waiting . . . next to her . . . the dead Yella. The light went back out. I was crouching on the last stair, in the dark, and . . .'

'And then? What did you do?'

'I carried her off,' Hofmeister said to his hands.

'Where?'

'Away.'

'Where?'

'Far away.'

'Far away?' She wanted to say more.

At that moment the strong offshore wind tore the impenetrable wall of fog apart like blotting paper and a few seconds later showed them the shimmering blue sea, the coast, the little houses, the water tower and the lighthouse, whose signal was not for sailors but island guests—if it was dark already and they had got their directions mixed up after too many shots of *Küstennebel*.

On that late afternoon, however, the lighthouse did not offer the man or the woman sitting alone on the sand any point of reference at all.

They had fallen out of the world.

CHAPTER EIGHT

Thirteen Years Ago

II

'Da Gino', where the two siblings had eaten pizza as kids, was right across from the Fehrmanns' guesthouse. Maximilian could have sworn that they were eating at the same table as the last time they had been, when their parents had told them that they would no longer be coming to the island. The almost ten-hour train and ferry ride had become too taxing, they wanted to spend the money they had saved for short trips to South Tyrol or Lake Garda instead, and, as far as their father was concerned, a trip or two to a motocross race. Nevertheless, he would be happy to know his children would stay true to the island and continue to spend their holidays there.

'You cried that evening,' Tania said.

'No way.'

'You thought we would never come here again.'

Maximilian took the last bite of his pizza *diavolo* and looked on to the street. Two young boys were recklessly riding their bicycles in circles and making motor sounds.

With a touch of surprise, he pushed the porcelain plate to the side. He had not thought he was that hungry and that he would even manage to finish the crust which was spilling over the edge. As for his salad, he had only eaten the tomato edges and cucumber slices. And, to be honest, he had only ordered it because his sister had insisted.

For her part, she contented herself with a tuna salad and pizza bread with garlic and thyme. While eating they talked about their parents, exchanged a couple of memories, silently looked at the tourists walking along the promenade, toasted each other—Tania drank white wine, Maximilian a wheat beer—and avoided any mention of what had happened that afternoon.

Even on their way back from the beach they had not exchanged a single word; they had just gone to their respective rooms and shut the doors. Maximilian laid down on his bed and immediately fell asleep, haunted by crazy dreams filled with strangers, while Tania sat at the small, round table in front of the window and tried to convince herself that everything her brother had told her was a ludicrous, unfathomable lie.

An hour later, she knocked on his door and persuaded him to go out to dinner at their favourite restaurant. Their bodies cast long shadows as they crossed the street.

In the meantime, they were the last guests. All the others were on the beach, marvelling at the sunset, just like every evening, well equipped with *prosecco*, beer and their mobile phones.

Gino stayed open until midnight. After a while, he would often sit down with his favourite guests from the south, offering them free *grappa* or Averna and telling them about when he ran a pub in east Munich, stories which over the course of the years had not really grown any more complex and from time to time even got on the Hofmeisters' nerves as well as those of their children; they had enough of their own material to talk about.

In Mathilda Hofmeister's eyes, however, Gino had a Mastroianni-like charm that, especially up there in the cold north, was impossible to withstand, nor were you allowed to.

Whenever she said things like that, Josef Hofmeister would cast his wife a glance that, in Tania's mind, sitting at the table next to her brother, expressed nothing but his utter doubt in her possessing any kind of healthy common sense whatsoever.

That evening, Gino Sandri, the son of a musician and a Venetian baker, did not find the silence between the two guests he had known for at least three decades to be an invitation to ask them how they were or to make a witty observation about the temperamental weather. On the contrary, he thought he could feel a dark tension between the two, hear a series of jarring notes and echoes from an ominous past. After a while, without being asked, he silently brought them two plates of homemade *tiramisu*.

'You're scaring me,' Tania said quietly.

'Now you know why I wanted to come here with you,' Maximilian said.

She looked towards the open door. Gino was out on the terrace, smoking, and looked lost in his thoughts. 'What did you do with her? With her body?'

Before he could respond, the waitress came to their table. Silke, a woman in her early thirties, regularly worked for Gino from June to September before going back to her hometown of Emden to be a cashier at a cinema. She asked if everything was OK and if they wanted anything else. They said no, and Silke carried the empty dishes and the mostly untouched salad back to the kitchen.

'I simply did it,' Maximilian said.

'What? What did you do?'

As if wanting to show them how tactful he was, Gino turned his back.

'Into the boot and then off.' Maximilian was bent forward, arms on his thighs. 'I didn't have any particular destination in mind, it just showed up on its own.'

He stopped speaking, seemed to be thinking about something intensely. With a nervous movement, he ran a hand through his dishevelled hair which he seemed to be letting grow longer, something that surprised her.

'There wasn't a lot of traffic. I didn't run in to anyone else on the Autobahn for a long time. Suddenly I knew where I wanted to go. By the time I got off the motorway and was driving through the villages, lights were already on in a few of the houses. Early morning, cows out in the fields, you know the place.'

'What place, Max?' She cocked her head to look into his eyes; he seemed to be even more bent over.

'The area around Lake Walchen,' he said, without returning her stare. 'I stopped on the southern edge, where the current's strongest. Where the boy drowned, the one who could supposedly swim so well. We were there, you remember? You'd taken me with you to see your girlfriends, I wanted to watch football instead. That's when the accident happened. I've never forgotten the landscape around there. Sometimes I've even dreamt of the boy treading water, no chance left. I wasn't there, you weren't either, we were in an ice-cream shop, you remember?

'Now I do, for the first time since . . .'

'Her body sunk immediately. I'd wrapped it in a blanket.'

'What kind of blanket?'

'In the old, red-wool blanket Mom gave me at some point because I was always so cold.'

Now he looked at her. His lost smile, Tania thought, did not have to do with her. 'And then I drove back home, the sun was just going up, and I remember I looked in the rear-view mirror to see if anyone was following me. There was no one there. It was like everyone was waiting for me to be gone again before they left their houses. Like the building where I live. Everyone just kept on sleeping until I'd taken the body away and cleaned up the blood, that's when they woke up. You just can't explain it any other way.'

She observed how he moved his upper body backwards and forwards, how his chin fell to his chest. As if he was going into a trance. She was afraid he would topple out of his chair and reached out her hand. He hesitated, then took it and gently placed it onto the tabletop.

The touch of his cold, bony hand frightened her, but she did not want to say the wrong thing: she wanted to say that she would accompany him to the police and stay by his side, no matter what.

She did not manage to get the words across her lips. Then she thought she was not allowed to pass such judgement and instead had the duty to protect him, to comfort him and to free him from the clutches of his interior life.

Looking at her brother, she saw nothing but a bundle of anxiety which she had always hoped he had got rid of on becoming an adult.

She said: 'Tell me about her, I know so little about her. On Christmas she was a bit quiet and then I saw her maybe two more times. Once, the three of us were together in a bar in Schwabing, at the Old Tankard.'

'At the Old Stove,' Maximilian corrected her. The movement cost him some effort. He had just about finished his beer and wanted a second one. That took a while. 'She doesn't drink, because of her figure. She works at a modelling agency, her friend Kira had set her up with the gig. They both were from Berlin. Didn't I tell you all that?'

'You did. And that she lives in Pasing.'

'Together with Kira in a two-bedroom flat. I visited her there once, otherwise she always came over to mine. Tuesdays and Thursdays, at eight-thirty, that was what we'd agreed. Twice a week, not more. Apparently she had a lot to do, she didn't talk about it much. Sometimes she mentioned appointments and receptions, she had to go and look good, that's how she made her money. I wanted to marry her, really, I made her an offer, she said yes. Nothing came of it. She switched to Dr Erker.'

'Who's that, Max?' Listening to him grew more and more difficult. She thought about suggesting a walk in the dunes. Perhaps that would relax them both, make talking easier and quiet the beat of their thoughts. Then she decided against it. No one was bothering them there in the restaurant, and Maximilian did not give the impression of wanting to step outside again unless it would be to go back to his room at the guesthouse.

'The father of her child,' he said. 'Most likely. There was a photo of the two of them on her mobile, I sent it to him with a note. *Love forever*. Maybe it made him happy, that would've been fine with me.'

'You kept her mobile phone?'

'Yes.'

'And the police didn't come to see you?'

'Her mobile's a piece of scrap at the recycling centre in Thalkirchen, it can't be located any more, it's not sending out any more signals.' He leant back and crossed his arms. 'All taken care of. But before that I sent the message with the photo.'

Tania was more concerned about other things—for example, whether or not her brother had planned the young woman's death, as meticulously as he had got rid of all the traces.

'I couldn't tell you where Yella got to know him. That was six months ago. He's got a law firm. Thanks to the phone book, I know where he lives too. She flitted back and forth between the two of us for six months. His family lives in Bogenhausen. I doubt they met up there, probably in a hotel. Yella from Berlin. At some point, she only started to see me on Thursdays. I wanted to marry her anyway. Did you ever think your brother was so dumb? Yeah, of course you did. That's fine. It's not my fault she's dead, you've got to believe me, I will not let myself be responsible for that.'

'You don't have to,' Tania said, feeling uneasy. 'She fell, right?'

He grabbed his glass, lifted it to his mouth, put it back down. 'Should I tell you something else? On the way here, I threw the rings out the train window, you'd just fallen asleep. I cracked the window and that was that. Two thousand euros, scattered across East Friesland. You want another glass of wine?'

Incapable of saying a word, she nodded. What she was hearing sounded like the ghostly confession of a stranger who had happened to sit down at her table and not the voice of her brother whom she had known for twenty-seven years. He had just confessed a crime—it had to do with nothing other than the elimination of a person who had died under mysterious circumstances—and made her an accessory. What was he expecting from her?

He waved the waitress over nonchalantly and in a good-natured tone—'If it's cool, Silke . . .'—ordered another Riesling and another wheat beer. He waited until the drinks were on the table before raising his glass and toasting his sister. 'To your health,' he said.

She did not like the taste of the wine, or maybe it just tasted different than the one before. She noticed her brother looking at her but did not know how to respond.

'Do you think I'm a criminal?' he asked.

'I don't know . . . no . . .'

'I'm not going to surrender.'

At first she did not know what he meant.

'Didn't you see the photo in the paper?' he asked.

'What kind of photo?'

'Of Yella. The police are looking for her.'

The longer the conversation went on, the more unnerving the fact that she was a part of it became. 'I don't understand,' she said. 'I must've seen the photo. Our parents, too. When was it?'

'Ten days ago, or two weeks, in the local section, Kira reported her missing.'

'Who's Kira?'

'Her friend, the one she lives with, I told you a second ago.'

'Right.' Tania had forgotten her name.

'I went to see her,' Maximilian said. 'We talked.'

He's lying, she thought. For some reason or other, he makes things up, and at last she wanted to know why. For some time already, a question had been on the tip of her tongue; she could not let herself forget it.

'Half a year ago, Yella told her we were through. After that, she never mentioned my name again. Kira told the police as much too. The best thing is that she doesn't know my surname. I'm Max and I'm a hairdresser. Nothing else. I've bet on the police knowing about me anyway though—they're clever over there at the CID. If you type Max and hairdresser into the computer, I come up pretty quickly. In fact, the police were already there, questioned me, wanted to know why I hadn't responded to the report in the paper, I told them I hadn't read it, and on top of it we hadn't been in contact for half a year, she'd dumped me. That was it. They left. Ever since then, it's been quiet.'

'But she had come to see you,' Tania said. 'Someone had to have seen her.'

'She only came once a week in the evening, and of late, only every two weeks. No one saw a thing.'

'It's hard for me to believe you, Max.'

'Why not?'

She did not have an answer. She thought about that afternoon when the fog had surprised her and forced her to stay put, and how she had been overcome by a sudden fear that almost made her lose her mind; and then about the fact that her brother was entrusting her with a secret that almost upset her more than her inner confusion. And now even more details were coming to light.

Looking at her brother, she did not detect the slightest hint that he was just experiencing a kind of temporary mania or playing some kind of cryptic game that, for whatever reason, he was using to wind her up.

Furthermore, that was one thing her brother had never been: a storyteller, someone who tried to make themselves more interesting by telling tales, a man who enjoyed playing. All of a sudden, it occurred to her that that had been true even when he was a kid; he had always seemed to be lost in his thoughts, a little bored, but never gave any indication as to what he wanted to do instead.

'Why are you looking at me like that?' he asked.

'I'm totally stumped.' Then the question came back to her, and she asked him despite her reservations. 'Tell me why you hit Yella. Why didn't you just tell her to go? You're not someone who hits women.'

'I lied to you,' he said.

Hofmeister took a long drink of his wheat beer, put the glass down, inhaled deeply then took another drink. After that he wiped the back of his hand across his mouth—a gesture Tania had never seen him make before. He crossed his arms again and fixed her with a challenging and unbelievably cold glance.

'If you're asking me why I didn't just tell her to go, well, let me tell you: I did. I stood in front of her and she got scared, I saw it, and I told her to fuck off, right there and then, and that if she ever crossed paths with me again I would beat her, in public too. It worked. She got dressed, still wanted to say something, but I forbid her from opening her mouth. She grabbed her purse, looked at me with her phoney eyes and went to the door. She opened it up and turned around once more. I was standing there in my boxer shorts, barefoot. And you know what she said? In all seriousness? "I'm really sorry." Of all the words in the world you can say at a moment like that, she chose the absolute worst. That's when I knew something was about to happen.

'I didn't react in any way.

'She went into the stairwell, it was dark, but she didn't switch on the light—the light from my flat was enough for her, I guess, the idiot. I can still see her putting her left hand on the railing and moving towards the stairs. Three steps and I was by her, she turned her head again, and I punched her forehead.

Strange sound, a dull plop. She lost her balance, swung her arms and down she went.

'And you know what was weird? Although her body and head hit the stairs or the railing or whatever, the sound of her fall was muffled. It was like she was rolling over a carpet or something. That's what I was thinking about on my way down to the ground floor where she was lying in her black jacket, all twisted up, not moving a muscle.

'But to be completely honest, Tania? I simply hadn't counted on her death. She must have made a wrong movement, or it was just bad luck. Fate. You choose.

'Now you know what really happened. If you want to report me, go ahead, you'd have the right. I'm a kind of murderer.'

He heaved a sigh that could be heard out on the street. Gino and his help, who were talking outside, cast their guests a quick glance.

'Forgive me for not telling you the truth from the beginning.' This time it was Maximilian who reached for her hand; she almost pulled it away out of a sense of revulsion she had never felt before.

Afterwards, for a long time, they were both silent.

In the meanwhile, Tania tried not to think about anything.

Maximilian appeared to have forgotten everything he had said in the restaurant and that afternoon on the beach. It was as if the fog had moved into his mind and wrapped all the certainties, lies, images and memories in merciful cotton.

He felt pleasantly freed from a weight he had wanted to be rid of for a long time and whose causes he no longer cared about.

It would take thirteen years for him to be overcome by boundless remorse.

He nodded to Gino and paid the bill.

Giving them their change, Gino refrained from offering them any more *tiramisu*. He watched the two siblings cross the dark street, hand in hand, enveloped by silence. He imagined having already seen them like that as children—two allies on the path through life's dark woods. Once again Sandri thought of his sister who had decided to move to a far-away continent, and he called over to Silke to bring him a double Averna over ice cream.

'Should I stay with you tonight?' Tania asked in the guesthouse hallway. She wished she could express all the things rioting within her.

'That would be really nice,' Maximilian said quietly.

They lay down on the narrow bed in their clothes, but barefoot, Maximilian on the side of the wall, wrapped in his sister's arms, while she continued to sniff at his hair which smelt of sand and hope for a miracle or some kind of redemptive and magic word from the wall.

She had only wanted to speak with Max about her incomplete, aimless life, about her almost thirty-five years which, for over the last ten, had concealed a disappointment every month and made her doubt her devotion, the malice of fate, the promise of happiness in which she had placed her trust since the moment she first got her period. That time was gone. From now on, she would simply age into childlessness and there was no consolation, no compensation.

She had not confided any of that to her brother. On that spontaneous trip to the island, she did not want to remain silent with the one person who would understand her. In a bashful way, she had even been a little happy about being able to talk.

But Max had his own plans.

Max had brought a horrible secret to their childhood island.

That afternoon, he had wiped out her old life and forged a new one from which there was no escape—just like her empty future.

She had become the accessory to a crime, an accomplice to a man she would never have thought capable of such an act. A violent lie weighed her down while simultaneously turning her into a liar, as she would not betray her brother under any circumstances.

For that night she understood this much: whatever truth there was in what Max had told her, no matter how the investigations and other police things went—she would not know a thing. If her brother would end up needing an alibi, she would provide him with one; she would do everything she could to make sure he did not end up in jail.

What else? she wondered, temporarily forgetting her own lost state.

'Sleep, my dear, go to sleep,' she whispered.

He wanted her to tell him a tale in which people could fly like storks and no one had to dream themselves dead.

'Sleep, my dear, go to sleep,' he whispered.

She wanted him to tell her a tale in which Lennard was still alive and collecting wondrous mussels on the beach of Juist.

CHAPTER NINE

Faces in the Mirror

On the list of those people whose mobile phones were logged in close to the school as well as to where the body was later found the night of Lennard's disappearance were the names of three men and one woman.

According to the findings of André Block's special unit, two brothers—the architects Marcus and Heiner Glenk—were visiting their mother on Schlierseestraße, just a few hundred metres away from Asam Gymnasium. Afterwards, they took her to dine in one of their favourite Bavarian restaurants in Grünwald and after that over the Grünwald Bridge, past Höllriegelskreuth S-Bahn station to Pullach, where they lived in a semi-detached house not far from Jakobus Church. Witnesses from the pub and a neighbour confirmed the brothers' times, but the investigators were unable to establish any connections whatsoever to the Grabbe family.

As to Bettina Zielke, known as Betty, the possession of a mobile in the relevant time period led to a charge of the illegal practice of prostitution and insulting a law-enforcement official the fifty-nine-year-old had referred to as a 'crazy nit-picker'.

Betty maintained that she had jumped in for a sick friend with the two gentlemen at Spitzingplatz and in Höllriegelskreuth, and for the first time. For 'reasons of privacy', she did not want to give her friend's name. To her benefit, thanks to their unproductive results in the Lennard Grabbe case, Block's inspectors had no time for sideshows and, in any event, were not responsible for pimping. Their colleagues in the department for organized crime said they were familiar with Betty—above all, because she offered special prices for Turkish men and those with an Arabic background, which she considered her 'personal contribution to integration and the propagation of love in times of general hatefulness'. In her own special way, a colleague said to Block, Betty was on a mission which, though illegal, was not harming any one; on the contrary.

It was not the first time Block had observed that, occasionally, interpretations of the law within the department were surprisingly divergent.

With the third person whose mobile had been located in the relevant area Jakob Franck set up a meeting at the Brückenwert pub below the Grünwald Bridge, along the Isar canal—on the other side of which the body of the eleven-year-old student had been found in a patch of woods.

As to why he had decided to leave his flat on Weißenseestraße and take, as he himself called it, a stroll through his neighbourhood in the pouring rain and icy wind, Siegfried Amroth explained to the investigators that he had intended to go to the supermarket by the new housing estate to buy bread, cheese and cold cuts. Halfway across the former Agfa grounds, he realized he was so wet that he turned around and went home to put on a few dry, and warm, things.

After that, he had 'got the desire to walk through the rain, just like when I was a boy', before taking off to meet up with his friends at the pub. And so he had grabbed his sturdy umbrella and set out one more time, this time 'vaguely' in the direction of Giesinger Station. From there he intended to take the suburban rail to East Station and switch to the S7. Then, at Höllriegelskreuth, as usual, he would take the bus to the Brückenwirt or be picked up by a friend.

'Probably because of the terrible weather or because I suddenly didn't want to be in the stuffy train,' as recorded in the files, that evening Amroth decided yet again to change direction and go back to Weißenseestraße. He took his coal-coloured Opel out of the garage and around forty minutes later arrived at the Brückenwirt.

According to the investigators it was 8.05 p.m. or 8.15; neither the pub owner nor the waiter could remember. 'Curiously,' Amroth had said, 'all of my other four friends had used public transport,' and they all reached the pub at just about eight, right before Amroth arrived.

He maintained that he had neither seen the boy that evening nor knew him at all, or at best 'in passing'. For it turned out that, until one year ago, the Grabbes had lived on Untersbergstraße, which crosses Weißenseestraße near the park. Tania and Stephan Grabbe could not remember the sixty-four-year-old insurance representative, but Amroth mentioned having seen the boy frequently playing football in the park. He never spoke with him.

The investigators could not find any witnesses who had ever seen them together. There was insufficient evidence for a search order allowing them to have a closer look at Amroth's Opel; he would not allow Block and his colleague Holland to have a look at the car's interior or boot. 'It's my right, and I take it seriously,' he said at the station.

As Franck fundamentally tended to take people seriously and, regardless of what they might have done, unconditionally conceded them their rights, he had to control himself whenever someone refused him, the investigator—who needed all the help he could get and who scrupulously followed his official duties—a request by insisting on a right that no one would ever have disputed.

That being said, in a murder case Franck did not believe any one was free of suspicion, even if they had only touched the most distant circles of the victim's life for a single second.

The older Franck had grown in his job, the more incomprehensible the behaviour of people who took themselves more seriously than death became.

'There is something I must ask you immediately,' Siegfried Amroth said. 'You called me because your former colleague—I've forgotten his name—gave you my number. Is he allowed to do that? You are no longer on duty. Or am I getting confused?'

Sitting upright on the wooden bench near the coat-check, Franck exuded an enormous sense of calm in the crowded, noisy pub. 'Thank you for asking. I would've given you the answers to your questions on my own. Thank you for being open to meeting up as well.'

'I like to come here, I know the people, in summer it's ideal.' Amroth smoothed flat his Loden jacket, which had a blue silk pocket square peeking out of the breast pocket; beneath it he wore a white shirt and jeans. A fit man in his early sixties, he seemed to be sporty and to pay attention to his weight.

Franck noticed his carefully cut fingernails which fit his well-groomed appearance, just like his carefully trimmed three-day beard and his short, dark-blonde hair, parted to the side. On the cardigan with the staghorn buttons and the green lining, there was not a single piece of lint to be seen. Upon coming inside, the pub owner had greeted Amroth by hand; the waiter and Amroth were on informal terms.

'I'm retired, that's true,' Franck said. 'Nevertheless, now and again I do some work with the criminal investigation department.'

'Really. And what exactly?' Amroth raised his eyebrows and made a curious face, which the inspector found contrived; for reasons that he would later come to express, Franck had to admit that his attitude towards the conversation was objective only to a limited degree.

Franck picked up the pen he had in front of him and drew a line straight down the page of the unlined notepad he had pulled from his pocket, like the pen, just in case. 'When there is a violent death,' he said, 'I deliver the news to the relatives.'

Amroth drank almost greedily from his beer, as if the words had parched his throat. 'And so what do you do? Do you have some kind of special training for that? How do you learn something like that?'

'I also visited the parents of the boy who was murdered, Lennard.'

'Full respect.'

'My colleague André Block, the one who questioned you, told me that you only knew the boy in passing, you were neighbours on Weißenseestraße.'

'Talked to each other a couple of times, not even worth mentioning.' Again Amroth took a long drink of his beer. 'All these questions have been answered. I thought you wanted to meet me so that I could tell you about the area because you believe the murderer could be hiding somewhere, camouflaged as a normal neighbour, and because you have more time for such probes than your colleagues do. That's more or less what you told me on the phone. But now you are conducting an interrogation. What exactly do you want from me? I don't have anything to do with this matter.'

On the right side of his book Franck wrote the word *matter*.

Amroth leant forward. 'What are you writing there? What does that have to do with the line?'

'Memory aids.' Franck had ordered a small lager; he wanted to drink but did not care for the taste. Every time he looked past Amroth into the room, the people talking over one another and their gestures distracted him—for the most part men, by the window two older couples, next to them two women around fifty, drinking wine spritzers, passing photos back and forth and making comments. No one was speaking in a particularly loud voice but occasionally Franck almost wanted to cover his ears.

'Once again.' The man in the traditional jacket pointed to the notepad. 'Please stop playing the official. You have no authority. We are sitting here to talk, nothing more. If I get the feeling that you're playing a game with me, I'll get up and go. This isn't a threat, I'm just saying what I think. It's tragic what happened to the boy, incomprehensible why I'm in the crosshairs. I am not responsible for the police's failures, and I certainly will not be the sacrificial pawn.'

Maybe it was just the one voice that was so difficult to put up with, Franck thought, the cultivated southern German of the model citizen seated across from him.

'You are neither in the crosshairs,' Franck said, 'nor would anyone like to see you as a sacrificial pawn. We are here, as you rightfully said, to talk. Once again, I would like to stress that I know how to appreciate your having agreed to meet. Every bit of information can help, every tiny observation could open a new door. Would you like to help me, *Herr* Amroth?'

'Everything I know I shared with your colleagues.'

'In the protocol, it says that you vaguely made your way in the direction of Giesinger station. What do you mean by "vaguely"?'

'What did I say? Vaguely? There's no way that I said that, never ever.'

'You signed the protocol.'

'Of course I signed it, or else it would not be valid. I cannot remember the word "vaguely". The matter took place a long time ago.'

'Two-and-a-half months,' Franck said. 'The weather was terrible that evening, which, however, did not stop you from taking a walk.'

'I like to go for walks. I need air, quiet too. As you know, I'm an insurance representative, I sit half a day in the office, the other half in the car or with clients. I talk a lot in closed rooms. It's understandable that I need to get out at times. Or is that difficult to grasp somehow?'

'What is certain is that you were close to Asam Gymnasium that evening.'

After a pause in which he took another drink and stared ahead as if lost in his thoughts, Amroth put the glass down on the coaster and raised his index finger. 'Obviously I did not make myself clear before, which is why I will now repeat: there will be no interrogation at the Brückenwirt pub. Is that explicit enough? No interrogation, a talk. If it is impossible for you to have a talk which is not an interrogation—because you continue to play the cop or because your colleagues have a bone to pick—then I ask that, for courtesy's sake, you pay the whole bill, pack up your secretive pad and pen and say goodbye.

'I am stating this as clearly as I am so that there aren't any misunderstandings. At the police station on Hansastraße I answered all the questions to the best of my ability, even when I was just about ready to call a lawyer. Some of the questions were simply outrageous, completely inappropriate—they were suggestive, to be precise. Your colleagues thought they finally had a clue to the murderer just because my mobile was logged in around the scene of the crime.

'How many other mobiles were logged in the area? No one answered that for me. I wasn't the only one, that much is clear. Case closed.

'I fulfilled my duty. I got in touch in accordance with the rules as soon as I found the official letter in my mailbox. I took almost an entire day off to listen to things that, in my opinion, have nothing to do with this case.

'I said to myself, "These people are just doing their job." Towards the end of the session, however, they began to become tedious, I must admit, and that was the moment I thought, "Now I've got to notify my lawyer." Which I did not do.

'I signed the protocol, you're right, after reading it all the way through, almost forty pages, if I remember correctly. Then I left the building the free man I was when I walked in. And you will not be able to limit my freedom in any way.

'Have I expressed myself clearly enough so that we can from now on deal with each other in a civilized fashion?'

'I did not state that you were in the area of the school the night Lennard Grabbe was murdered on account of the boy.' Franck lowered his voice. When he was on the squad, he had often gleaned information from the contrast between the stridently presented *Suada* of a self-important witness and his own, hushed tones.

'The crime of the poor boy's death is something of marginal interest to me in my discussion with you. I am interested in *you*, as I told you on the phone. You sparked my interest. And as far as the concept of freedom is concerned: as opposed to my investigative colleagues, I am allowed to express presumptions without any fear of legal repercussions. I can assume that you will lie. I am not obliged to objectivity. I am meeting you on a personal level. At that point you are no longer able to handle me, you can simply get up and go, I have absolutely no claims on you, and you do not have to fear being taken into custody. Are we agreed?'

'Why are you saying all this to me? Are you trying to intimidate me?'

'Your mobile was logged in to the cell tower which is closer to the school than to the suburban rail station where you wanted to get the S-Bahn before deciding to get your car instead.'

'Are you starting up again? Are you trying to provoke me? Do I need to notify a lawyer because of you?'

'I don't know,' Franck said.

His response took the strength out of the insurance representative's inner gale. He placed his hands on his lapel, tugged and seemed as if he had to hold on. The inspector's unblinking stare made him shake his head a number of times. Amroth contorted his mouth into a sneer which was meant to be superior but only betrayed insecurity.

'You never wanted to have anything to do with these things either,' Franck said, carefully letting a silence grow between the two of them. He liked how Amroth, incapable of hiding how much the past haunted him even when confronted by nothing more than a hint, chewed on his every word and how his self-confidence had shrivelled to the size of a pocket square.

In an extensive late-night call, Block had mentioned a number of details. Franck had continued to ask questions until he was convinced that his ex-colleague had not overlooked a single item—at least as far as the verifiable facts in connection with the actual search went. As for Franck, the question as to whether all the statements they had collected until now actually corresponded to the truth when placed into other contexts remained completely open.

During murder investigations without any suspects or clear evidence, often every new perspective held crude but decipherable secrets and, if lucky, completely useable surprises. For the exploration of remote possibilities, the investigators had to put in an unbelievable amount of overtime—that or they asked one of their own, now retired, who happened to be blessed with a lot of time.

Franck pulled out a red folder from the shoulder bag he had placed on the bench next to him, laid it on the table and placed his folded hands on top. 'A few years ago, you were arrested for being a notorious flasher in the English Garden. You were also known as a voyeur, you watched children in the schoolyard, approached them, gave them gifts. You secretly took photographs at swimming pools. Nevertheless, you were never convicted, not even charged, your lawyer was good, and you showed remorse. Until the next incident, that is. Witnesses claim to have seen you around Asam Gymnasium several times, speaking to students. I am convinced that you were in contact with Lennard Grabbe, quite probably on the day of his death as well.'

Amroth slammed the wooden table. 'Lies!' he yelled. 'You're a liar.'

Franck found the guests' abrupt silence to be a blessing.

Aside from Franck and the two women at the next table who for a minute interrupted their exchange of family photos and cast the agitated man frightened looks, no other guest noticed the change in Amroth's face. Sitting with his back to the rest of the pub, he flew into a rage that seemed to discolour his skin and throw his expressions into disarray.

He braced his wrists on the edge of the table and stretched his crooked fingers as if wanting to strangle someone. Trying to temper his voice, all that came out was a hoarse croak that sanded down his words.

'I will hold you to account,' Amroth managed to splutter. Then he paused and observed the inspector, who just looked at him calmly, schooled by hundreds of similar moments. 'They will cut your pension, you will have to go before a court, you will not insult a respectable citizen with impunity.

'What you are alleging is scandalous. You consider me a paedophile and are accusing me of little Lennard's death too. He could have been a star football player, in my opinion. But that's unimportant now. What you just did is a crime. We are here in public and you have pilloried me. The police should never have accepted a person like you. You are a disgrace to your profession and, aside from that, a detestable fellow citizen. I am going to pay now and go, and tomorrow morning I will inform my lawyer. I will probably go to the press as well so that people in this city will be warned of who you are.'

Franck took note of the mute boiling. Then he reached for his pen and on the left side of the line wrote the words *star football player*. He laid his pen parallel to it, looked at the man across from him without showing any kind of emotion at all, and waited. Amroth attempted to grin, then let it go; his upper body jerked impatiently.

'The best thing for you to do,' Franck said, 'would be to give your lawyer my number, then I can talk with him directly as to how to proceed.'

'What does that mean?' The insurance representative finally relaxed his hands. He frantically turned his head right and left to see if anyone was watching him; then for a while he just nodded. 'Do you think you can intimidate me? You don't stand a chance. I'll finish you.'

'Then let me explain the situation to you: nothing you have told me sounds so convincing that I can exclude you from suspicion. Do not say anything, *Herr* Amroth, just listen.

'You knew Lennard Grabbe better than you let on to my colleagues. You knew which school he attended, and you waited for him out front—there will be evidence of that. You watched Lennard play football and noticed that he was indeed excellent.

'One moment, it's not your turn, *Herr* Amroth. It would be a good idea for you to listen, then you would get a reasonable— or to use your word—*vague* idea of how my colleagues will meet you during the next round of questioning.

'I will find a witness that saw you on the night or on the day of Lennard's death in his presence, I will ask every single person whose statements are already in the protocol one more time.

'And as far as you are concerned, I am convinced that you accepted to meet me not because I asked you for help but because you wanted to learn something about the state of the investigations. You wanted to hear if you were still coming up as the stalker of a murdered child. Let me give the answer myself: you've been discovered. Give your lawyer a call, he has probably been waiting for a call from you for days. What do you think?'

At that moment the waiter arrived, asked if they wanted another round and chummily laid his hand on the regular's shoulder. Amroth winced, almost imperceptibly. He indecisively looked at his glass where only a flat bit of beer remained. Without saying a word, he decided on another. Franck ordered a coffee.

'All good, Sigi?' the waiter asked.

'All good, Chris,' Amroth answered. Shortly thereafter he looked at Franck and said: 'He used to be an animal keeper, Chris, the waiter, then he lost contact with people. You understand? He trained gibbons how to play with balls, he built them frames to climb, he sang with them—gibbons don't sing all that frequently. Chris wanted to teach them songs, 'Happy Birthday' and such, to entertain visitors and make them aware of the fact that animals are at risk of extinction. The gibbons liked him. Whenever one of the young ones would get ill, he'd spend the night at the zoo . . .

'Chris spent more time with the gibbons than with his wife. She divorced him. He took his guitar into the pen with him and played for the animals. Not good. They let him go. Now he's a waiter and all day long is in contact with people, people he doesn't really like, with a few exceptions.

'You cannot ask about his past, otherwise his mood changes, and he tends to get depressed. He spent his fiftieth birthday last year at the zoo, alone and ignored. No one knows that, just me, he trusts me. He skulked through Hellabrunn for five hours in a houndstooth hat and sunglasses, and do you know what he says? He says he did not visit the gibbons, he avoided them because they would have recognized him and he would've been ashamed. He told me he would've broken out in tears, right there, in public.

'Do you know what I think? I think he lied to me. He was definitely with the apes. Why do I think so? Because he seemed happy when he came here and served us—he didn't give anything away; but when late that night—all the other guests had already gone and Hubert, that's the pub owner, was outside with a friend smoking—he told me about his trip and over and over again mentioned how he hadn't visited the gibbons, it was clear. I also learnt that it was his birthday just that night, it was shortly after midnight, once it was over already. That's what he's like, Chris . . . '

'What am I like?' Chris placed a coffee, a little pot of milk and a lager on the table; he was wearing a bright white shirt with a red-and-black striped vest on top. He had hardly served the drinks when he crossed his hands behind his back and asked if they wanted anything else.

Amroth turned to him. 'You're a real head waiter, with your style you could even work in Vienna.'

'They've got enough of their own waiters,' Chris said, who, Franck noticed, hid his teeth when speaking and smiled with his mouth closed.

Little by little, the other guests asked for their bills. The two women, who had attempted to garner details from the men's discussion in vain, cast their last, critical glances over at the table and then left.

As per his usual, Franck added a good deal of sugar and milk to his coffee. He would have liked to smoke a cigarette as well; he always kept an open pack in his shoulder bag. Ever since giving up smoking completely some years before, he never touched more than five a week.

While Amroth silently picked up his glass and put it back down a number of times, Franck drank his lukewarm coffee with relish. He thought about the animal-loving waiter and decided to visit the zoo again. Then it occurred to him that he entertained the idea at regular intervals but, until now, had done nothing about it.

'Don't forget to call your lawyer,' he said.

'I will not be doing that.' As if disgusted by it, Amroth shoved his glass to the edge of the table.

'Don't you like your beer any more?'

'You are looking for a perpetrator and are focusing on me because I had something to do with the police in the past. Those are nasty methods.'

'Complain to your lawyer, *Herr* Amroth.'

'Be open with me: do you think I'm a murderer? A paedophile? A dangerous man? Come out with it.'

'As far as I've been informed,' Franck said, 'you are not registered as a paedophile. You observe, take photos, speak to boys—we do not know what you have saved to your computer . . .'

'Because there is nothing to know, *Herr* Ex-Inspector.'

'Perhaps. I also do not know if you're a murderer, but I by all means believe you are a dangerous man. But that doesn't need to concern you further. As you quite rightly point out, I am an ex-inspector, even if I continue to work on investigations and question people. I feel obligated to do so. When you live here and want to stick to your lies, go right ahead. I told you what will happen. The police will show up at your office at Goetheplatz and ask you to come with them. You can say no, you can babble something about your lawyer but in the end you will be sitting in the station on Hansastraße, just like before, and won't have the chance to serve up your story another time. No one believes you any more. If you're unlucky, you'll receive an arrest warrant, and the press office at police headquarters will not wait a second to say that at long last a suspect in the little Lennard murder case has been found.

'Your old life ends here at this table. Or you can pull your-self together one last time and pretend that I'm a mirror and you can see that face which for two-and-a-half months you have hated, and for good reason, but from which you no longer want to hide. Think about it until I get back.'

While washing his hands in the bathroom, Franck looked at his own by-now-old face and had a hard time handling the gouges of time; the dark circles beneath his eyes which did not have to do with insomnia or too much alcohol, but most likely sheer stress; the bushy eyebrows that darkened his glance; his narrow mouth that lacked any kind of mischievousness; his crooked shoulders that made his expensive, rather perfectly fitting dark-blue linen shirt look misshapen; his tousled head of hair.

What's all this self-flagellation about? he asked himself, wadded up the paper towel, threw it into the bin next to the sink and walked back into the pub.

'He gave me 10 euros,' Chris said, standing by the table. 'You've got to cover the rest.'

Franck paid, put on his leather jacket and bag, and made his way to the door. The waiter whizzed past him and reached for the door handle. 'One more thing,' Chris said, 'Sigi is a dear guest, but you can't believe everything he says. I never sang with the apes, I'm not totally nuts. OK?'

'OK,' Franck said.

Chris nodded and opened the door.

Two hundred metres from Brückenwirt a figure was standing in the darkness, facing the slope.

'Where was he found?' Amroth asked as the inspector came nearer.

CHAPTER TEN

'You're Almost Likeable'

Chief Inspector Elena Holland and the leader of the special unit, André Block, led the insurance representative into the interview room with the large windows through which, that Friday morning, the light fell bright and mild. In the middle of the room, three square white tables had been pushed together, on them were two water bottles and four glasses, on the right-hand wall a flat-screen TV with both a DVD and a video recorder, and on the other side of the room two flipcharts which had already been started and whose front pages were covered in writing.

The last time they questioned him, Siegfried Amroth thought, they had brought him into a narrow, windowless room lit by uncomfortable neon light. The proximity of the inspectors would have intimidated him had his lawyer not been by his side, giving him a sense of security. Even the secretary's ceaseless typing right behind his back had made him feel unreasonably nervous the whole time.

Today, on the contrary, the atmosphere seemed almost welcoming. Following the inspector's gesture, he sat down on the long side of the table on one of the eight upholstered chairs. The inspector and his colleague sat across from him. The woman, whose name he had forgotten, offered him a glass of mineral water; he declined. He would have to be patient for two, three more minutes, she explained, one of the two recording clerks was ill and therefore the other had to take care of all the actual examinations.

None of the two, Amroth noticed, had a file or paper in front of them; they just looked at him indifferently, nothing more. Yesterday, when the inspector had asked him to come in for another round of questioning, Amroth had considered informing his lawyer, Dr Fender. After thinking a moment, however, he decided that he did not want to unnecessarily make it out to be more than it was. He was innocent, that was all that mattered.

Two nights earlier, together with Jakob Franck and not far from where the young boy's body had been found, he admitted to having stopped at the Asam Gymnasium on that rainy November day as well. Out of respect for the place they were standing—he had emphasized in particular—he admitted to having lied.

Yes, he had even spoken with Lennard because he wanted to know if the student would be coming to the park on Weißenseestraße again at the weekend to play football with his friends; he, Amroth, loved to watch them, especially the exceptionally talented Lennard.

Yes, they had spoken often about football in general and a possible career for Lennard in particular.

Yes, he knew where Lennard and his parents moved after leaving Untersbergstraße.

Yes, he had liked the boy because he exuded a zest for life and always had a good word to say about him.

And no, he had never touched the boy in any illicit way nor did he ever want to seduce or coax him into anything.

No, on the evening of Lennard's disappearance he did not visit the school a second time, he had been there in the afternoon and spoken with Lennard, afterwards nothing else.

Then he and Franck had said goodbye to each other in the car park near the Brückenwirt. That he would soon be receiving a call from the station was clear.

Block wanted to know what he understood 'a good word' to mean. In the meanwhile, the recording clerk had arrived—Amroth guessed early fifties, black ponytail, denim jacket on top of a white blouse—and had begun to write on her laptop; next to the computer was a notebook and a pen. Every now and again—the reason remained mysterious to Amroth—she quickly scribbled down a note.

Seeing as that he assumed Franck had shared every detail of their entire talk at the Brückenwirt and his admission thereafter by the patch of woods to his former colleague—in retrospect he had suspected that Franck had secretly recorded their conversation—Amroth did not pay too much attention to being precise. He increasingly felt the need to contest and suggest to the, in his opinion, overly motivated investigator that their duty as public servants paid by the people consisted in catching homicidal criminals and not in interrogating innocent fellow citizens.

He expressed himself such about twenty minutes after they had begun. Block immediately took a short break. To him, Amroth appeared nervous and unable to concentrate, and he suggested he have a glass of water or green tea, which would be no problem. He could also, Block said, have some bread and rolls brought in if Amroth had not yet had breakfast. 'I'm fine,' Amroth replied. He was once again wearing his traditional coat with the pocket square. Sweat had broken out on his forehead, but he did not think of taking off his jacket or accepting the offer of a glass of water.

Amroth steadily fell into an undertow of self-complacency which remained untroubled by his whirling thoughts and which watered down his feelings but did not cause him to feel afraid or bring him to his senses. More than anything else, he felt the noise inside himself to be the triumphant howl of a superior man, a victor over the village idiots of the police and other lackeys of the law.

What the law was, Amroth thought, pulling his jacket lapels straight and then keeping his hands there, was decided by the law books and in no way by simple clerks driven to insanity by biased opinions and pathetic statistics on success.

'I am completely fine,' he said and made a smacking noise.

Over the course of the afternoon Amroth managed to manoeuvre himself into a region of contradictions, vacillations, lies and half-truths over which he lost all grip. It took him almost three hours before he realized what had happened. He had struck a conversational tone that to Holland and Block's ears sounded like a thought-out, more or less memorized strategy.

After hearing what Franck had told his friend Block, the insurance representative was certainly juggling self-deceptive reasons based on his double-life and his tendencies; but neither Franck nor his colleagues would ever have believed that his statements could take a relevant turn as far as the crime was concerned.

From a certain point on—the clerk noted 12.45 p.m.—the two interrogators no longer looked at the babbling man as a witness, but as a suspect.

Before informing him of the fact, they wanted to grant him one last chance to provide them with a truthful, believable statement. Amroth shrugged his shoulders and sat for a while with a sunken head, seeming to think intensely. Then he looked at Holland and Block and even the clerk and asked if he could in fact still have a roll with cold liver pâté and a cup of coffee with milk. Thereafter, he would be ready for further questions.

During the pause—a co-worker from the canteen brought the coffee and the roll in on a tray—Block opened one of the windows. He watched Armoth, immersed in reflection, drink his coffee in small sips and slowly take bites from his roll at regular intervals. Elena Holland had remained at the desk; the clerk had gone to the bathroom.

A cold wind blew in. Out in the back courtyard, mountains of grey snow had piled up and did not want to melt. Block answered questions from the press office by SMS. In truth, another press conference had been scheduled for that Friday, but the investigating public prosecutor had cancelled it at the last minute due to a lack of new findings; logically, that led to further enquiries from the journalists. Block stated that the special unit was following up a new lead, but that details would not be released before Monday.

'I'm ready.' Amroth dabbed his mouth with the paper napkin, wadded it up and tossed it onto the tray.

The clerk was ready too. Since entering the room that morning, she had not uttered a word. She was not surprised by what was to follow, she was used to remaining impassive no matter how appalling the details of the crime or inhuman the perpetrator's statements. Chief Inspector Block explained that Siegfried Amroth was no longer considered a witness but a suspect according to paragraph one hundred and fifty-two—one of the criminal procedure code; he was being accused of likely being involved with the abduction and murder of eleven-year-old Lennard Grabbe. The public prosecutor would decide whether or not to initiate a criminal investigation. As the accused, Amroth had the right to refuse to give a statement, to procure a lawyer and to request evidence. 'Do you understand what I am telling you?' Block asked.

'Yes.'

'Would you like to refuse to give a statement?'

'I am willing to give a statement, just as I was before. I do not need a lawyer.'

Block asked him again whether he was aware of the different nature of the situation; Amroth said yes and said no to any legal assistance.

After that, Block and Holland began their questions once more from the top. To some degree the same ones, they were surprised to receive the same crude answers which clearly did not contribute to exonerating him whatsoever.

To the decisive question of whether on the evening of the eighteenth of November he had waited for eleven-year-old Lennard Grabbe at the school, picked him up in his car and later murdered him, Amroth responded in a flat voice: no. He admitted—which differed from what he had told Franck—to having been in the area around the school at about seven o'clock, when the football match in the gym was over; he was sitting in his car, feeling ill; he no longer knew why he could only remember feeling that way; the rain had crashed against the roof and the storm shook his old heap. He had not seen the boy again.

He could not explain why he had driven back to the school one more time, even though his friends were waiting for him at Brückenwirt. Did he yearn for Lennard? Holland asked. It was possible, Amroth answered, avoiding the inspector's eyes.

'Were you in love with Lennard?' the inspector asked. Amroth shrugged his shoulders, rocked his head back and forth, smiled sheepishly—the clerk noted his reaction in her book—and pushed his chair away from the table; he crossed his legs and took a deep breath. He was fond of him, Amroth said, he thought about him all the time. When the boy moved away from Untersbergstraße, he felt like he had been stabbed in the chest. However, he took heart when he saw Lennard in the schoolyard and was able to speak to him; Lennard had always had a kind word for him.

What kind of good word? Chief Inspector Block asked for the second time. This time around Amroth said something different from the first time a number of hours earlier. He claimed that Lenny—for the first time he referred to the boy by his nickname—had told him that he did not have to hide when he came to visit. That was a good word, Amroth said, and it made him happy.

Towards the end of questioning, the sixty-four-year-old seemed tired; he had difficulty speaking clearly, had to start over from the beginning multiple times; he screwed up his eyes for seconds before continuing. Trying to supress a yawn, he made an effort and sat up straight.

He was now finished with his statements, he said, and would like to know what was going to happen with him. The different colour of his face—a fibrous grey—was impossible to ignore, his right hand trembled slightly; he had only managed to get out the last words sluggishly.

What remained for him to complete were a number of files, and he, Block, would apply for a search order, and not with the investigating magistrate but with the relevant public prosecutor, due to the threat of imminent danger. He told Amroth that it would be a good idea to have a lawyer there when they searched his flat, garage, vehicle and offices. The searches would take place that very evening.

'I have nothing to hide,' Siegfried Amroth said, more to the clerk than to Block and Holland.

For the veteran investigator, the man was one of the strangest suspects he had ever questioned. Though he was by no means convinced that he was sitting in front of Lennard's murderer, he had no choice but to present him to the judge and request the search warrant. He was also considering having Amroth examined by a psychologist, as long as he agreed.

Before leaving to fill out the paperwork, Amroth shook everyone's hand. Then he put both of his own hands into the pockets of his jacket and paused.

'I feel quite relieved,' he said. 'Recently I have been stumbling around a lot . . . inside myself. I no longer know what I did. No doubt nothing terrible. Or did I? I talk with clients and afterwards don't remember a thing. I take notes, just like you . . . '

He nodded at the clerk. ' . . . and when I read what I've written, I get scared. Because I forget that I'd even written it down. Today was a good day. I'm going to drive home and wait for you. Two rooms, there's simply nothing else to search. I'll call Dr Fender, he'll need to make sure that nothing gets messed up and goes missing. After that, we can drive to my office at Goetheplatz. What the law requires must be done.

'I'm well aware that you do not believe me and desperately need someone to be guilty. People will point at me and call me a paedophile, things move pretty quickly these days. Bad for my job, I'm counting on the worst. My pension is tiny, but I won't end up under the bridge, I promise you that much. No one will be turning off my water.

'You questioned me, and I answered all your questions. I am already curious to see the protocol . . . '

Once again he nodded at the recording clerk. ' . . . I'm going to double-check every word. There will not be a thing I did not say. You've squeezed me dry. I know quite well that you were trying to put me in a bind. That is what your job requires—I accept that. Your former colleague *Herr* Franck skilfully danced around me too, and I answered his questions as well, and in the end even admitted something to him, just as I did to you.

'I admit that Lennard gave me the courage to be honest and to show my face and to be good to myself, and I have been ever since the day he spoke to me. Ever since that very day. Arrest me, embarrass me, I won't hide.

'Could you please call me a taxi? I'll pick up my car tomorrow, after you have X-rayed it. You've demoralized me with your questions, the way you ask questions borders on torture. I will inform Dr Fender so that he can undertake the appropriate legal steps.

'Be that as it may, I am not criticizing you, you are simply following your nature, you cannot be held to account for that. Am I right?'

'He likes to be right,' she said. 'And he's convinced that he always is.' Hanne Amroth brought a glass of freshly squeezed orange juice into the living room and offered it to her visitor; she sat down next to him at the table and took a sip from her glass. 'We got separated for specific reasons. I don't want to say anything else about it. Has he already been interrogated by the police?'

'He has been questioned,' Franck said. 'Interrogations have not taken place since forty-five.'

A devilish smile flitted across the painted lips of the grey, curly-haired woman. 'As far as these things are concerned, I almost have to say that he is indeed right, my husband. He believes that the police fundamentally just follow a single goal: to arrest someone once they've got them in their claws. Heavy interrogations are inevitable, no matter what you call them. An interrogation is an interrogation, and the fact that questioning sounds more harmless makes absolutely no difference to those concerned.'

In her words, Franck felt he could recognize the voice and the opinions of the man he had spoken with at Brückenwirt; if he was not mistaken, the woman even used the same expressions.

'Above all,' Franck said, 'questioning serves the discovery of the truth and not the collection of evidence for or against someone who has been accused of a crime or is a suspect. But we can discuss that another time. What I'd like to know from you is how well your husband knew Lennard Grabbe and what kind of impression the boy made on you over the years.'

She smiled again and trained her quick eyes on Franck through her round, rimless glasses. 'I like you, yes, you're almost likeable, and yet we've just met each other for the first time. You exude calm, and that's worth a lot. I work in a department store, it's nothing but chaos, everyone wants to be first, everyone's always in a rush, not only on the weekends. When you called me, I thought, "No, no visits, and certainly not from any strangers, I want to be alone, I don't want to see anyone." I'm on sick leave from work because of my tooth operation, I told you that on the phone already. And now you're sitting here and not bothering me in the least. Are you sure you wouldn't like a coffee?'

'Yes,' said Franck.

'So, you're retired but still work as a detective. How so?'

'I was the one who told the murdered boy's parents that he was dead. I have been responsible for delivering such news from when I was still on active duty. Did Lennard come to visit you often on Weißenseestraße?'

'It's possible. I'm not sure. Why is that important?'

The remark could have come from Amroth, Franck thought, and said: 'What interests me is what kind of individual the boy was to you.'

'Please don't think I'm being cruel but: he's dead. Nothing I say will bring him back to life. He was a kid, what else should I say?'

In the red-and-yellow dress generously covering her body, with her seemingly uninhibited and girlish manner which seemed to have received a special touch from the lisp produced by her operation, she seemed kindness personified. From his time in homicide, however, Franck was familiar with all the varieties; he knew that such people never noticed the armour they had at some point slipped on, out of the most varied and sometimes even completely understandable reasons; at long last, they felt comfortable.

His hands folded on the table, he nodded deliberately. 'Would you say that Lennard was a bright boy, one who was unafraid of adults?'

She flicked her fingers. 'Absolutely,' she said.

Franck had to force himself not to stare at her hand; he had not heard or seen that kind of movement in a long time. Hanne Amroth seemed exceptionally cheerful.

'You couldn't have fooled him,' she said emphatically. 'The kid was on the ball, as they say. Whenever he talked to Sigi about football, there was no stopping him, they would just talk about football, the whole time, without a break. I'm not interested in football. Now and again I watch dance competitions, I used to dance myself, long time ago. Football? No. Sports bore me. But the boy and Sigi, nothing but football in their heads.'

So she did know the boy well, Franck thought, and knew when he and her husband would meet. He said: 'Lennard played in the park nearby.'

'As often as he could. Sigi thought that one day he'd play for the national team. I can't judge—I still wouldn't watch a match. What is it again you wanted to know exactly?'

'The boy was often over here.'

'We were neighbours, it happens. Whenever I baked a cake, he naturally got a piece. He was always very polite, I have to say. For the most part, though, he really just went on and on, he knew everything better. Perfect. Sigi is the same. Maybe that's why the two understood each other so well. There's just one risk: when two people always want to be right, at some point there's going to be a fight, just like in a marriage. Then things go flying through the air, or one of the two gets violent, or both. Then there's nothing you can do. We never threw things at each other, that much I can tell you. I moved out, end of story.'

'Why did you move out, *Frau* Amroth?'

'As I said already: I had my reasons, and I prefer to keep them to myself.'

'You refused to give a statement to police,' Franck said. 'You were asked if you knew about your husband's tendencies—that he observed boys, took photos of them and approached them. That he's a stalker, not just in schoolyards but also at swimming pools and on private property. You stayed silent.'

'That is my right as his wife.'

'Do you believe it possible that your husband murdered Lennard?'

'That is preposterous.' For a split second, Franck thought he saw a shadow flit through her clear eyes. 'He had his tics. Who doesn't? He doesn't have an easy time of it at work, the insurance branch isn't booming at the moment, he needs diversion and has to charge his batteries, what's wrong with that? And, I have to admit, sometimes he talks a big game, as men do. But that's it. Murder someone? Are you totally clean? You're starting to squander the sympathy I had for you, *Herr* Inspector. *Ex*-inspector. My husband didn't kill anyone, certainly not a young boy, and one he liked on top of it. Yes, he liked him, still met up with him after the family had moved away from Untersbergstraße. They're buds. Is that illegal? I think you've learnt enough. I have to rest, the wound in my gums is starting to throb again.'

For a few seconds it was deadly still in the small, simply decorated flat. Hanne Amroth held her hand to her cheek; in the meanwhile, her smile had begun to strike Franck as a kind of tic. Siegfried Amroth needed the presence of children; his wife needed comfort in innocence.

At the door Franck said: 'Good luck with your tooth.'

'It will heal, nothing tragic,' Hanne Amroth said smiling.

Franck wanted to call his friend Block from the car to ask about their questioning of Amroth. At the exact same moment his mobile rang.

'Just imagine, *Herr* Inspector,' Max Hofmeister said. 'My sister's just had her hair cut. There's almost nothing left. And she didn't come to me to do it. Why is she doing this? Why?'

CHAPTER ELEVEN

A World with No People

II

One of the fifteen investigators who had remained in the special unit—ten men, five women—must have given the tabloid a tip. Referring to a source at the police department, the paper reported the arrest of a suspect in the Lennard Grabbe case. A former neighbour, the man had known the student well. Speculation about possible sexual abuse was referred to as such, and yet, without any concrete evidence, emphasized.

According to the reporter, the questioning had lasted all night, even the suspect's wife and other people in the immediate vicinity were questioned. At least that part of the full-page article—the boy's fate was once more extensively detailed and expanded with photos of the place the body was found and which was also most likely the scene of the crime—was truthful. André Block had to admit that much, as difficult as it was.

The fact that with unusual, and especially unsolved, murder cases information always leaked out of the department belonged—apparently unavoidably, as he in the meantime had to state resignedly—to the everyday life of a head investigator. They were responsible for every procedure, every colleague, every piece of paper and every public coughing fit of their shared work.

What angered Block the most had nothing to do with indiscretion—it was bad enough not being able to trust one's own people one hundred per cent. No, what he found far worse was that such press coverage had an adverse effect on the search by publishing details of the investigation.

If Lennard had indeed already been killed on the night of his disappearance between, at the earliest, eight o'clock and, at the latest, midnight, aside from the murderer who could know that with any certainty? After reading the article, the perpetrator would have an incredible amount of time to construct an alibi and to get rid of any traces that they had possibly overlooked.

Even when an experienced investigator like André Block never asked questions that implied some kind of insider knowledge about the crime—Where were you on this or that day between eight and midnight, or something similar—he habitually refrained from making any chronological enquiries until a suspect made a mistake, delivered a clue to a possible time on their own or stumbled over their own inconsistencies in their self-constructed labyrinth of lies.

For the general public, the announcement of an arrest led to a form of reconciliation with the, as far as many citizens were concerned incompetent, police. This apparent success put the investigative team under extreme pressure, for the available facts as far as Siegfried Amroth was concerned did offer much cause for optimism in terms of a definitive solution to the case. After searching Amroth's flat on Weißenseestraße, the garage and the car, as well as his office at Goetheplatz, the inspectors, accompanied by investigators from the state criminal police, found no clues suggesting complicity whatsoever. That stated, the technicians in the laboratory did find DNA traces of Lennard Grabbe on two coffee-table books about the World Cup championships, as well as on a small-format imitation of a Champions League trophy that, according to Amroth, he had bought for Lennard at the Auer Dult market. On his last visit, in his haste, the boy had forgotten to take the piece of painted plastic with him.

Asked when Lennard had last been to the flat, Amroth said: 'Shortly after the fair in October, something like that.'

Based on new statements from Siegfried Amroth ('Lenny could never get enough of photos and stories about the old heroes out on the pitch, he'd sit on the sofa and leaf through the books for hours'), Block and his colleague Elena Holland attempted to question the boy's parents one more time about his relationships with adults in the neighbourhood, especially with the enthusiastic football fan of the insurance representative.

Their attempt failed.

Tania Grabbe refused to talk; she did not even open the door to the inspectors but called her brother who was once again supposed to tell her husband that the police were outside the door. Stephan Grabbe then called the chief inspector on his mobile and asked for his understanding, his wife did not even want to have any kind of reasonable talk with him, their home situation was extremely difficult.

So they met at the Café Beach House, which, with a second pastry chef, extra help in the kitchen, his waitress Claire and the Afghan student, Grabbe was 'halfway managing to run', as he put it. To his displeasure, the curious as well as many just plain gawkers continued to stream by, shyly asking about Lennard's mother or taking a picture of the photograph on the wall, knowing that it was of Lennard thanks to the paper.

The father's scanty declarations did not provide the inspectors with any insights that could lead to any conclusions as to the concrete guilt of the suspect being held in custody.

Although the public prosecutor had signed off on a detention order because of the photos of children found in Amroth's flat—he did not dismiss the danger of absconding or suppression of evidence—Block was counting on the fact that Amroth's lawyer, Dr Fender, would have him released within seventy-two hours. Despite all the suspect's contradictions and coarseness, and his wife's meagre, one-sided and consciously general statements, due to the unsatisfactory body of evidence the investigating magistrate would have no choice but to set the suspect free.

For the time being, Block ignored thinking about the media frenzy that would descend on the special unit when that happened. The varnish of his hope remained intact. Experience had taught him that the need to confess could overcome any suspect regardless of what strategies they believed to have internalized.

As much as Chief Inspector Holland pushed to be allowed to exchange even just a few words with Lennard's mother, Stephan Grabbe flatly refused. The reasons were vague; he reacted curtly to any and all enquiries. The police had failed and were looking to pass it off on the victims, he knew about such things. As long as Lennard's murderer was free, the criminal police had no right to rummage about in his life and to put insinuations into the world that he and his wife had neglected their son and even allowed him to come into contact with the wrong people.

To the repeated question as to whether he could in any way find it possible that his former neighbour, Amroth, might be involved in Lennard's disappearance or that ill-fated night's course of events, Grabbe, more emphatically than before and with a kind of great indignation, said no.

Not even five minutes later, Block and Holland were once again out on the street in front of the cafe, deflated and furious with disappointment.

'I need a drink,' Block said.

'I'll come with you.'

An hour after receiving the call, Franck found himself walking into Gasthaus Weinbauer, a Bavarian restaurant close to Münchner Freiheit and just a few steps away from the Grabbes' cafe. As Franck was stepping through the door, Block was already ordering his second beer. They shook hands. Franck sat down on the bench next to Elena Holland. From there, they had a view of the entire restaurant which at the moment had only four other guests, two old men and two old women, each at their own table.

At first Franck regretted having been torn away from his work; then it became clear to him that his job that day consisted of juxtaposing empty spaces and an admission whose veracity seemed doubtful. On his S-Bahn ride into the city, he thought that a bit of distraction might air out his mind a bit, stuffy as it was with thoughts.

Block told him about their meeting with Stephan Grabbe, making no secret of his incomprehension at the man's behaviour.

'It's all the same to him, even the fact that we have a suspect, someone he even de*fends*, if you can believe it.' Beads of sweat shone on Block's almost cleanly shaven head; on his throat, above his tight shirt collar, the veins stood out; the colour of his face shifted between tones of dark red. Rarely had Franck seen him like this. In his opinion, Block almost felt personally offended by the Grabbes' behaviour, as if they not only considered his work a failure but he himself too.

'Their child is dead,' Block said, his voice full of suppressed anger. 'The boy was murdered, and it's our fault, or what? We were with them every day . . .' He looked at his colleague. 'You did everything to try and establish a basis of trust with the mother, you went to visit her nights and comforted her and told her about the state of the investigations. We were open and available although we didn't have to be and, in fact, aren't allowed to be.

'Objectivity, decorum, incorruptibility, an absence of feelings, that's the basis of our work and the reason for our success when solving crimes. We learnt a lot from you, Jakob, you were always the first to warn us not to lose sight of the facts for even one second, of what's demonstrable, of what's right in front of our eyes, of what's possible and even probable, of every individual detail that holds the key to the whole picture, and that we just have to look carefully enough.

'And by no means can we allow our eyes to be obscured by feelings, from too much pity and too much closeness to the victims and the victim's loved ones. We're detectives, we are those who are responsible and bound to reading clues and grasping, analysing connections as well as coming to the right conclusions.

'We aren't paid to hold people's hands or to allow ourselves to be plagued by doubt. Our work would suffer for that, and we really would be the idiots wasting people's tax money instead of catching the murderer, at best within a few days. Sloppiness is forbidden. Your words, Jakob.

'And when the investigations take longer because the circumstances are particularly chaotic or the place the body's found doesn't coincide with the scene of the crime, or the weather has destroyed all the traces or when there's not even the tiniest verifiable connection between the victim and the perpetrator, or we don't get hold of any witnesses who've seen anything or when neither the mobiles from the area or the CCTV cameras deliver a usable clue, well, then after three months we can also still be digging around in the dirt for a truffle of truth or, as you like to put it, Jakob, the fossil.

'We can't do anything *but* keep on looking, keep on digging, and we don't do anything else, either.

'And no one has the right to accuse us of sitting around, and that a child's death doesn't matter to us and we're nothing but losers and that we just ask questions to keep people from noticing we sit around our offices all day, doing crossword puzzles.

'I won't let anyone treat me that way, and I won't let anyone in my department be treated that way either. I just wanted to make that all clear. This Stephan Grabbe will be surprised.'

Block stood up, wiped his face and sat back down. Not one of the four other guests at their tables even raised an eyebrow when the shaved head shot up into the air; they had other concerns.

He paused and waved to the server. He ordered a beer for himself and one for Franck. Holland still had some ginger tea left.

'He's suffering because of his wife,' she said. 'He's talking and taking care of things in her place, we've got to accept that.'

'Not me.' Block took a gulp of his beer and pointed his glass at the man across from him. 'Give us a suggestion, Jakob. How can we get the parents to talk? And who, in your opinion, told the press?'

Franck had already thought about that, without getting particularly upset at all. 'No one from your team is responsible for that,' he said. 'Unless someone's trying to get back at you for something.'

'Yeah, me,' Holland said with a serious look on her face.

'Sure.' Block shook his head. 'But to do that you don't need any help from any journalists.' He looked at Franck. 'She's just angry because I didn't allow her to join the questioning on our last case.'

'A little trust would've been nice.'

'It's done and over with. The man threatened you before we arrested him, he grew violent, have you repressed all that? You were light years away from being able to lead an objective round of questioning.'

'You know for a fact that I can turn off my feelings when it has to do with work.'

'Who knows that better than I do?' With the next swallow, Block had already finished his third glass. He waited for Franck to take up the thread again.

'Among the uniformed cops, there are always colleagues of ours who have a good connection to certain journalists,' Franck said. 'Indiscretions are unavoidable. Thank goodness no photos were passed on this time. When Sedlmayr was found beaten to death in his bed, one of the crime-scene photos of the naked corpse ended up in the paper; I knew who was responsible, but his own people covered for him and even contested his appearance before the chief of police. Of course, the fact that they published the presumed time of the crime in Lennard's case is frustrating.'

Franck paused; without drawing attention to himself, he inhaled the smell of Elena Holland's perfume which reminded him of the first time they met. After going to the pub one night, her cousin's husband, a patrolman, was hit by a lorry and mortally wounded. After the inspector had said goodbye on the street in front of the cemetery and gone to her car, Franck had felt the helpless desire to see her again; later that evening, in his flat, he had imagined that he could still smell her perfume.

When she looked at him upon greeting each other there in Weinbauern, he had almost avoided her glance out of bashfulness.

'As far as the family goes,' he said, 'you'll just have to accept what they give you. Already after her son's burial the mother began to sink into her pain, it seems to me that she's refusing any kind of help, either that of her husband or her brother, with whom I had a long discussion, by the way. Tania Grabbe is only able to handle reality because she shuts herself off from it. We don't know if she blames the police. I suspect that her state wouldn't be too different even if in the meantime the murderer had been caught. Her son was the centre of her life. What should she do? Keep on living like she did before? Incomprehensible for her. She's closed the door on her old life, but she doesn't know how to begin a new one yet. She's alone—when she looks into the mirror, she doesn't recognize herself.'

'What do you mean by that?' Elena Holland asked.

'There's no way the woman she sees in the mirror is the same as the one from half a year ago, from three months ago. Three months ago, she was the mother of her eleven-year-old son, and, now that he's dead, she no longer exists. In any event, I imagine that, for her, her very being is a mistake, an optical illusion, an insult to nature.'

'But she's not guilty of her child's death,' the female inspector said.

'In her eyes, if anyone's guilty of Lennard's death, it's her. In her eyes, she should never have allowed him to be alone that night, what with the rain and storms lashing the city. She was at home in the kitchen and did not protect him. No one was there when he left the school. Lennard didn't have an umbrella, no poncho, and some guy stole his bike. He had his book bag on his back and his football under his arm. His mother was at home on the other side of the cemetery, his father was still at the cafe, his uncle in the salon, not a friend far and wide, no one to accompany him. He took off and never arrived. What does a mother think when she imagines a situation like that? What should she feel but this inextinguishable memory? What else *is* there of that November eighteenth inside her but guilt?'

'Her husband,' Holland said. 'And her mother. And her brother. There are people around her who can help her. She isn't alone. We know how close she is to her brother. What's with him? Why hasn't he got through to her? You mentioned having talked with him. What's he got to say? What kind of impression did you get?'

'He's carrying around some kind of secret.' After being silent a moment Franck added: 'He believes that neither he nor his sister were born to live.'

For a while the table was quiet. Then André Block stood up and went outside, disgusted by being drunk.

CHAPTER TWELVE

After Sunset

This time he had put on sturdy leather shoes with a thick rubber sole, clean jeans that were not frayed at the ends, a black down jacket and a dark-red wool hat—from which his braid stuck out—down over his forehead. The hat's colour matched his scarf which he had wrapped around his neck numerous times. As opposed to when they were at the Fraunhofer pub, if Franck was not mistaken, this time Lennard's uncle seemed focused, determined, confident, almost downright euphoric.

'Free on a day off,' Maximilian Hofmeister said. He had trimmed his beard and not skimped on aftershave.

Franck hid his surprise—not only about the man's tone of voice and cologne. After barely a minute, though, his behaviour began to seem artificial and odd, which sparked Franck's interest and gave a distinctly anticipatory feel to their planned walk by the river in the cold and invigorating snowy air.

Three days earlier, after he had expressed outrage at his sister's haircut, Hofmeister asked whether they could meet again.

From Reichenbach Bridge they walked south along the high bank. After his initial momentum, the hairdresser's flow of words began to ebb for a while before he abruptly came to a halt, took his hands out of his jacket pockets and balled his right hand into a fist. 'Maybe I've been wrong about my sister all my life.'

'Tell me,' Franck said.

'I don't know who she is any more. Have you spoken with her recently?'

'No.'

'I haven't either, no one has.' He rubbed his head, pushed his hat back and forth. 'And when I went to see her yesterday, the day before yesterday, I barely got a word out of her. She just sat there and stared at me, with that ragged hair, who does something like that to their hair? I don't know, *Herr* Franck. And Stephan doesn't know where she went to get it done either. Isn't that nuts? Good Lord, what's going on inside her?'

'Do you know what I'd really like to do? Get out of here. Up north, to the North Sea, where we used to go, all of us, the whole family. In the good old days.'

His pale lips curved into a smile. 'I'm talking like an old man. And when I'm standing in front of Tania and looking at her, I *am* an old man and she's an old woman. Life, *Herr* Franck, has cast us out, and we were probably never really born to live, that's just something we imagined. But I know there was a time . . .'

Hofmeister looked towards the torrential river; on its surface branches, shreds of uprooted trees and rubbish rushed northwards, in the direction of Stauwehr. 'Back then it was spring the whole year.' In order to cover up how moved he was, he smiled again and shook his head. 'Don't listen to me too closely, or else you'll think I'm starting to go out of my head, just like my sister.'

With an angry jerk, he turned away from Franck. 'I'm her brother. I always told her everything. I always took care of her. I took over the business although I didn't want to. I was never mad at her for that, not a single day. I wanted her to be free and to be able to live and move out into the world and not go to waste in a salon. Everything, everything could've gone well but didn't. Why not?'

He had yelled the last words so loud that a walker on the iced-over surface close to the bank with his dog stopped in alarm and shielded his eyes with his hand to get a better look; the dog began to bark.

Bent forward, mouth wide, Hofmeister began to cough. Because of the convulsions of his body, his hat slid off his head and landed in the snow. His tightly knotted braid swung here and there, his face had turned a dark red; he looked as if he could not get any air. When Franck took a step closer, Hofmeister shooed him away.

Little by little, the hairdresser got his breath back. He bowed down to get his hat, put it back on, pushed it into position and once again let out a heavy sigh.

'Where were we now?' he said and closed his eyes for a moment. 'Sorry, I got lost for a second.' He clearly wanted to add something else. He looked at Franck, cleared his throat and briefly touched his arm; shaking his head, he pointed to the path in front of them. Franck was not sure what exactly Hofmeister wanted to express, so he folded his hands behind his back.

'Please keep walking with me,' Hofmeister said. As Franck showed no reaction, the hairdresser once again took a step towards him. 'What's up? I said that I was sorry for being so rude. Are you angry with me?'

'Of course not. You weren't being rude. On the contrary, you were being honest and direct. Please tell me more about you and your sister, about your connection.'

Franck spoke in a soft voice. His face did not give the slightest hint of how shaken he had become over the last few minutes nor how overwhelmed and trapped his intense listening had made him feel.

He performed the indefatigably unemotional analyst and police expert, one who was additionally qualified to impart comfort and assurance to those who had been touched by a murder, to walk a bit of the way with them, reasonably approachable, understanding, drawing on experience and attentive not to ever make any promises about catching the criminal.

Unobserved by his partner, that frosty Monday morning Franck was stumbling through his own world. In that world, he had lost his sister and had never stopped missing her; it was as if her death had not occurred almost a lifetime ago but maybe only three months—as long ago as the murder of eleven-year-old Lennard.

Franck would have liked to join Hofmeister in his outcry.

He would have liked to turn around and flee, without another word.

'I don't know if I like this,' Hofmeister said. 'In spite of everything, you're a stranger.'

After a moment's confusion, Franck found the thread again. 'What do you think about just continuing to walk until talking comes naturally?' he said. 'Until I seem less of a stranger to you, as if we were just two men from the neighbourhood who've taken the day off and gone for a walk together.'

As his words did not cause his fifteen-year-old sister's voice to stop, Franck pointed to the river where the walker was talking to his dog which was crouched down in front of him and continuing to bark. 'It looks like the two still need to get used to each other as well.' He turned to Hofmeister. 'Help me understand your sister, maybe then I'll be able to find some way to reach her.'

'No one's going to find that.' Hofmeister took off, but Franck kept up with him. 'I think that you can only understand someone else's sister if you have one yourself. Do you have any brothers or sisters?'

Franck felt a lie on the tip of his tongue. Believing he was not misappropriating the truth if he only interpreted the question in terms of the present, he shook his head. He wanted to repress Lily's name and went through great pains to do so. The effort etched furrows into his face which Hofmeister noticed but ascribed to the biting wind. How could he sense that Franck's budding feeling of shame tormented him more than the cold?

'Single children have their issues too,' Hofmeister said understandingly and pulled his cap down lower over his forehead.

Now and again hooded figures came towards them, swinging ski poles with sweeping arm movements—probably thinking it was a healthy type of sport, Franck thought. With a tinge of a pointless feeling of superiority, he was amused by the thought that he could not remember the last time he had done anything athletic. Back when he was together with Marion, they had regularly played table tennis, and later, after he had had a number of ailments and provisionally given up smoking, he had gone jogging a few times; it bored him immensely.

That had to have been at least twenty years ago. Since then, he had contented himself with walking as often as possible instead of taking the car, avoiding escalators and lifts whenever possible, not drinking alcohol all that often and smoking at most five cigarettes a week.

He ignored his ex-wife's regularly reoccurring plea for him to make an appointment with a doctor or specialist for a medical check-up; his unavoidable trip to the dentist was enough though over the last number of years—most likely due to his hyper-modern equipment in the otherwise antiquated rooms—his dentist expressed a somewhat overly motivated haste to repair things. Indeed, he had already convinced him to have three implants—a procedure whose necessity Franck to this day had difficulty understanding and whose financial consequences bordered on downright robbery. Marion thought he was astonishingly petty-minded and urged him to be thankful for his doctor's attentiveness instead.

As they were walking beneath Wittelsbacher Bridge, his sister silently returned through the trapdoor of his memory.

'What did you talk about with her?' Franck enjoyed the cool air. 'What did your sister confide in you?'

Hofmeister stopped for a moment before starting to walk again. 'She says she doesn't want to see me, she *can't* see me, she says. She apologized for it. What am I supposed to do with that?'

'Were you alone with her?'

'Yeah, in Lennard's room. She's rarely anywhere else. Day and night there's a candle burning on the windowsill, and a vase with a white rose, too.'

'She replaces both, the candle and the rose,' Franck said. 'Once the old candle has burnt down and the rose is dried out.'

'She does, yeah.'

'She leaves the flat and goes shopping.'

'I don't know.' Hofmeister looked at Franck helplessly. 'I need to ask Stephan some time. Until now, I'd just imagined she never left the house. Maybe that's not true.'

'You were with her in the child's room, and the door was closed.'

'The door is always closed.'

'What happened between you and Tania?'

'Nothing.' Once again Hofmeister stopped; he let his arms hang down, looked towards the river, bowed his head to the side, as if he were listening to music or the silence. 'She was lying in bed, in Lennard's bed, the blue blanket up to her chin. She was looking up at the fishnet with all the animals, it's been hanging there for years. Lennard had always brought back new mussels and stones from their holidays and carefully sorted them and made sure that nothing fell through the mesh. And me? I just stood there, talking at her—she simply did not respond. Then I sat down on the piano stool. I don't know how long I sat there.'

'No one said a word.'

'No one.'

'But at some point,' Franck said, 'she did in fact speak with you.'

'Could you call it that? Speaking? Her voice was so thin and strange, I wanted to get up and go kneel in front of the bed so I could understand her better. I didn't trust myself. Does that make me a coward?'

'No.'

'I'm not so sure.'

'What did Tania say?'

'She asked me why I was still there. She'd closed her eyes, was just lying there, her face snow white, her scruffy hair. I thought, My sister's not talking with me, she must have confused me with someone else.'

'What did you do?'

'I can't tell you that.' Hofmeister kept on walking. Franck stopped.

'Go on.'

After taking two more steps Hofmeister turned around, stopped and put both of his hands in front of his face. He lifted his head, let his hands sink and then dangle while he continued to speak. 'I closed my eyes, like a kid. I do that often. I catch myself but by then it's too late.'

'Your sister did not react,' Franck said.

'I don't know. When I opened them back up, she was lying there just like before. Maybe she reacted, I'd been sitting there with my hands in front of my face for at least a minute. I remember the whole flat being quiet. Stephan was there, probably sitting in the kitchen, as always these days, sitting there and staring at the ground. He's powerless, Tania doesn't pay any attention to him—it's like he's air, just like me.'

'Did you say anything to your sister after that?'

Hofmeister looked around like someone who was wondering which direction to go. 'Let's keep on walking, please.' He waited until Franck was next to him. 'I asked her if she could remember something in particular, the last trip we took together, before Lennard was born.'

'Where did you go?'

'To Juist. We used to go there with our parents. We'd go there every year, for us kids it was paradise, the soft sand, the North Sea, the food, the sun, the wind and the fog which shows up all of a sudden and makes the world disappear. That's where we'd gone, Tania and I.'

'What was the occasion?'

'I don't remember any more,' Hofmeister said, running a hand through his beard. The gesture triggered complex thoughts in the innately wary ex-inspector; he decided to pay more attention than before to the nuances of the man's so seemingly straightforward confessions of uncertainty and hurt.

'But the trip occurred to you again,' Franck said.

'I'd thought about Lenny, then I saw my sister and me sitting on the beach again, in the heaviest of fog, it had come so quickly that we couldn't find our way back to the village. We just sat there and held on to each other and talked and were close.'

'What all did you talk about?'

'Everything. Life, passing time, the people we do or don't like.'

'Didn't you have a girlfriend at the time?'

Hofmeister stopped suddenly. 'What makes you think about my girlfriend? What does my girlfriend have to do with anything? We'd just broken up. You wanted to know what I talked about with my sister, and now you know.'

'Did she like the memory?'

Once again Hofmeister ran a hand across his face. He sniffed a few times while appearing to search for words. He could feel that he had revealed something he had wanted to keep a secret at all costs but was unsure as to what. He wondered whether something else could have driven him to call the inspector and ask him to meet.

The longer Hofmeister thought about it, the more oppressive the idea that he had lied to himself and used his sister's drama as a pretext for revealing his own nightmare, which had been living deep inside him for years, became.

That could never be true. 'No. No,' he said aloud.

'She didn't like the memory.' Franck was curious how many twists and turns the man's change would take.

'No.' Hofmeister became aware of how false his voice sounded and, as if acknowledging it, shook his head. 'What am I talking about? Yes, she liked the memory, she smiled at me and said that she'd had to think of our trip a few days earlier as well, and that it had been a lovely week.'

'She said that.' Franck appeared convinced. To tell the truth, however, he did not believe a word though he would have been hard-pressed to explain why not.

'Yeah, and then we talked about the trip a little while longer. I think I want to go back home now, I'm not feeling so well, I hope I haven't caught a cold.'

'Let's turn around,' Franck said. 'And that was it.'

'Sorry?'

'You didn't talk about anything else, you and your sister.'

'No.'

'Did you feel reconciled in the end?'

'What do you mean?'

'At the beginning, you felt cut off and ignored, that your sister treated you like air. And at the end of your visit?'

'I don't understand you,' Hofmeister said. His steps were heavy, his boots scraped the frozen snow.

'Did you hug each other when you left?'

'I . . . no . . . I gave her a kiss on the cheek, she was still in bed and didn't want to get up.'

For a while, they walked next to each other in silence.

'What surprises me,' Franck said, as if at random, 'is that you didn't ask her about her haircut at all.'

'Sorry?'

'Which colleague of yours cut your sister's hair?'

'I don't know.' It sounded dismissive, offended. 'Doesn't interest me any more.'

'She didn't tell you?'

'No.'

'Your brother-in-law doesn't know either.'

'So? What's the big deal?'

'That was the first thing you told me on the telephone,' Franck said. 'And how much the fact that Tania went to some-one else to have her hair cut hurt your feelings.'

Hofmeister waved a hand through the air, then buried it in his jacket pocket; shuffling onward, he moved more quickly than before. Franck let him go and fell into a kind of saunter appropriate to his thoughts.

In front of the playground beneath Reichenbach Bridge, Hofmeister turned around. Surprised by the distance he had put between himself and Franck, he just stood there, defenceless against the thought of having been a pitiful coward ever since that day thirteen years ago.

He watched the man with the short grey hair, the well-kept leather jacket and the upright, unwavering step come closer and felt just about ready to go up to him, drop to his knees and confess.

Back in his stuffy, overheated flat later on, he asked himself what had kept him from doing so.

'What do you think's behind the brother's secret?' Elena Holland asked him a day later at the Gaststätte Weinbauer pub.

'His sister knows it too, I'm sure of it,' Franck said.

'Yes, but what is it?'

They were silent until André Block came back in, trailing cool evening air. 'We're overlooking something,' he said. 'The riddle's right there in front of us, and we're not getting it.'

The same thought had been robbing Franck of sleep for days. That and the thought of Tania Grabbe turning into a shade in front of everyone, a shade that one evening in the not-too-distant future might disappear forever.

CHAPTER THIRTEEN

The Outcast Apostle

People were staring at him. Some of them were standing at a distance and waiting to see if something was going to happen; if he would move; if maybe a boy from the school across the street would walk by and steal the ball; if the police would show up and take him away.

The checkout woman at the supermarket, who was out on the pavement smoking with a colleague and would not let the man out of her sight, put him at around sixty or even older and thought he was confused or senile or simply lonely; like her grandfather who back home in Split would walk down to the sea every day, a wicker basket with a bottle of red wine and white bread under his arm, and pray for his wife to return, his wife who had drowned twenty-one years earlier. She would gladly have offered the man at the intersection—who she imagined she had seen before or even spoken with—a pretzel or a cigarette, but she did not have enough time. Going back inside, her colleague tapped a finger against her temple while the cashier turned around again and cast the man, standing there motionless with his back to her, a compassionate glance.

With his hands in the pockets of his leather jacket, Franck had been standing in the same place for three hours. Between the tips of his boots was the black ball with the orange pattern and the puma which the neighbourhood boy had found on the playground at Spitzingplatz and which had belonged to Lennard Grabbe.

Furious about his bicycle being stolen, Franck thought, Lennard had left the school grounds, crossed at the light, and, for a reason still to be explained, set off home on the path across the playground instead of the south side of Eintrachtstraße, which was closer.

Franck believed that the boy—despite the rain and the storm—wanted to get rid of his frustration and kick the ball a few more times before heading home.

Which is why Franck had positioned himself at the southern entrance to the playground, there, where Lennard must have passed.

It was only a paltry attempt, an expression of his flagging hope that was threatening to slip away completely. Maybe someone would remember the peculiar leather ball, a passer-by, a driver, a supermarket client, a neighbour, a guest from one of the nearby pubs, a pizza-delivery guy from the other side of the street, a lost stray. Maybe someone would be looking out their window and the ball would jog their memory. Maybe a new, ground-breaking thought would suddenly occur to him.

Maybe he was just ridiculous.

Franck noticed the people's looks, saw them whispering and shaking their heads. Maybe it would be a good idea to bring the ball back to the Grabbes' and apologize for his childish and fruitless behaviour and then break off all contact, to which they did not attach any great importance to begin with.

He was unsuccessful.

At the moment Lennard was leaving the building—how many times had Franck already thought about this, thirty?—the rain was beating down on the schoolyard and the five bicycles with their frames and U-locks; the storm whipping leaves and rubbish across the pavement. Lenard immediately saw that his bike was gone. Maybe he hesitated a few seconds, looking for someone—his mother, his uncle—who had come to pick him up. Seeing no one, he took off for the intersection; he definitely did not wait for the green. He crossed Werinherstraße over to the Turkish greengrocer's and from there ran over to the tram stop, behind which was the playground. He could have—Franck wished the question would stop nagging him—waited for the next tram and ridden it to the end of the East Cemetery, not even ten minutes away from his house.

Like an unquiet spirit, the subjunctive mood haunted Franck. Lennard could have done this or that; he should have acted this way and not that; the shortest way would have been the one on that side of the street; if someone had been standing at the tram stop, if Lennard had been standing next to them; if he had locked up his bicycle nothing would have happened; if Maximilian Hofmeister had not preferred his regular client to his nephew . . .

That November evening was pitch black. No one was going outside by choice. No one was waiting for the tram—or at least no one had come forward as a witness, and even the tram drivers working in the area had not seen anything out of the ordinary; the driver who had reached the Werinherstraße stop shortly after seven-thirty and who had been questioned by André Block's colleagues could not remember anyone getting on.

No one. Nothing. Dark. Storms. Not a soul.

On that cold, dry Thursday evening in February, Franck stubbornly stuck to his place in the dim light, a crime scene behind his back that, like one of death's apprentices, kept its secrets to itself.

Giving up was impossible. Franck froze. Yet again he had forgotten his hat; the lined gloves Marion had given him on his birthday two years before were lying unused in his drawer. Nevertheless, he had thought of taking a scarf which, as it turned out, seemed more appropriate for a cool autumnal evening than a frosty winter night.

Franck's growing bad mood angered him. He was afraid his body could not take standing still for so long and would thus force him to move and destroy his plan: to go drink a schnapps against the cold, eat a soup, go to the bathroom.

He was startled to realize that he was moving back and forth in place, and that his legs were twitching; he wanted to stop. He should have eaten something substantial that afternoon, he thought. The spirit again. He should not have done anything but what he did.

He had come here to reclaim time.

Looking around for the first time, from the corners of his eyes he noticed a woman across the street, standing in front of the illuminated supermarket sign, watching him; she had tossed a coat over her shoulders and was smoking a cigarette. Bending down to pick up the ball cost him a lot of effort, he winced more than flexed, his bones hurt and it was hard for him to stretch out his fingers.

After casting another hasty glance at the woman from the supermarket, who he thought he recognized as the cashier, he turned to face the bush- and tree-lined playground. With clumsy steps, clutching the ball in both hands over his stomach, he went on his way.

He was completely alone. The ten wooden benches in the process of becoming completely rotten were abandoned, as was the climbing frame with its red-yellow slide and the sand covered with patches of frozen snow. Gnarled, dead-looking branches jutted out from black tree trunks.

He could not hear the hum of traffic from the nearby high roads. Franck perceived nothing but silence—that deceitful silence which camouflaged itself with everyday sounds and that, even after hundreds of similar moments, he continued to find malevolent and slanderous.

For a long time he observed the trunk to whose bark belonged the particles that the forensic pathologist had found in Lennard's scalp. Here, not far from one of the wooden benches, is where the boy must have met his murderer. But no matter how many hours Franck would spend in this place or nearby, its silence would mock his ignorance—like back then . . .

Like back then on Friedenstraße, behind East Station, where the nineteen-year-old prostitute Valerie had been stabbed with a screwdriver before bleeding to death behind a garbage container. Around forty of her colleagues made statements, trying to remember any shady, violent customers; a lot of clients even told them their, as far as the case was concerned, irrelevant stories; their questioning of neighbours and visitors to the station did not bring to light any definitive clues. Valerie, born in Untermenzing, was buried, and her picture disappeared from the papers.

For as long as Franck was a homicide detective in Department 11, he had to put off Valerie's parents until a later day when he would catch the murderer . . .

. . . homeless Yockl Zeiss was probably murdered by one of his buddies. At the end of the wine and the night, Yockl was lying in a pool of his own blood not even one hundred metres away from the bridge by the zoo; his companion had disappeared into thin air like an elephant's gas. For weeks Franck had hung around rough sleepers, under bridges and in decaying shelters, talking with people who had banished the dawn from their eyes. He collected fingerprints and DNA; sometimes he felt guilty, believing that the genetic traces of most of those men and women would be eliminated from the thoughts of urban society more efficiently than from any police computer.

He extended the search to the country next door. The perpetrator must have wandered off to the North Pole.

In the end, Yockl's mother, old *Frau* Zeiss from Peysingstraße, had hugged Franck and said that God the Father must have known why he smacked her son, a trained roofer, with vertigo and forced him to land out on the street. Over and over Franck returned to the crime scene near the bridge by the zoo, over and over he deplored the silence . . .

. . . Karla was her name, he thought he remembered, she was found lying in her flat, fifty-two years old, strangled with a nylon cord from her sewing box. No one had missed her for four weeks, not even her son, who she slipped a hundred euros every month since his degree in self-discovery required a certain amount of doing nothing, as he extensively explained to the detectives during his questioning.

Franck had never suspected him but caught himself hoping—most likely because of his growing frustration. Neither her neighbours nor her friends, acquaintances, fellow workers at the health insurance company or her sister or mother offered any clues as to a compelling motive for the crime.

The divorced clerk lived in a humble three-room flat on Harras Square. Once a year, she travelled to the Baltic Sea for two weeks, now and again with her sister who was also divorced and constantly on the prowl for a new, respectable partner, as opposed to Karla who clearly got along just fine on her own.

Nevertheless, the genetic traces of a man were found in Karla's flat, among other places on a toothbrush and a pillow. The data, however, could not be matched to anyone, no one in the building or in the pubs close by seemed to have ever seen Karla in the company of a man.

After eight months, all the investigators' confidence was gone. Franck wanted to keep on visiting the flat regularly, just as in the weeks immediately following the crime—in order to have the chance at grasping a new detail and to counter the silence with his steps and breaths. In the meantime, a new tenant had moved in.

Franck was left with trips to the general area, the inner courtyard, at times the stairwell whose ugly, mute indifference upset him . . .

. . . silent twelve-year-old Azra sat on a chair in Franck's office next to her Turkish father and his lawyer who repeatedly extolled the work of the German police and judicial system and expressed his conviction that the officials would soon find the murderer and put him before a court.

Franck had listened, watched the girl, handed the father paper tissues, nodded to the lawyer and knew that both of the men's statements—they were wearing ready-made suits and ties—consisted of customized lies which served one purpose only: to divert attention from the true motive and pull one over on the state investigators.

One Sunday afternoon, Azra's younger brother Berat, four years younger than she was, was found dead in his parents' bathtub. Following the examinations and autopsy at the forensic institute, it was unclear whether the boy, while splashing wildly in the tub, which he loved, slipped and hit his head against the rim and subsequently drowned, or whether there was a crime behind it.

As Franck learnt just a few hours after the corpse was found by colleagues in the department for organized crime, there were ongoing investigations of Berat's family as well as two other families in the area of small businessmen on Landwehrstraße for blackmail, abduction and illegal prostitution. The suspect had been under surveillance for months; after the violent death of a family member, a witness confided in a patrol officer that she had seen who her uncle had stabbed. Shortly thereafter, the witness rescinded her statement; the search for the perpetrator remained fruitless. The witness was the young student Azra.

The more the lawyer on the one hand dismissed every accusation against the family as absurd and impossible to prove while steering suspicion towards individuals connected to organized-crime groups in Turkey, the more sceptical Franck became.

The lawyer's speculation that certain circles could have treacherously killed little Berat—when, that is, he did not drown because of his romping around, which, of course, was to be assumed—as the family categorically refused to enter into criminal ploys with their fellow countrymen caused Franck to leave the room in shame.

Due to traces on the victim's body, neighbours' statements and a single, tiny hint from Berat's sister, Franck was convinced that it had to do with a family drama that most likely had to do with an argument between the boy and his father or his uncle.

Franck could not exclude manslaughter. But Berat was buried in Anatolia, the state criminal investigation office's leads disappeared into the sand, the families on Landwehrstraße went silent in Franck's face. Azra, quite possibly a witness, was apparently transferred to a school in Istanbul. Franck never saw her again . . .

Four fatalities remained unsolved when he left the department. He would not allow a fifth crime in whose undertow he had fallen—or to which he had freely given himself—to end up in a file with the other cold cases.

That is why he was standing there, on that lousy evening in early February, twelve weeks after the night of the murder, with a black football between his hands like a globe where an all-knowing God in the form of a cat of prey was jumping over an exploding sun.

If he held the ball long enough, Franck thought, maybe the earth would speak to him.

He stood there as if at prayer. Then he noticed a dark, stooped figure carrying four plastic bags at the other end of the play-ground. The man placed the bags on a bench and turned towards the shrubbery, fumbling with his trousers under his anorak. Just then Franck himself was overcome by a pressing need.

He got himself together and left. He reached the pub at the next intersection where Lennard's wake had been held just in time. The waitress recognized him, but did not show it. Before going to the bathroom, he ordered noodle soup and a beer.

After he had eaten and drunk, he crossed himself, folded his hands on the table and closed his eyes.

He had no idea why nor how long he had sat that way.

By the time he raised his head and opened his eyes, Tania Grabbe was standing in front of him in a long, dark-blue coat. Her shorn blonde hair was a ragged nest.

'You?' she said with a timid voice.

'I've been waiting for you.'

In that world in which he had been wandering like an outcast apostle, the statement was not a lie, Franck thought.

CHAPTER FOURTEEN

Nightly Escapes

She hesitated to speak. Once the owner had brought her a black tea and a small glass of rum, she turned her back to the guest at the next table as best she could while unbuttoning her coat.

She was sitting by the window, like him, but was angry with herself for not having chosen a table further away. They were the only guests, they could sit anywhere, and she had not taken advantage of it.

Don't complain, she thought, tipping the rum into her tea. At first, the strong taste bothered her, but then the alcohol's warmth reconciled her to the ice-cold night that had stung her face as she made her way through the neighbourhood.

The old man, she thought, could not do anything about the fact that he was old and alone. He had no children, no wife. No doubt he was afraid of going home and that was why he was having a quick beer to steel his nerves. In the meantime, Tania had almost looked at him again. She felt sorry for him but did not know why. She took the tea glass in both hands, and, with her eyes closed, breathed in the smell of the rum as if she had been waiting for it a long time. She decided she would order another round as soon as the old man left.

For some reason, she thought, he must have aged tremendously over the past few weeks. Maybe something bad had happened and that explained his emaciated appearance and his transformation into a grey form, he was so bent and thin, staring at his flat beer, hands folded on the table, almost pitiful. He reminded her of a homeless man who would sometimes come to the cafe and was allowed to sit at the table by the window without having to order anything; she would bring him a coffee and a glass of mineral water, he would always thank her very politely and take his time. Once he was finished, he would stand up, bow towards the counter, no matter who was there, and go back out into the anonymity of the city. Supposedly his name was Freddy. He was old and grey, and she often wondered if he had ever been young and colourful.

She did not wish the grey man at the next table anything. Perhaps, she thought, she should have turned around as soon as she saw him. He had no right to be there. His presence overwhelmed her.

Tortured by the thought that he might have been waiting to ambush her, she turned away with a stiff movement, knocking over the schnapps glass with the arm of her coat in the process.

'Couldn't you go?' she said to Franck. 'I'd like to be alone.'

He did not waver a second. 'As I already said, I've been waiting for you.'

'Why are you lying to me?'

'May I sit with you?'

'No.'

'Would you like to sit at my table?'

'Why?'

'Because I'd like to speak with you.'

'Well, not me.' His gaze kept her from reacting.

She wanted to turn her head to the side and look for the owner; or to set the schnapps glass, which thank goodness was empty, back up; or to drink the rest of her tea; or to maybe take off her coat and look towards the back wall of the pub, where there was a framed engraving of a cityscape which during her speech following the funeral—she now remembered with painful clarity—had possessed an almost magical allure. She did not know any longer what she had said, not a single word; but back at home, alone in Lennard's room, the black-and-white image never left her mind. She had no idea what city it was; she could just see the outlines of the houses and churches, as if from a hill or a tower.

'Why are you doing that?' she asked, incapable of even squinting.

'I'm happy to see you,' he said.

Tania did not understand what he meant. Her headache returned; she had a bad taste in her mouth and felt sweat on her forehead, on her neck, under her arms. The light in the room, it seemed to her, was getting dimmer.

Once she finally managed to tear her eyes away from the glance of the man sitting there as if turned to stone to order a glass of water, she was gripped by a feeling of dizziness that caused her to reel.

Her upper body swung back and forth; her head jerked so strongly that she got scared. Her mouth open, she gasped for air. She held on to the edge of the table with both hands, convinced that she would otherwise fall to the ground.

At the very second her eyes wandered to the bar, she became aware of an object on the bench next to the inspector; it catapulted her back into the crypt of a room from which she had escaped two hours before, with all her might—and despite her husband's pleas not to.

And she felt like the inspector had kicked the black leather ball, a tenth of a second after she had discovered it, against her heart as powerfully as he could.

Disturbed by her delirium of thoughts, she dug her nails into the white tablecloth and listened to her own whimpering like a foreign, threatening voice. The yellow spot swam before her eyes. For a while she thought the ball would start to spin rapidly.

Then she saw Lennard in his white jersey and red shorts, standing on the pitch, laughing. She let out a cry and waved her left arm through the air to scare away the hallucination while the other hand tore the tablecloth with the tea and schnapps glass and the little porcelain vase with three red carnations to the floor.

In shock, she let out another cry.

Neither the glasses nor the vase had broken. Watching the glasses roll across the floor, Tania began to laugh, and kept on laughing until someone took hold of her wrists and refused to let go.

From her blurry eyes she recognized a man bending over her and gently applying pressure, to which she gave in. She could feel her back against the bench's upholstered backrest. She wanted to say something but did not have the strength. Her convulsions slowly faded; crazy images triggered a new throbbing in her temples when, following someone's request, she briefly closed her eyes.

All that she could recognize were distant noises, a soft rattling, a woman's incomprehensible voice and a man's short reply; quick-sounding steps; and again the unobtrusive smell of beer close to her face. She liked the smell, and gently took it in.

Once her tears had ceased, she noticed that she had put her hands in her lap. No one was holding on to her any longer. She raised her head.

Sitting across from her was the old *Herr* Franck, whose name she finally remembered again, with a soft expression. She

looked at him for a minute or even longer, filled with an almost
forgotten sense of peace.

She let out a sigh and, almost unconsciously and with a
light shrug of the shoulder, slipped off her coat. She looked next
to her on the bench.

'Oh,' she said to Franck. 'You've brought Lenny's lucky ball
back. That's a lovely surprise, thank you.' Her smile was directed
at the ball and stayed there even after she had turned back to
the inspector. 'When you call my husband, tell him that I'm
sorry.'

'I have no intention of calling him.'

'No?'

'No.'

Once more her glance went to the ball, to the leather bag
Franck had placed on the bench, to the empty beer glass on the
table. 'That was you,' she said as the smell of beer that she had
found familiar came back to her nose. She did not expect any
reaction; Franck did not grasp what she meant.

In the meantime, he no longer excluded the idea that he had
indeed been waiting for Tania Grabbe or had at least considered
her showing up a possibility. The pub was hardly fifteen minutes away from the Grabbes' flat, and as they had held the wake
there she probably came fairly often.

'What are you looking at?' she asked.

She was wearing a tight black roll-neck sweater and a pair
of slim-cut black trousers, and, since their last meeting, Franck
estimated, must have lost eight to ten kilos. In her snow-white
face, jutting cheekbones, lips that seemed to have been formed
by a practiced smile and her turquoise eyes, he recognized a
similarly fascinating and unsettling beauty.

The longer he looked at her, the more he felt the need to touch her, not only—as before in her brief moment of shock—on the wrists, but in her face and her mangled hair which, he imagined, gave her the aura of a girl living in a self-imposed wilderness, far from the sun.

'You look really sad,' she said. 'I don't want you to worry because of me.' Once again, her lips formed a timid smile; he continued to look into her face as if entranced. Out of embarrassment, he tried to think of some kind of harmless question.

'Shall we have something else to drink?'

'That would be nice. I'll have another tea with rum.'

To his ears, her voice sounded like that of a child speaking foreign sentences. 'Is something wrong, *Herr* Franck? You have such a strange look on your face.'

'No,' he said.

He turned towards the bar where the waitress had been waiting the whole time. She had picked up the glasses and the now-empty vase and put them into the dishwasher and then taken the carnations off the table and thrown them out. Franck ordered a large beer and the tea.

'Your husband doesn't know that you're here?' he asked.

She put her hands under her thighs and looked at the door. 'I got up and went. I needed air. He wanted to stop me, you can't be angry at him, he's at the cafe from early to late and makes sure that everything's going well. Without him, I'd have to close. Were you ever in our cafe?'

'Yes.' Franck hoped she would remember the day and he could spare her from having to bring up those hours in December again.

'Did you like it? Did you try our cherry pancakes? That's a specialty of ours.' The thought of the pancakes seemed to brighten her up a bit. 'The recipe comes from Vera, Stephan's mother. As a kid, he used to look forward to his favourite dish every Friday. At his house, on Fridays, there wasn't any meat, just fish or something sweet. As long as I've known him, he's always gushed about the pancakes. When I opened the cafe, I wanted to have Vera's pancakes on the menu at all costs, which made him incredibly happy. And he's a master at baking. What did you eat when you were with us? A toast? They're good too, and always fresh. Or didn't you like it?'

The girlish way she was speaking to him forced him to tell the truth. 'I delivered the news of your son's death to you.'

'Oh, I know that already. I didn't mean that day, but any other. I'd like to invite you but at the moment that won't work. I only go there at night, when it's closed, then I'm all alone.'

'What do you do nights in the cafe, *Frau* Grabbe?'

'I clean, what else am I supposed to do?'

The owner brought them their drinks—the tea and the schnapps on a little wooden tray—and put her hand on the woman's shoulder. 'You've got to eat something, Tania, I still have some chicken fricassee left over. Can I bring you a plate?'

'No, thank you, I'm not hungry.'

'You look pale and exhausted.'

'Maybe the *Herr* Inspector is hungry.'

'If you're eating something,' Franck said, 'I'll have a plate, too.'

Tania poured the rum into the tea glass. 'Today I'm drinking alcohol, like I used to back on our island, I don't need anything else.' She inhaled and licked her lips. 'I'm getting warm,' she said to the waitress. 'Sometimes, we really froze up there by the sea. Thank you, Inge.'

The door to the pub opened. Accompanied by a gust of wind, a married couple of around seventy came inside. Holding the door open the whole time, they looked around, cast the waitress and the two guests a glance but did not move. Both were wearing down jackets, the man had a hat pulled over his face, the woman a colourfully sewn cap with earmuffs. 'Are you open?'

'Of course.' The waitress walked up to the two of them. 'And we're still serving warm food.'

'Ice cream isn't really what I had in mind at the moment,' the man said, making his way between his wife and the waitress over to a table he had probably chosen as his goal. Franck had turned around to look at the two of them and asked himself what was keeping the man from closing the door. Within seconds, the cold air had gone all the way through the pub.

'Have a seat wherever you like,' the waitress said with sweeping gesture. The woman seemed to be considering; in the interim, her husband did not prove to be a windbreak.

Franck, shivering inconspicuously, turned back to Tania, who was watching the newcomers with wide eyes. Then, like a child, she held her hand to her cheek and whispered: 'I know them, they live in the same complex and walk through the neighbourhood all day long, arguing most of the time.'

Franck heard the door click shut and the two walked to a table where they noisily took off their jackets. The owner brought them the menu.

'Are you sure you really don't want to eat?'

Tania shook her head. She carefully sipped her hot tea and closed her eyes; she took two more and looked at the man across from her, bent over the table. 'You're not drinking. To your health.'

He raised his glass and toasted her. Taking a drink, he heard the woman behind him say: 'You don't eat *gulasch*, it doesn't agree with you, you know that.'

'Apparently he used to work for the federal railway company, the Bundesbahn,' Tania's voice flit through the vapour coming off her tea. 'Like Emil, my father-in-law. I don't think they knew each other, though, and I don't remember the man's name either.' She peeked past Franck and, as if caught, immediately looked away again. 'She's kept her cap on.' He could barely hear her whisper. 'She's got two floppy ears.' A suppressed giggle came out of her mouth, which was over before Franck could even catch it.

What he saw was a face gone pale by being lost, its eyes—despite the sparkle triggered by occasional, fleeting, chance looks—simply like mechanically functioning organs.

When she looked at him, Franck felt that that eternal light he now and again thought he could see in the eyes of those left behind as proof of the indestructible connection to a beloved dead person had gone out during those nights of her icy loneliness and no prayer, no zest for life, no passing of time would ever cause it to flame again.

Tania Grabbe had lost her son to whom she had dedicated her life, and he, Jakob Franck, retired chief inspector, and many driven colleagues could not manage to shed light on the eleven-year-old's death and thus give the mother some sense of closure; maybe then she could once again find the courage to have a thought about opening the door to the silent child's room.

'Sometimes,' she said in an unbelievably strong, indeed almost loud voice, as if for her listeners, 'sometimes I think that if Lenny were still just missing, there'd be hope for us all. That would be eternally beautiful.'

From time to time, she wished that the inspector would not notice her hellish agitation. All day long she had had to think of a woman without the slightest idea why. The woman did not play even the tiniest role any more, in her brother's life or her own. She had not even known her well, almost not at all, they had met just once or twice, then she was gone and never returned.

Had her brother not told her the story of her death, Yella Hagen would have long been dead to her.

Yella Hagen from Berlin.

She had lied to Maximilian and cheated on him. Lived with a girlfriend somewhere at the edge of the city, worked as a model or in the red-light district, who really knew? Why had she shown up again all of a sudden, out of the blue, at night?

Tania had lain awake for hours, thinking about the young woman who no longer even had a face, just a name, and the story of her death that her brother had apparently caused.

Then something had occurred to her: hadn't her brother said that, standing by the railing, he'd only heard the falling body as if muffled somehow, like someone rolling over a carpet?

For a while Tania wondered whether he had lied to her; nonetheless, on the beach, without being asked, he had served up all the variations possible, almost exuberantly at that, and later in conspiratorial tones at the pizzeria.

He had confessed to an accident, an accident with a deadly result. Or was it indeed murder? He had pushed Yella, she had lost her balance; afterwards, he got rid of the body.

Her memories would not stop. Was her brother really capable of something like that, she wondered, and put her hands in front of her face, like he did sometimes and as a little boy had done whenever he could not handle the world around him or his annoying sister any longer.

In the certainty that, since that short trip to the North Sea thirteen years ago, she had never spoken with her brother about the woman or the situation again, Tania spent a night that did not want to end.

She apologized to Lennard numerous times for her disloyalty.

The following day came, and Tania continued to think about the island in the North Sea and her brother's confession and that all of it had been forgotten as if behind an impenetrable patch of coastal fog.

As twilight began to fall, she could no longer handle being at home. The name Yella echoed through her head; she could not get it to stop, even when banging on the keys of the piano with both hands and with her husband yelling at her. Not once did Stephan's voice chase off the cursed intruder.

She pulled on her coat, freed herself from her husband's embrace and walked down Welfenstraße in the direction of East Station, and finally through the dark, icy streets around Bordeauxplatz. Then she turned back towards Rosenheimer Platz along the tramlines.

She waited impatiently then set off on foot when the loudspeaker announced a service cut due to an accident, walking past the brightly lit windows of her building to the fast-food restaurant where she stopped, wanting suddenly to warm up with a coffee.

She walked east along the cemetery wall accompanied by the biting wind and the scattered thoughts of her brother; his unfaithful lover; her husband alone in the silent flat after his yells had faded away; Lennard who, no matter how many burgers he wolfed down, did not gain a single gram; the starless night; the frozen snow at the side of the road; her cafe which she still had to clean so that the guests would have nothing to complain about.

The bright light above the entrance to Inge's Berghof pub made her happy. But she was neither hungry nor thirsty; she wanted to keep on going and maybe take a bus from Giesinger Station to Münchner Freiheit, to her cafe.

She looked up at the sign. The yellow light hurt her eyes and she wondered whether Inge had put in a stronger bulb or had just scrubbed the frosted glass clean. Suddenly she wanted to feel a strong tea with rum on her gums. The thought caused her to open the door and go inside.

That is how it all came about.

Out of the fear that, in her state, she might make a thoughtless remark, Tania Grabbe reached for the inspector's hand and met his surprised glance.

'Snow was falling outside the window,' she said. 'On the day my son came into the world.'

He had seen her pass by on the street below and decided that, when she came home, without any reproach or questions, he would just say hello and suggest they go to a nearby Turkish restaurant. He stood in the hallway and waited. After five minutes, he realized that she would not be coming and was probably following some new crazy idea of hers—this time outside their house.

'Can we meet?' Stephan Grabbe asked into his mobile. In the background, he could hear music, voices, the sound of glasses, car horns.

'Come on by.' Maximilian Hofmeister was standing by the half-opened door. In front of it were two young women and a thin young man in a hoodie, cigarettes in one hand, beer bottles in the other.

The bar just a few steps past his house served his favourite beer; all the same, he did not go there too often. At forty, he felt a bit out-of-place and unhip among all the dynamic twenty, at most thirty, somethings and his conventional hair salon and his fifty-hour week made him feel locked into routine. As he saw it, his somehow fashionable beard and bun did not ultimately change his thoroughly uncool, middle-class vibe.

After closing up at exactly seven o'clock, he did not need too long to consider how he would spend his evening. The day's conversations had worn him out more than the work. Sarah's ceaseless questions—Can I do something good for you, boss? Should I pick you up some Chinese? Something bothering you, boss?—reminded him unfairly of childhood friction with his sister. He began to glance at the clock every half hour, angry with himself and unable to relax with trusty old platitudes or pleasantries.

On top of it all, for two days a thought had been keeping him awake at night, a thought whose origin was a single, terrifying riddle.

He sat in bed, miserably cold.

Then he overcame his motionlessness and smacked his hand against the switch. Blinded by the sudden light, he closed his eyes; when he opened them back up, the ghost was still there.

He sank onto his cushion and, as when young, longed for his sister to come and lie down next to him, touching his nose with her eyelashes.

After that, he thought incessantly about Yella, and for a long time did not understand why.

The pub owner handed him his third beer. Hofmeister found his brother-in-law's calling to say he would come by to be the perfect diversion from the corruption of his past.

A little while later they were toasting each other with their bottles. Grabbe drank half of his in one go and then exhaled exhaustedly. 'At least here there's something going on,' he said. 'Not a tomb like our house.'

'Wasn't my day either. How's Tania?'

'I don't know, she left.'

'I was afraid she'd never leave the kid's room again,' Hofmeister said.

'She didn't tell me what she was planning to do.' Until Grabbe finished his bottle, he went silent and stared at the women by the bar. He ordered two more bottles, paid, handed one to Hofmeister and stuffed his own into his jacket pocket. 'Come outside.' He pulled out a pack of cigarettes.

'When you start smoking again?'

'It's the only way.'

Out on the pavement, Hofmeister zipped up his down jacket; Grabbe left his open.

'You can't be angry at her,' Hofmeister said.

Grabbe nodded, took a drag, watched the tram go by. He grabbed the bottle from out of his pocket and took a drink. 'She's in mourning, I get it. I'm in mourning, too, we're all in mourning, day and night. We sit around our place and mourn. What else are we supposed to do? Our child is dead, was murdered. Our son is lying in the East Cemetery, his bed is empty. Wrong. His mother's in his bed now, night after night, during the day too, as far as I know. We don't talk, I don't go snooping around to see what she's up to. She wants to be alone, as far as I can tell. Can I tell you something?'

'Of course,' Hofmeister said. He did not consider hiding even a syllable that someone said about his sister from her, not even a relative and told in confidence.

'The day we learnt . . . ' Grabbe needed another drink; then he flicked the butt over the street and pointed at Hofmeister with the neck of the bottle. 'When the inspector came to the cafe, you know this already, I'd gone for a walk, alone, for three hours. Tania was at the cafe, sitting around, waiting for something. Then someone came, the inspector.

'I couldn't be with her. You want to know why? I'd been thinking about getting a divorce. You hear what I'm saying? That was the very day the police came to tell us that Lenny had been found dead. I wanted to say we were through. Of course, I couldn't talk about it on that special day. You understand, Max? It's got nothing to do with how she's acting now, the insanity she radiates, the fact that she crawls into Lenny's bed, that she doesn't talk with me any more, that she goes to the cafe almost every night to clean.'

'She still does that?'

'She does, and every time she's there longer—she scrubs and polishes and cleans the windows in the middle of the night. You can't live like that, despite the situation, despite the sadness.

'And I'll tell you something else: even if Lenny were alive, she'd still be that absent with me. She's been that way for a long time, and I don't have any explanation. I touch her and she flinches. I ask her what's wrong and she says, "Nothing, everything's OK." I even asked Lenny once, little Lenny, if he thought his mother was acting strange at all. What was he supposed to say? She took care of him, she was always there for him, she worshipped him, he had no reason to feel ignored.

'I'm not bitching. I tried to talk to her, quietly, lovingly. Yeah, now and again we slept with each other. In retrospect, I always thought she was just fulfilling a duty, wanting to do me a favour. That's no life, Max, no marriage, no companionship. It was like that before Lenny's death and after it things have just got worse.

'What should I do? I'm telling you: I'm going to get a divorce. I'll continue to look after things, I'll pay her alimony, I hope we can continue to run the cafe together, I'm not going to take off and screw her over. Nothing binds us together any more, there's just mourning and isolation. Where's the future in any of that, Max? And we still have a future, all of us. Right?'

Hofmeister would have preferred to leave, to put the empty bottle into his hand and go back to his home two doors down, lock the door, turn on the TV, grab another beer from the refrigerator and turn up the volume until his brother-in-law's voice disappeared. He felt such an aversion to everything he had just heard that he only reacted when Grabbe punched him in the shoulder.

'Honestly?' Hofmeister asked. 'You want to know what I think?'

'Say it.'

'I'm not sure we *do* have a future.'

'What?' Grabbe made a face like someone about to vomit. To Hofmeister, the sight was unbearable. He looked to the intersection where a line of people had formed in front of the 24-hour cornershop.

'Lennard's dead, where's any future there?'

'I'm not talking about Lennard!' Grabbe yelled. 'I'm talking about myself! It's got to do with me! Don't you get it, you git? Of course you're standing by your sister. You always have, nothing will come between the two of you. It's been clear to me for a hundred years.

'You go on holidays together, you talk on the phone for hours, you know everything about her and she knows everything about you, and if she's got a problem, she talks to you before she remembers she's got a husband and a business partner she could discuss and clear things up with.

'Do you all just think I'm a pawn you can push around here and there depending on what you need at the moment? From the beginning I've made an effort to compromise, in everything, in my daily life and at work, raising a child, being together. That's how I was raised. You don't always need to be right, you can do without it sometimes without making yourself small. My father was a model for me. My parent's marriage would still be a stroke of luck if my father hadn't had to die all of a sudden. You forget? Goes to the hospital, dies. Five months before Lennard was born. He'd really been looking forward to his grandchild.

'What do you all think with your intimacy, your secrets, your sibling bond that no one can reach, your secret circle you keep everyone out of, even those who just come into your proximity? Who did she go to church with after just coming home from giving birth to light candles and to pray? With me? No. She called you when she got back from being with my mother who, out of despair, had stopped eating and drinking and was just lying around in bed, wanting to die. I wasn't good enough for comfort, she made that abundantly clear, I was there to take care of the business, that was my part, nothing else.

'She let me down, Max, and I didn't get it. No compliment for a man, clear evidence of incompetence. I was a wimp, not any more. She's lost her power over me, you can tell her yourself if you call her tonight.'

'Tell her yourself.' Hofmeister was already by the door. He desperately needed another beer. 'And her name is Tania. T-a-n-i-a.' With a grim expression and crooked movements he pushed his way through the guests to the bar.

Grabbe had lit another cigarette and pulled out his mobile. He dragged his thumb across the screen until the name Claire appeared.

'You at home? I've got to spend the night.'

'Where's Tania?'

'Away. I'll be there in fifteen minutes.'

'Wait . . .'

He stuffed his mobile back into his pocket, took the empty bottle out, put it against the wall of the building and flagged a taxi that was coming over the bridge with its sign lit.

CHAPTER FIFTEEN

The Problem with Fish

The story about the snow on the morning of April twenty-fifth was still bothering him the following day. Franck had been sitting in the room, which had never become a child's room, for hours, leafing through his sloppily written notes from the Berghof pub, trying to figure out why he felt so uncomfortable when Tania Grabbe told him about the birth of her son.

He did not doubt the truth of what she said. What bothered him was the way she conjured up the experience and constantly embellished it with new details, like someone who felt they had to convince the person listening to them that *that* was precisely the way things had gone. In the meanwhile, eleven years had passed and a mother giving birth—at least in Franck's mind—would be concerned with other things than intense observations of the weather or her mother-in-law's cherry-red earrings.

Something about her description had made him sceptical. Considering the circumstances, he felt a bit ashamed. But the longer he thought about it there in his study, the rougher his assumptions became. It had taken hours for him to even halfway lose the armour he immediately donned during questioning and return to his unofficial role as support to the police and listener in times of need—as impartial as possible.

Nevertheless, he could not find any peace of mind.

To concentrate better, he repeated an exercise which during his time on the force had brought him new impulses during seemingly hopeless investigations; in a couple of cases, it had even led him to the definitive clue, what he liked to refer to as 'the fossil'.

Lying on the floor on his blue wool blanket—arms and legs extended, barefoot, breathing evenly—and, with his eyes open, falling into a state of relaxed concentration, his thoughts and the related feelings came into order as if on their own.

That was the way he attempted to bring a bit of clarity to the mess of provable facts they had as well as some kind of heat, without letting himself be overwhelmed by the horror and the brutality of the crime.

He called this process, which could last two or three hours, 'thought-sensitivity'. Later on, in a state of buoyant exhaustion, taking a cold shower, he would mumble his newly won insights to himself, fully aware of how unorthodox his methods would be for any officer-in-training at the academy. On the other hand, his colleagues at the department rarely found anything to disagree with in his approach or suggestions as to how they might look at the crime scenes and statements from another perspective.

After having successfully solved one case, Franck rejected any analysis of his unconventional method. Now and again, however, he would make a suggestion to his friend and closest colleague, André Block, who for his part placed great importance on remaining the only one being privy to such insights; otherwise, Block told him flatly, he would fear for the department's reputation.

Franck did not allow himself to be distracted. Even after leaving the force, he had let the details of the files work on him in the proven way—with the result that a girl's death appeared to him in a new, unexpected light.

And now he was trying again.

The morning after running into Tania Grabbe at Gasthaus Berghof, Franck was lying on the floor of his study, listening to the voice following him and passing him information whose meaning he did not know how to gauge. He summed up his former colleagues' reports and projected all the facts related to Lennard's murder that he could upon the ceiling so that he could trace his inner convulsions, his doubts, his bewilderment at a body of evidence that did not seem to lead anywhere.

His perspective, he thought over and over, was off. The fossil he was looking for like someone lost in the dark was not there. He was convinced of that much and, after his attempts that morning, all the more.

The thing he was looking for had to be in a parallel universe, beyond all that he had understood up until now, far away from the witnesses' statements and declarations, as well as those of the relatives and chance individuals and onlookers who showed up in every crime.

More likely than not—due to back pain, he ended his research after an hour and a half—Franck would have to pay more attention to someone previously unknown or ignored, or something that had been there but for some dubious reason or other had lost its form.

Like a shadow that—unnoticed by anyone or, on the contrary, taken for granted—wanders across a square and, at sunset, suddenly disappears.

Just like the boy, Franck remembered on his way to the bathroom, who had been nearby, unseen, when the schoolgirl died, the schoolgirl whose final hours he was able to reconstitute only twenty years later.

This time he did not have that long.

While he was in the shower, then while getting dressed and then while drinking coffee in the kitchen, Franck wondered what was so important about the snow falling beyond the hospital window the day Lennard was born.

And what did Vera Grabbe's red earrings mean? That woman who had been present at the boy's birth just like his father?

What was the importance of Tania Grabbe's having emulated the Slavic inflection of the midwife without any change of expression, and then continuing to talk, empty teacup in her hands, as if repeating a text she had learnt by heart?

Why was it important for him to know there had been a framed copy of a painting by Cézanne on the wall and that Tania Grabbe had learnt the painter's name as well as the title of the picture—*The Bay of Marseille*—from the doctor, who, with his twisted moustache, looked like an artist to her? And that he generally wore green instead of white cloth shoes?

As a young woman—Franck had just left his home and was on his way to the S-Bahn—her stepmother Vera had been a passionate bowler. Stephan, her son, had loved going with her, and, after every round, would set up the pins on the old wooden lane again and serve the adults their drinks. His father Emil, on the other hand, was a train driver and often not at home for days; in his free time, he would sit in front of the TV reading the paper, but otherwise had nothing to do with raising his son or household affairs. On all the saints' days, Tania Grabbe said, he would bring his wife to the pub to meet her bowling friends and he would play cards with Stephan, which bored the boy to death.

Furthermore, Franck also learnt that—on his trip to the centre city he had to think about Tania Grabbe's extensive descriptions again—after Emil Grabbe suffered a 'completely surprising' heart attack and died not even five months before the birth he had been looking forward to, Tania and Stephan fell into silent spells which often lasted for days. Her father-in-law's death reminded her of her grandmother—Eleonore was her name, she told Franck—who, just in her early sixties, 'from one day to the next fell over dead'.

While Franck was busy watching the simple and monotonously constructed commercial buildings along the side of the tracks from the train window, as he often did, it occurred to him that Tania's brother, Maximilian Hofmeister, had also mentioned his grandmother's death.

In general, Franck thought while walking through the tunnel beneath the main station, Tania and Maximilian's psychological connection seemed to determine the greatest part of the familial bond, it was stronger than the Grabbes' marriage; and Hofmeister himself led a constant, and probably happy, life of being single—as if his sister were enough of a partner.

Falling once again into the sceptical mode he thought he had overcome, Franck had almost missed getting off at East Station. From there, he had to take another train to St-Martins Square, which was close to the crime scene.

People were hurrying everywhere. The voices of the train announcements rang out across the platforms.

The ceaselessly meandering monologue of Lennard's mother would not leave his head, all of the individual details of that twenty-fifth of April; suddenly church bells began to toll, she said, and she noticed a gold tooth in the midwife's mouth; her ardent emphasis of certain phrases, which most likely did not have to do with the two glasses of rum; the way she had sat in front of him, avoiding his glance and dreamily rubbing the blue stone on her necklace before unexpectedly reaching for his hand.

Looking into his eyes as if forced, she had begun to tell him the episodes of her memory. Concentrating on listening, Franck felt the narrow, hard fingers encircling his own. He had needed a few minutes before he was able to pull his hand away and, bending forwards a bit, shake it off beneath the table.

She talked. He wanted to take notes but hesitated out of concern for something he could not quite name. After the first few sentences already, he felt that her desire to tell stories was a kind of diversion.

Although she was talking about the birth of her child with all the intensity she had left, and about the things which had to do with it both directly and indirectly, Franck began to think she was following a plan which had nothing to do with her present need but one that was as mysterious to him as the motive behind Lennard's murder.

In the short street that led to Spitzingplatz and the adjacent playground with its shrubbery and trees, Franck stopped to catch his breath. Driven forward by his tumbling thoughts, he had walked too quickly and almost passed where the road branched off. What he desperately needed was a moment of complete silence.

He pulled a bottle of mineral water out of his shoulder bag and, while drinking, looked at the place where the boy and his murderer had most likely met.

What concerned Franck most of all at that moment was the eleven-year-old child, not his father and mother, not his class-mates or relatives. Nothing was more important than the handful of time required to extinguish a life from the living world.

Thousands of murders and deaths later, and despite the incorruptible sobriety of criminology, whenever Franck thought silently about the victim the only image he saw was that of the midday sun letting an Easter candle melt away out of pure jealousy.

He was not a particularly religious man. The names of the saints were unfamiliar to him. And yet, for a long time, a person's violent end set loose a kind of Abrahamic piousness within him, one which probably allowed him to attach a greater meaning to the murdered one's destiny.

Maybe, he thought, pressing the bell of the corner building by the playground, it was just that his own death concerned him more than before, when he had not had any time for it.

'I see everything,' the old woman said as she led him through her one-room flat to the window and pulled the curtains to the side. Franck could smell washing powder. 'Down there, that's where the kids are, running around screaming all day long. I don't mind, I like to hear them, though I don't understand any Turkish or Greek or what-have-you. Would you care for a coffee?'

'Do you remember November eighteenth?'

'Not at all.' Her name was Irmgard Zille and she was seventy-nine. Franck had learnt as much from the files of those questioned as well as the fact that, at first, she claimed to have seen someone, which she retracted upon later questioning; she had been confused about the day.

'Do you often sit at the window in the evenings?'

'Where else? I don't have a TV, I don't need to know what's going on there. And anyway, I used to work in TV myself.'

'Are you an actress?'

'God forbid! I was a gameshow usher, at the end, on talk shows, but I might as well have been working at the zoo. Would you like a schnapps? *Blutwurz.*'

'Are you trying to poison me, *Frau* Zille?'

'What do you mean? My son's still alive, and he drinks it all the time, even at work.'

'What does your son do?'

'He works in a funeral parlour. It's a steady income. Aren't you warm in your leather jacket?'

He asked her a few more times about her observations, and, once he realized that he would not be learning anything new, said goodbye.

'Thank you for your visit,' she said at the door. She waited until he had disappeared in the stairwell, then locked the door, went into the kitchen, took the bottle of schnapps out of the refrigerator and poured herself a full shot. With the glass in her trembling hand, she walked over to the window. She toasted the afternoon and finished the drink in one go.

She had no idea what her son liked about its taste, to her it was worse than the absinthe she had sometimes secretly taken sips of when yet another sweaty politician was up onstage, holding forth for the camera.

Down on the pavement, two dark-haired boys were yelling at each other, but no sound made it through the soundproof window. Irmgard Zille wondered whether she should go out to the balcony in order to catch a little of the day's hustle and bustle before it turned pitch black again.

'Thanks to the dull light from the streetlamps you can hardly see a thing.' Ralf Lahner, the man who lived above the old woman, was leaning against the balcony parapet. 'And that evening it was really coming down, I can still remember that. Later on we didn't talk about anything else. After they found the boy's body, I mean, supposedly he was murdered right here, in front of our door. I told your colleagues everything I know, and I don't know anything. I racked my brains, of course, everyone wants to do their part.'

'You were at home that evening,' said Franck.

'I was, it's all in the files. I was there, I know I looked out the window too, or was out on the balcony to smoke, one hundred per cent. If there was a murder, I would've noticed. Or no?'

'You were alone.'

'Yeah.'

Franck cast a quick glance at the file he was holding in his hands. 'You left your flat around eight o'clock.'

'Definitely. I had to get to work. It was my shift at the car park. It's in all your notes there.'

'You drove.'

'Definitely. I went down to the underground garage and then I left.'

'You drove right past the playground.'

'I have to, up to Eintrachtstraße, then right.'

'No one was there, not a single person, a single car.'

'There was a storm, and it was raining, I had to be careful in order to see anything through the windscreen. Why are you even showing up after such a long time? I thought the whole thing was solved.'

'What thing?'

'The thing with the playground. I read that, in the end, the investigators didn't find anything. You doing this on your own, or what?'

'As I said: I am not investigating, I am just asking questions. I am looking for clues.'

'That's a good thing, but aren't you a bit late?'

'No.' Franck closed the file and stuck it into his bag, which he had put on top of a weathered wicker chair. 'Were any cars parked in front of the playground that night?'

'There are always a few down there, as you can see.'

'At night, too?'

'Think so. Didn't I say anything about that? It's not in the files?'

'It says that you mentioned having seen parked cars.'

'Then it should be right.'

'Everything went smoothly,' said Franck. Once again, he felt the cold on his head. It seemed to him that in a matter of minutes the dark had fallen like a stiffly frozen drape across the early evening.

'What was supposed to have happened?'

'You came out of the underground garage, turned right and then at the corner down here took a left.' He gestured towards the intersection a cyclist was passing through.

'Exactly.'

'There were cars everywhere.'

'Think so, yeah. One was sticking out. I had to swerve. I honked, yeah, or maybe not. I don't know any more.'

'Where was the car exactly?'

'On the corner.'

'At the entrance to the playground.'

'At an angle,' Lahner said. 'He was probably coming from Schlierseestraße and had just backed in so he could hurry out to buy something.'

'What?'

'Sorry?'

'What did he want to buy?'

'What kind of question is that? No idea. A paper, something at the supermarket.'

Franck stuffed his hands into his leather jacket; he had read the protocol, three or four times, paying particular attention to what the local residents had said. And they were the people he wanted to speak with again.

'Everything OK?' Lahner asked.

'Did you tell my colleagues about that particular car?'

'I'm sure I did.'

'There's nothing about it in the files.'

'Really?'

Inside a light was on. Franck went in to be able to read better. In the meanwhile, Lahner smoked another cigarette, tipping his ashes into the empty flower box the entire time. Franck came back, looked down onto the street, held the file behind his back and waited for Lahner to stub out his cigarette. 'What else did you notice?'

'Nothing. What's up? What's so important about the car?'

'I don't know yet. For a start, I'm wondering why the driver parked there, almost on the street, so that you had to go around it.'

'As I said, he wanted to buy something, I gather.'

'The newspaper stand was already closed,' Franck said. 'And when someone wants to go into a store in that kind of weather, they don't park their car a hundred metres away when they can just double-park out front.'

'You've got a point.'

'You did not see anyone around the car or inside it?'

'I don't like to repeat myself. First of all: dark. Second of all: rain and storms. Third: leaves and crap were flying through the air, end of the world and all that. Wipers at full blast. The car doesn't mean a thing, believe me. The guy probably just had to have a quick piss. People go off behind the bushes, not only bums, it happens here all the time. It's disgusting. It's a playground, for God's sake, no?' He stopped short. 'You got something else to say?'

Franck thought about the man with the plastic bags he had observed the night before when he had had to go to the bathroom badly himself, after waiting for a miracle for hours. The man, most likely a rough sleeper, had put all his bags on one of the benches before heading off for a screened place to do his business. 'So, no one around at all,' Franck said. 'What kind of car could it have been?'

'Just about anything. Not big, not small.'

'Not a van?'

'No.'

'An SUV?'

'No. Normal size, there are tons of middle-class cars down there, this one was too. That was a long time ago. Didn't I mention what kind of car it was in my statement? What's in your secret file?'

'It says that you didn't see a thing. Which clearly is not the case.'

'You trying to stick something on me?'

'On the contrary,' said Franck. 'I'd like for you to remember better. Concentrate.'

'I'm thinking.' With the index and middle fingers of both hands Lahner drummed on his last remaining wisps of hair; he pursed his lips and rocked his head, a laboured expression on his face.

Franck did not move his eyes from where the previously unknown automobile was said to have been, its rear end sticking out into the street. Thanks to the rain, no one had bothered themselves about it; perhaps even *Frau* Zille had noticed the car but not thought a thing, which meant that she could also have seen a person that evening and not another one, as she later said. Franck knew from innumerable question sessions that memories consisted of fissures, ellipses, misperceptions, loose sensory connections.

Turning back to Lahner, he played with the idea of once again questioning all the witnesses in the files, no matter how insignificant their perceptions might have seemed the first time round.

Shaking his head, Lahner fished the packet of cigarettes back out of his pocket. 'I have to disappoint you, but I'm not coming up with anything else.' He pulled his lighter out of the pack, covered the flame with his hand and inhaled deeply. 'I really hadn't thought about it any more, you saw so yourself, and if I had thought about it earlier, it would've been the same. It doesn't mean anything.'

'Was a light on in the car?'

Lahner shrugged.

'Yes? No?'

'Yes and no.'

'Sorry?'

'I'm not sure.'

'Could the light have been on?' Franck asked.

Lahner raised his shoulders, took a drag and exhaled. 'The streetlight's right over the corner, it was probably reflecting off the windows. What did Shorsch have to tell you? He saw the car, too.'

Back when he was still on active duty, these kinds of surprises coming right out of the blue were like sudden bumps on a trip across otherwise completely flat ground.

'Shorsch,' Franck repeated. 'Shorsch what?'

'What do you mean "what"?'

'The man doubtless has a surname.' Franck had not counted on the force of his impatience. 'You've got to know it.'

Lahner flicked the butt into the flower box. 'I do. What's wrong with you? You aren't a police officer any more, just a private citizen, so relax. The man's name is Ritting, Georg Ritting. Over there.' He pointed to the corner building across the street with a hair salon and an empty storefront on the ground floor. 'On the third floor, tell him I said hello, it'll make him happy.'

Ritting did not seem to pay much attention to his neighbour's greeting. He led Franck down the hallway, which was filled to the brim with moving boxes, chairs and various objects, and into the living room, where he offered him a seat in a recliner. Then he shoved all the crossword-puzzle books he had open on the table over one another and put the two pens and the bent reading glass on top; with a snort he fell onto the couch and crossed his arms above his prominent belly. Aside from saying hello at the door, he had not said a word.

Franck guessed Georg Ritting to be in his late fifties, a stooped man with a wide back and strong upper arms whose fat had probably once been muscle. He was wearing a large, red-and-white checked shirt that hung out of his trousers and white socks, no house shoes. Two blue eyes cast gentle glances into the world from out of a round face.

'I'm disturbing you in your free time,' Franck said, sunk deep within the thick chair.

'No, you aren't.' Next to Ritting was a pair of black-and-yellow earmuffs; the colours reminded Franck of Lenny's football. The TV was on but the sound was off. There was a show with historical recordings of the construction of the first skyscrapers in New York. 'Should I turn off the TV? Work-related illness.'

'Did you also work in television?' The question just tumbled out.

'What do you mean by "also"?'

'Earlier I was speaking with an older woman who . . .' He interrupted the statement with a playful grin. 'As far as I'm concerned, you can leave it on.'

'I can watch these documentaries over and over,' Ritting said, holding on to the earmuffs in his lap. Franck noticed that Ritting often blinked one eye when he was listening. 'Actually, it's embarrassing. I was a road-maintenance manager for the state. Whenever and wherever there was a road to be built, I was there. I'd already loved construction when I was a kid. I'd stand at a site and watch the workers bustling about, heaping one stone on top of another, or huge cranes lifting slabs of concrete through the air, and the wires and cables being laid down. And all of a sudden you'd have a foundation, the first window openings would go into the walls, the smell of stone and concrete throughout the air. Other kids would go swimming or go to play football but I would climb site fences and stand there with my mouth open wide. I wanted to be a master builder, but then I became a road-maintenance manager. That was good too. But you're not here for my life story.'

'This ear protection here,' Franck said. 'You use it at work because of the sound of all the machines.'

With a strangely gentle hand movement, Ritting lifted the earmuffs up. 'No. I don't work any more, I had to quit.'

He looked at the TV. Enveloped in a grainy, grey half-light, workers with unnaturally white glowing faces were carrying steel girders across vertigo-inducing depths.

'The doctors diagnosed an illness, suddenly I could no longer handle any kind of racket. I flinched at every noise. The sound of a colleague's snowblower almost caused me to have a heart attack. Then I did in fact have a heart attack, not a bad one but a clear sign. I suffer from phonophobia. That's why I have these things. Ear protection, just like you use to go to shooting practice. They go down to thirty decibels and even less. Without my ear protection I can't watch TV, most of the time I also turn off the sound, just in case. Pitiful, but unavoidable. No one was ever able to explain where my phobia came from, from one day to the next it was there and didn't go away. I live off the state, I was a civil servant, like you. But hopefully you don't have any phobias.'

'I don't know if I do.'

'Then you don't.' Ritting put his headphones down next to him on the couch, bent forward, picked the remote control up from the table and turned off the TV. 'Did you know there's a phobia of clowns?'

'Very funny.'

'It's true. I've forgotten what the phobia's called, but some people suffer from it, even children. And I'm not talking about evil clowns and all those kinds of idiots.'

For a while both men, their faces turned away from each other, seemed to be wondering how the appearance of colourfully dressed figures could cause people of various ages to experience terror while others could not stop laughing.

A dog barking in the stairwell ended their silence. His right eyelid flickering again, Ritting looked into the corridor. 'That's Hugo, the yapper from next door. His owner, *Herr* Tell, is deaf, which he denies. The dog barks the whole day, thankfully, most of the time, down in the park. I can hardly hear him through the thick windows. I can't walk around all day long with my headphones on. And I haven't excused myself for all the mess. My ex-wife just divorced her husband and is leaving her things here with me until she can move in to her new place, which is undergoing renovation. I understood correctly: you don't want anything to drink?'

To his own amazement Franck did not feel the slightest hurry. He still did not want anything to drink, but when he looked at the yellow-and-black headphones, he liked the idea of putting them on and settling into a silence in which there were no more lies and the furious sounds of November eighteenth ceased. Then, he thought, as Ritting's blue eyes watched him, he would perhaps be capable of hearing eleven-year-old Lennard's voice, which up until then had been slumbering in a knothole—an Easter-time gift from death, who was not holding his hand over any murderer.

'I desperately need your help,' Franck said, slowly getting up. He went to the curtain-less window and looked down at the street, where here and there a car passed by or parked; now and again someone left the supermarket, their arms full of bags.

'As I mentioned, your neighbour across the way believes that you saw something the night the young boy was likely murdered. *Herr* Lahner and you spoke about it.'

'We're not all that special, I'm afraid. We meet every so often over at Grandl's, that's the bar on the corner, next to the pastry shop on Werinherstraße. That's true, the day the police and all those people showed up here to close off the playground we spoke to each other; especially once all the other neighbours had been questioned. Not me, I must tell you that immediately.'

'Why weren't you questioned?'

'I don't know. Maybe I wasn't at home. In general, I don't go out much. In any event, no one knocked on my door.'

'Incredible,' Franck said. 'My colleagues went to every building in the area, to every flat, everywhere.'

As if excusing himself, Ritting raised both his hands. 'Naturally, I would have opened up.'

'You must have heard something, my colleagues must have rung the bell many times.'

'That doesn't matter one bit, I deactivated my bell, I used to get scared to death every time the mailman rang. I haven't been able to handle that in a long time. People simply knock at my door when they want something from me. And I'll tell you: No police officer knocked at my door.' He placed his hands on his thighs and stared blankly ahead; then he raised his head and pointed his index finger into the air. 'One second. False. Let's start over: at Grandl's, a woman started to talk to me, she had black hair, I think, I can see her in front of me now, she was wearing a clip shaped like a butterfly in her hair, could that be? What's your name again?'

'Franck. And the woman was from the police.'

'Yes, because she asked me about that evening in November. It was Christmas day, that's when I was at Grandl's to have lunch. What all comes back to mind when someone insists on asking. That's why no one knocked. I did make a statement! Now I feel better.' Snorting again, he leant back and stretched out his arms and legs.

In his mind, Franck returned to his table; getting ready that morning, he was sure he had not read Georg Ritting's statement. 'What did you see that evening?'

'Nothing in particular. Some cars around. A few people in a hurry, what with all the rain. My statement did not produce any results, that's certain.'

'You talked with *Herr* Lahner about having also seen an unusually parked car, in fact, right in front of the entrance to the playground. The car was sticking out into the street so that Lahner had to swerve to avoid it.'

'Correct. And I also said that a man had got out of the car beforehand.'

Franck felt that he had just stumbled over another bump. 'A man,' he repeated to win some time. 'Did you tell the police officer that?'

'What a question. Probably not. I first talked about it later on with Ralf. Or did I? That wasn't important either; I just happened to have looked out the window. A man getting out of a car, not exactly a sensational observation. Who knows if that's even the same car that Ralf was talking about. Pure speculation. Not to mention a month had already passed.'

He watched Franck bend over and pick up the leather bag he had leant against the back of the chair to pull out a black folder.

Franck leafed through the papers inside, went through the same pages a number of times, looking for the definitive point. Then he closed the folder, ran a hand across the cover and let out an indefinable sound he usually only made after getting up from his quirky concentration exercise and shaking out his limbs.

'Your friend from the bar did not mention the man in his statement,' Franck said. 'I do not have your statement with me, *Herr* Ritting, but I would know if I had encountered that detail. You did not mention the man to the police officer. What did he look like?'

'A man in the dark,' he said, blinking wildly. 'And today I would no longer say I had really seen him that particular evening. Perhaps I made a mistake, it happens, time goes by, I never really look at the clock and rarely look at the calendar. We were chatting down at the bar, or rather, Ralf was talking and entertaining people and I was listening. Maybe the idea with the man came from him and I just agreed with him so that I could have some peace; it happens. I like him, basically he's the only one I regularly go and have a beer with. Well, sometimes my ex-wife, we're used to that from when we were married, we never argued at the pub, on the contrary, there we were something like one heart and soul. Back at home was where things were rocky, that was the problem zone.'

Franck's old impatience rose up and he wanted to begin pacing; instead, he sat back down in his chair so that his host would not have to look up at him. 'Please describe the man.' And as with Ralf Lahner in the building across the street he added an urgent: 'Concentrate.'

Ritting closed his eyes and for a few minutes remained as if frozen, his stomach almost upright, hands again on his thighs, mouth half-open. Franck could do nothing but watch. Out of tension he had not noticed that he had folded his hands over the file folder.

Ritting's eyes popped open; he blinked. 'A black shadow,' he said. 'He hurried off and was gone. I can't offer you anything else.'

After a moment of puzzled dismay, Franck picked up his bag from the floor, slid the folder inside and took out his unlined block of paper and a pen. He put the bag back, next to the chair, turned the first page and drew a straight line down the middle of the empty leaf; on the right he wrote 'car (normal sized)', on the left 'man hurries off'. He wanted to write down more of Ritting's brittle memories, to put his observations into his own words but the pen slipped out of his fingers and onto the carpet.

Ritting turned his head in fright. 'What's with you?' His nervous tic had begun to affect both of his eyes. 'I'm very sorry if I disappointed you. I did not intentionally lie to you about the statement, I just forgot . . . '

'The man,' Franck said. 'Did he hurry off onto the playground or across the street?'

'Across the street? No. That's impossible, I would've seen that. He must have . . . I didn't stay at the window. Do you think I saw the murderer? That can't be. And . . . and . . . ' His massive upper body began to sway back and forth. 'One hundred per cent, there was no child, no boy, there was no one else, that much I can say. I swear to you, *Herr* Franck, I didn't see anyone, just that shadow. I cannot do anything else for you.' He let himself fall back onto the cushion, and then stayed put, snorting and fingering his headphones.

'Should I get you something to drink? Do you take medication?'

'I don't take anything,' Ritting said tiredly. 'I would just like it to be quiet.'

No noises found their way inside, no dog was barking in the stairwell. Right when Franck was about to stand up, Ritting turned. 'I'm not asking you to go,' he said. 'Do stay, we don't have to talk.'

Franck rose and extended his hand. 'Thank you for your help. I may get in touch with you again.'

'It was a pleasure.'

'You don't need to accompany me to the door.' He stuck his notepad into the inner pocket of his leather jacket, picked up his bag, slung it over his shoulder.

'Do you have any pets?' Ritting asked abruptly.

'No.'

'My ex-wife thinks I should get an aquarium, fish don't make any noise, but I'd still have someone to talk to. Would you speak with confined fish?'

Franck had never thought about it.

'The fish can't hear you through the thick glass,' Ritting said. He shook his head and the hesitant smile that crossed his pale lips—once again Franck was looking at him as if transfixed—seemed to flow into the blue of his eyes.

From the place in front of the playground where the car the two neighbours had mentioned supposedly stood, Franck looked up at the third floor of the corner building.

In the faint light of the flat, he recognized the road manager's silhouette at the window. Then his glance fell onto the brightly lit hair-salon on the ground floor; he thought about Tania Grabbe's brother who he had gone walking along the river with and who was obviously carrying around some kind of secret—just like his sister.

Facing the deserted little park in that normal neighbourhood, Franck asked himself for the first time what gave him the right to stick his nose into the siblings' private affairs when he and his well-experienced colleagues had failed so miserably to solve the crime.

No family member was complicit in the child's death. As opposed to most of the cases when a child violently loses their life, Lennard did not die at the savage hand of a relative but that of an absolute stranger. And right there.

Walking in circles through the dark on the gravel path and its patches of icy snow, Franck stretched out an arm to point at a bench beneath one of the trees; there, in the middle of all those buildings and heavily trafficked streets, that is where the boy had been killed.

At an increasingly fast pace, Franck rounded the playground equipment growing out of the remaining bits of black snow like foreign objects, his voice growing louder as if there were people listening just behind the trees. 'We've failed!' he yelled. 'We're blind and deaf and dusty, our routines have made us uninspired . . .'

After the second round, he stumbled back onto the pavement. He spun around and around, waiting for a car that he would recognize—however that might be—and did not know where to go.

A driver honked. Franck was standing in the middle of the poorly lit street. The driver honked again and, after Franck moved to the side, a third time.

He walked on. Ralf Lahner, the car-park security officer, out on his balcony smoking, watched him go.

Unawares, Franck reached Grandl's bar on the corner of Werinherstraße. He was in the mood for a beer. Before that, however, he had to make a call.

Breathing heavily, he took his mobile out of his jacket and leant next to the door; first he wanted to calm down; then he did not see the point. He typed Chief Inspector Holland's number. She barely had time to answer before he began speaking.

She was sitting on her swivel chair, arms over the neck rest, legs up on the desk, looking at the computer. Police announcements from the entire region appeared constantly on the screen in the form of a table. She listened to the caller. The smartphone from which Franck's slightly distorted voice, accentuated by traffic sounds, came was lying on her stomach. Three minutes and forty-eight seconds long. Then he said: 'Did I make myself clear?'

Holding the phone in her hand, Holland pulled her feet off the desk and put her elbows in their place. 'Acoustically speaking, absolutely,' she said. 'Content-wise, the case seems to be as follows: In and around Spitzingplatz, in nineteen of the nearby streets, we questioned a total of six hundred and forty-five people and checked out a number of them . . . '

While Franck had continued to talk, she had, without changing her comfortable position, clicked away from the INPOL news ticker and called up the data on Lennard Grabbe's murder case.

'Not one person came under suspicion to our investigators, not a single man, woman or teen. We double-checked the lease and ownership agreements multiple times and, with a number of people whose statements seemed a bit shaky or even bogus, we contacted relatives or work colleagues, partly in the area, party in other cities and regions, all the way to Switzerland, Italy, Serbia, Croatia and Finland. No indications of complicity, no connection to the boy's family or school.

'Let me repeat the number for you one more time: six hundred and forty-five people. We were relentless—not a day's rest, you can imagine. All the observations that had to do with the suspected night of the murder did not bring us one step further, not one.

'And we followed up every lead, every detail, no matter how absurd, every windbag's crap, every assertion and every rumour. We typed our fingers raw.

'Oh yeah. This helped us catch five crack dealers, two sommeliers working illegally in a brewery and a voyeur, who liked to watch and take photos of old women and justified everything by saying that they didn't have anyone else who looked at them and wanted them. And to come to your two special witnesses: the first, this night security guard . . . '

'Car-park security guard,' said Franck.

'I know, I just wanted to make sure you were listening. The car-park security guard talked my ear off when I questioned him at his place, telling me over and over again the story about the strangely parked car; every time nothing came out of it, *nichts*, zero, neither a halfway usable description of the car nor anything else; he likes to listen to himself talk or whatever. Which is why, in the protocol, I reduced his statement down to the essentials.

'The other guy, the friendly *Herr* Ritting . . . Did he really remember my hairclip? That's incredible considering his usual powers of recollection . . . I did indeed meet the gentleman in the bar, and he said that he had possibly seen someone that evening, but he was by no means certain. He wanted to talk with his acquaintance from across the street, *Herr* Lahner, first, the two had talked about the evening a lot. But nothing else came of it. We were at his flat, like you, and everything he had to say was just half-baked, I can't put it any other way. I think that the car-park man just talked his ear off with his story about the car so that poor *Herr* Ritting convinced himself that he'd also noticed something.

'With that kind of investigation just constantly leading back to nothing, our guys get grumpy too and don't want to hear any more crap. You know the phases. The man was honest with us, I recognize that, you met him yourself, he's a good guy at heart. But as a witness he's useless.

'So, Jakob: thank you for your attempts to bring a bit of light into the darkness, we appreciate it. André and I both. No reason to curse us or accuse of us of . . . how did you put it . . . *juggling soap bubbles instead of engaging in well-grounded policework and taking our witnesses seriously.*

'For the last time: there aren't any witnesses. The night at Spitzingplatz is as good as dead. A very rare and terrible state, but—as you know from other cases—sadly not an impossible one.

'Have I made myself clear?'

'As always,' said Franck.

The silence that followed lasted too long for Holland. 'Where are you?' she asked. 'What's all that noise?'

'Traffic jam at the intersection, a car's sticking out into the road, chaos. I need some earmuffs.'

'Sorry?'

'What's going on with Amroth, the insurance rep?'

'After luring him out of his reserve in that special way of yours, he was compelled to, as you know, pull down his trousers with us, so to speak,' Holland said. 'Sadly, with no positive effect on the case. In the meantime, he's back at home. It wasn't him either. Would you like to meet up and have something to drink?'

'Not today.'

A man in a thin brown suit and worn blue trainers stepped out of the bar. He shuddered, cast Franck a wry glance, pulled up the collar of his suit and crept along the building to the corner where nothing was going on any longer.

'Do you want to talk with André? He's just coming in the door.'

'Not today,' Franck repeated.

They said goodbye. Franck opened to the door to Grandl's.

For a while, Holland and Block looked at each other without saying a word.

'What was it?'

'Like us, he's starting to lose the ground under his feet.'

She hugged the ball the inspector had pressed into her hands when leaving and smelt the leather. Carefully, she ran her fingertips over it; she put it down next to the pillow and held it tight. Then she fell asleep. When she woke up from a dreamless slumber two hours later, she brushed her cheek against the football and thought she could smell Lenny's shampoo.

'I've got to take off at twelve tomorrow, on the dot.'

'That means that, until we close, I'll be alone in the cafe for two hours,' Claire Wiest said.

'Nothing to be done.'

'What's so urgent?'

'I've got a date with a killer,' Stephan Grabbe said.

CHAPTER SIXTEEN

Men's Confinement

His insomnia, she thought, was not to blame for the unease he exuded, his flighty gestures, his tangential statements. Her ex-husband, that much was clear to her shortly after he showed up unannounced, was thrashing about in a net of memories, just like the last time he had visited. He smelt of alcohol and admitted to having had four quick beers in a row. Marion knew him well enough to know that alcohol never drew him out and made him say things he later regretted.

Franck—she could see it and did not ask—was extremely stressed. The only thing that seemed to give him any relief was meeting someone he could take his shoes off in front of and walk around, as if entangled in nothing but his own thoughts.

At Grandl's bar, Franck had just sat silently and after the second beer simply raised his empty glass to order. The other guests were of no interest. And yet, it was because of them that he had come inside in the first place. While accusing Chief Inspector Holland of all kinds of things on the phone, he wallowed in the thought that, that night, he would encounter some kind of information that the shoddy investigations had not given enough credit.

His inner pleading for answers in Lennard Grabbe's murder case had suddenly and unconsciously changed into a form of hubris in whose wake his reproaches had almost gone too far.

Only when Elena put the facts in front of him and unambiguously put him in his place did he come back to a sense of reason.

Nevertheless, he still thought conducting a round of questioning in the bar was a good idea; he thought he was on the right path. But hardly had he sat down at the table next to the door and looked around at the five male guests that he realized he was wrong and that every talk would be destined to fail from the start.

The intoxicated men did not give off an air of anything but apathy. Staring straight ahead, full of ragged thoughts and angry at his terrible mood, Franck drank one glass after the other. Then he stood up—he had not taken off his jacket—put a bill down on the table and walked to the door. No one said a thing; someone loudly blew their nose.

He did not know what he would have done if the woman he had been married to for nine years and for a while now had been sharing a new intimacy with had not been there. He probably would have walked from where she lived on Pariser Straße to East Station and got on the S-Bahn. At the same time, the idea of hanging around in his study alone with the incomprehensible files or giving in to the need for mindless distraction by playing hours of online poker made him so uneasy that, instead of going home, he probably would have gone to the station bar and started up a conversation with one of the regulars instead.

'Another?' Marion asked but did not make any move to get him a fresh beer from the refrigerator. Stretched out on the sofa in her red kimono, she followed his movements throughout the room. Whenever he directed a question at her, she did not answer; she had understood that he needed to be listened to, here and there maybe receive a compassionate nod.

She learnt about his encounters with the two men in the buildings facing each other, his apparently pointless efforts at establishing outlines and precise timeframes. The black holes of the past few days in which he had intended to do so much but which, in his words, had just treated him like an unwanted guest.

Again and again Franck evoked the boy's form. He described the place where Lennard had most likely suffered his deadly injuries; then, at the next moment, he jumped decades back because—as Marion had come to realize—the eleven-year-old's destiny for him was inextricable from that of the fifteen-year-old Lina whose murderer the police had been alerted to by a witness.

Just a short while ago, Marion had told her best friend Elke it was as if, through the crime at Spitzingplatz, the death of Franck's sister had come crashing back into his life and once again ripped open a huge crater at his feet.

'Come on, sit down a moment,' she said.

He was propped up against the back of the chair and felt a vague need for sleep, for absence; for him, the world around him was made up on a single, soundproof child's room.

He knew that he was obsessed but did nothing about it.

As unsettled as he was by the fact that he had to admit that his thought sensitivity had not brought him to any deeper understanding of the circumstances but, on the contrary, had catapulted him of his trusty coordinate system, he unwaveringly swore by the logic of a labyrinth.

'Let us suppose that we accept there are no witnesses,' he said, once again leaning against the balcony door. He had stretched out his left arm, turned his hand palm up and spread his fingers as if balancing an invisible ball. 'What's left? What do we still have in our hand? On this side, there isn't anything, see? Assuming we're happy with this. And so?'

Marion looked at him. He stretched out his right arm and made a fist. 'We have to hold onto what's in here.' After looking back and forth at both hands, he let his arms sink, moved off from the glass door and began to talk again while moving back and forth.

'Traces, data, forensic evidence: truth's clear and incontro-vertible patrimony. That's what we've got to recognize, that's what leads us to the hidden door behind which the perpetrator thinks they're safe. Uwe Nawrath thought so too. You remem-ber? He went to work and on the weekends holed himself up in his room and listened to music. Had little contact with his peers.'

Standing in front of the sofa, he looked into Marion Siedler's face; she stood up. He folded his hands behind his back. She noticed the sweat on his forehead and the bags under his eyes, the pale, stubbled skin. She did not ask him again if he wanted anything to drink, maybe water for a change.

'Naturally he was questioned,' Franck said. 'His responses sounded convincing, what else? Who would've thought that a nineteen-year-old could come into question?'

'You hadn't excluded it.' She wanted to encourage him. The pained, policeman-like look she knew so well and did not care to have in her private life upset her.

He seemed to be considering her observation. 'He was a good liar, the kid, at work too. He was apprenticing at a garage and was robbing his boss, he wasn't a suspect for a long time. Talented guy. Not one of us realized that Lilly knew him. They would meet on the sly, she probably liked him because he was a raw dog that didn't take any crap . . . '

'Please, Hannes, don't beat yourself up about it any more.' She did not notice that she had addressed him with his nickname.

(They had first seen the film with Hans Albers decades ago and been both impressed and touched; since then, they had watched it countless times on DVD. At some point, Franck had begun to call her Gisa and she had begun to call him Hannes. The habit continued after their divorce.)

'She played recorder,' he said, walking back and forth in front of the table. 'The most difficult pieces, a real pro. Just like Lennard, he played with dedication and talent, and most recently even piano and guitar too. Maybe they both could have become musicians . . . '

'Hannes . . . '

'Well, they're just dumb things that distract us.' He stopped and sunk his head, gasping.

'Please, sit down, please . . . '

'She would give him butterfly kisses,' he said before going silent and moving back into the past. 'Lilly would kiss me softly on the head when I wasn't feeling well, and Lennard's mother would brush his cheeks with her lashes—no doubt his heart skipped a beat every time. What do you think, Gisa?'

'No doubt,' she said. 'Let me get you something to drink.'

'Don't go. I'm telling you . . . ' Again he curled his right hand into a fist. 'They aren't recognizing the facts, they've got them in their hands but they're coming to the wrong conclusions. Therefore, and I have to say this one more time, the assumption that there are no witnesses is false. I have run into at least one. They did not question the man intensively enough two months ago, they spoke to hundreds of people but did not listen.'

'There you go again, insulting your colleagues. The inspector explained everything to you, and yet you still don't believe her.'

'I believe her and am convinced the decisive clue is in the files.'

'Why are you so sure? André's special unit isn't made up of idiots.'

'No.'

'So why are you criticizing their work so vehemently?'

'What am I supposed to tell Lennard's mother if I see her again? How can I look her in the eye? She's falling out of the world, soon she won't need us any more, she won't need anyone, not her man or her brother and not her family, we've all pushed her away. We've left her alone with her son's death and there's nothing for her to do but sink away inside it. We are no longer responsible because we have no witnesses, no evidence. Millions of people in the area but no suspects. I delivered her the news of her son's murder and she is waiting for me to return and deliver her the news of having caught the murderer. Like back when the inspector told us that a minor by the name of Uwe Nawrath had admitted to killing my sister. That's how it's got to be. Do you understand that, Gisa?'

'I would like,' she said, 'for you to sit down next to me and be quiet for a bit.'

For a time he avoided her stare.

At five minutes past twelve, Grabbe left the cafe in Schwabing. At twenty minutes to one, he was standing in front of the killer's door and could hear his footsteps.

When Siegfried Amroth unlocked it with his jangle of keys and grumpily stuck out his head, Grabbe punched his shoulder, pushed him back into the hall and shut the door with his other hand.

In the half-light, the insurance representative did not recognize the intruder straight away.

'You ruined our life,' Grabbe said. 'You think you can screw around with us like you have the police. Why did they let you go again? I can tell you: because you're an amateur.'

'Herr . . . Herr Grabbe . . . '

'You seduced my son, you're a child fucker, and you were always a killer, says so in the paper. But now you're going to confess something and on paper so my wife can read it too, and then you're going to say goodbye.'

Amroth did not understand what the man meant; he was wearing his inexpensive cloth trousers, as he always did at home, and the fuzzy, indestructible wool sweater he wore every winter which kept him so warm that he never had to turn up his radiators more than two notches.

'You mass murderer, you dog,' Grabbe said. 'How many kids are on your conscience? Tell me the truth. Or do you want me to beat it out of you? What are you staring at?'

Taking a step backwards Amroth ducked into the kitchen, his hands on the doorframe; his right foot slipped out of his felt slipper; when he tried to edge back in, he unintentionally kicked it under the table where his plate of potato salad was still waiting. He looked over and got angry at being disturbed; by his former neighbour, by a psychopath.

By the time Amroth realized the man had put both his hands around his neck, he was already gasping for breath. He wanted to yell for help. For reasons he could not explain, it occurred to him that he had never done something like that before; he felt small and cowardly.

But the pain triggered by the two thumbs bearing into his skin dispelled any other thoughts. Amroth let out a loud wheeze; spit ran down his chin, his legs buckled. His head bent back he stared at the ceiling but could not see anything because his eyes were wet with tears. Close to his ear was a voice whose sound made him break into a compulsive smile of grotesque hope.

'You'll never be able to pay for what you have done.' Grabbe felt a strange kind of sweat running beneath his fingers. 'The only thing left for you to do is kill yourself. Before that, though, I'm going to bring you to my wife. Lately, she's been spending most of her time buried in the kid's room. You know why? Of course you know why. You listening to me?'

Grabbe abruptly let him go, turned, took a step forward, paused. Then he spun back around and threw his fist.

Caught above his breastbone, Amroth stumbled back against the wall and crumpled to the floor. In shock, he thought he was going to suffocate. But when the other man sat down on the chair he had just been sitting in himself and rubbed his hands together with a relaxed expression like someone who had just come from the cold into a warm room, Amroth came to his senses. He mumbled a few words that seemed to interest his listener; Grabbe bent forward and let his arms dangle.

'Why . . . why are you doing this . . . to me?' The attempt to prop himself up on one hand, to bend his legs and stand was unsuccessful. Using his other hand to help, Amroth just barely managed to keep from falling over like a wet bag. He grew furious, just like when he was questioned by the police and the decommissioned inspector. He greedily wanted more.

'Is that a joke?' Grabbe asked.

'Please . . . please . . . I don't know . . .'

'You've got to speak clearly, I don't understand a thing. I tell Samira all the time too, every word's got to be clear, no one likes a mumbling waitress. Mumbling. Sigi?'

'Who . . . who . . . Samira . . .' The wall behind his back gave him an unexpected feeling of relief. The dull pain in his chest where he had been punched seemed to be lessening. Sitting as upright as possible he tried to breathe evenly; whenever he moved his upper body even a centimetre, though, he winced. 'At any rate, I'm swelling,' he thought confusedly, though the fear of death no longer came out of his pores, which made him a drooling old man but one who would not be defeated by a short-legged burglar.

Whatever the man had said to him Amroth had already forgotten. After a few seconds, he took this to be a sign of his willpower returning—even if he could smack himself for it otherwise.

'Understood,' he replied, putting his palms on the floor, stretching his arms and lifting his behind. Not a good idea. His arms buckled, and he fell forwards. He felt as if a bolt of lightning had shot out of the depths of his arse and into his back, setting off a thundering in his skull that refused to stop.

He had never let out such a fervent cry before, he was sure of that immediately, not even at the height of his youth.

'Pull yourself together,' Grabbe said emptily. He did not have any plan. Nevertheless, for days he had been unable to think of anything but visiting his former neighbour on Weißenseestraße. He wanted him to talk; he wanted him to accept responsibility; he wanted to spit in his face; to ask him whether what the paper said was true: that Amroth was a voyeur and a stalker.

But if Grabbe was being honest, his scheme was of interest to him for one single and grotesque and squalid reason: visiting the old man's home, which he had imagined in all shades, gave him the chance to escape his ceaseless soliloquy.

The endlessly closed door of the child's room, his own now-immeasurable incapability for lenience, empathy and patience had placed Stephan Grabbe in a state as black as the grave, and he could not find his way back out; not even with his employees or his secret lover Claire, with whom he spent the night ever more frequently, bored, passive and surprised by his body's impulses which he would have preferred to have prevented.

Again and again he would repeat the story of the longed-for day in his head, the day he would deliver a cosmically sweeping blow, after which the world would be healed.

For days, there was nothing preposterous to him about this idea at all.

Conjuring up the neighbourhood, the building, the way the flat was decorated, all the possible encounters in the stairwell and out front in his awesome rage, it only occurred to Grabbe much later that he had forgotten his victim's name.

'He' is what he had named him, he—the who was clear. He, the dog, the killer; the one who belonged in the ground, in the hole of the damned; he who, not suspecting a thing and then begging for mercy the rest of the day, would remain unheard.

Grabbe had almost accidentally asked his wife for the name.

For hours—at night after Tania had once again left the flat without a word to, as he called it, dedicate herself to her self-imposed penance of cleaning—he would indiscriminately leaf through folders full of correspondence with business partners and friends' holiday postcards. Dig through drawers full of notes and unnecessary things.

Egged on by alcohol-induced ambition—hardly would his wife be out the door than he would open a bottle of white wine, then a second—he did not hesitate in front of Lennard's room either. His search through the shelves and in the wardrobe brought him nothing but a wave of sadness as soon as he saw the orderly made bed and the black football on the pillow. Afterwards he would grumble to himself why he had gone in to the room in the first place; where his wife was; what day it was; why the candle was burning on the windowsill.

Full of anger at his stupidity, he would walk back into the kitchen and drink wine out of the bottle, knocking it back like water. He had no idea what to do any more.

Wobbling, holding onto the empty bottle, he stared at the open door of the child's room. Then he sniffled and started to hiccup, which did not bother him until the bottle slipped out of his wet hand and exploded into pieces on the floor.

The loud crash did not bother him. He stubbornly waited for another sound.

All of a sudden he found the silence less oppressive.

After a while, he reached for the dishtowel and wiped it across his face. 'You'll pay for the broken bottle,' he heard himself mumble. That is precisely when his former neighbour's full name came to mind.

'I'm sorry.' Amroth coughed and was afraid his head would explode. He frantically searched his mind for the man's first name; he had remembered his surname, which was logical: Lennard was named Grabbe.

'The guy's shown up because of Lennard,' shot through his mind. Why did that occur to him only now? Lenny was dead and his father believed that he, his neighbour, was the murderer because that was the easiest solution.

The realization hit him as unexpectedly as the punch. He bent over again and spit; he spit onto the kitchen floor in the same way he would have at the edge of the pitch, watching the boy kick the ball. He speechlessly looked at the drops of spittle on the ground and felt some left over on his chin. He was overcome by disgust—with himself and especially the man with the greasy curls and bloodshot eyes of a drunk, who was just sitting in the kitchen chair shaking his head, looking like a milky-faced loser.

Amroth wiped the back of his hand across his mouth. He gathered up all his strength, swung his upper body forward, took a deep breath, reached for the refrigerator and, pressing his hands against it, centimetre by centimetre, lifted himself into the air, snorting, with a pulsating pain in his buttocks and wobbly knees. The blatantly obvious fury he felt mobilized his reserves.

Determined to put up a fight, after having turned his back to Grabbe during his torturous getting up, he turned back around. The first thought that came to mind was that he didn't give a shit what the man's first name was. 'Why . . . why?' he asked for a second time. 'Why are you doing this, *Herr* Grabbe?'

'What?'

Amroth noticed that his right hand was trembling; it had been happening ever more often, and he had no idea why. 'You have . . . you have no right to be here.'

Grabbe noticed a smell of sweaty clothes and musty air. His reason for coming to the narrow, poorly ventilated flat now struck him as pure vanity. 'I should never have provoked the old man in such a heavy-handed way and let myself go,' he thought, and grew extremely angry. Looking at Amroth, he experienced a bout of physical disgust at the thought that he had lowered himself to the level of a man who attacked young children and lured them into his flat with slimy promises, the spawn of dirt. It was no wonder the walls stank.

The two men—mid-sixties the one, early fifties the other—stood across from each other in the disordered, unheated kitchen despising one another to a cosmic degree.

Neither Stephan Grabbe nor Siegfried Amroth was familiar with the feeling. Both of them, each in their own way, felt they were capable of committing an act they would later regret. Amroth, who for days had not left his house out of the fear of running into reporters or neighbours asking unnecessary questions and casting evil glances, was cultivating his contempt for the state, the authorities and public opinion with obsessive devotion and the arrogant patience of a convict sentenced to pointless gardening.

Grabbe's contempt fed upon a dark pool of tedium and boredom that overcame him when in the mornings he woke up alone and, in the evenings, went back to bed alone, condemned to leading a life whose meaning had become a personally offensive mystery and whose solution remained barred to him like the touch of his wife or even a word.

The longer the two dissimilar and yet, in their self-actuating fury, similar men shared the silence, the more absurd and incomprehensible the situation appeared to them.

For minutes they silently exchanged threats. They audibly snorted their built-up desire to destroy each other and would have sneered at anything else as unmanly posturing.

Their faces were impassive. Amroth had crossed his arms in front of his chest; Grabbe, his hands in his pockets, did not raise his head once. Most of the time, Amroth looked past him to the tear-off calendar on the wall which still showed the day before.

As Amroth began to think about his wife and all the ridiculous stuff she had probably told the press and police about him, Grabbe stood up and went into the hall. Then the door closed behind him.

Through the small kitchen window came the barking of a dog.

'Shut up, Bongo!' Amroth yelled.

She was already at the door when she noticed a small brown spot on the tablecloth. She put the salt and the pepper shakers down on the chair, pulled the starched and normally bright white tablecloth off the table and brought a new one out of the cupboard in the office. She smoothed it flat, placed the shakers in the middle, cast one last glance through the cafe and opened the door.

The air was icy. No one was out, no light on in the windows across the street. Tania Grabbe locked up, put the key in her coat pocket. She only needed a few minutes to reach the underground. At Münchner Freiheit, she suddenly stopped at the top of the stairs down to the basement level. The illuminated clock at the bus stop said one-fourteen.

Young people were standing around or walking through the nearby streets, some with bottles of beer in their hands, others with slices of pizza of kebabs from the takeaway stands where lines of hungry, thirsty partiers formed and reformed without cease. Tania looked over and wondered if she should go stand in line—not because she was hungry or thirsty but out of a desire to belong.

She turned and looked to the taxis; even the cars were standing in rank and file in the taxi stand in front of the department store.

With an awkward hand movement she waved to no one in particular and crossed the street. Strolling in the direction of the city centre, past the taxi drivers waiting, smoking and leaning against their cars, she smiled and wondered: Where would she have told a taxi driver to go?

She did not know. She had no goal.

CHAPTER SEVENTEEN

'It's a Dead Lead, My Friend'

'The city's always so beautiful at night,' Tania Grabbe thought, stopping whenever a group of vivacious partygoers came towards her, laughing and talking.

On the way from Münchner Freiheit along Leopoldstraße to the Victory Gate the name she had been trying to think of the whole time came to her. Partygoers. People attending parties, something she had last done around twenty years earlier. It's always so beautiful, she thought, life raging everywhere one looked.

Based on a misunderstanding, she was sure of it immediately, a man in his mid-twenties wearing a colourfully patterned, teardrop-shaped hat and a green wool coat returned her smile. She guessed he had taken it to be a comment on him and his lively step; in truth, she was simply relieved to have noticed the spot on the tablecloth at the last minute. Otherwise, on Monday, Stephan would have berated and blamed Claire or, worse, poor innocent Samira. She knew her husband: it was always someone else's fault.

'I shouldn't think like that,' she said to herself. Then, clearly knowing the way, a cyclist shot past with his lights off, spooking her. By the time she turned around, he had already disappeared into the distance with his billowing black cape.

She imagined him having forgotten an appointment and hurrying to the edge of the city, to a bar that was already long closed while his girlfriend waited on an abandoned park bench across from it, writing one unanswered SMS after another. When he arrives, out of breath, and jumps off his bike and she hugs him and begs him to tell her where he's been and why he didn't respond to any messages he says: 'This morning I fell out of time and needed till now to find my beloved's shadow again.'

For, and this much Tania knew, he had long been dead and the girl a lost creature.

As when the great murderer had held court.

At the traffic light by the Victory Gate, she glanced about.

She saw the dead exchanging kisses and secret gestures; she saw them listening to loud music in their cars and crossing the street against red. For what could really happen to them?

Back at the cafe where, because it was a weekend, she had also cleaned the windows and rubbed the panes of the cake displays with a new glass cleaner, she had thought two or three glasses of the lovely artichoke liquor would be good for her; it had almost made her joyful.

For the first night in ages, she looked at the photo on the wall across from the beach chair as something other than a window onto the Dead Sea. Suddenly people appeared behind the dunes, waving; she could hear children's cries and gulls; a yellow kite fluttered over the beach; kite-surfers balanced themselves like acrobats over the powerful North Sea waves; she could not see them, but she could hear the hiss of their boards; she was not deaf.

Holding onto the framed photo carefully with one hand, she dusted off the glass, breathed on it and held it to her eye for an ample butterfly kiss. Then she hung it back on the hook. The shimmering afternoon light from the beach fell onto her;

she closed her eyes and licked her lips, which tasted both sandy and sweet. When she opened her eyes back up, Lenny was doing somersaults across the sand in his fire-red bathing trunks.

Tania could remember how, up until he went to school, he was the quickest and most flexible somersaulter that ever rolled across the earth; even Stephan agreed. When they would watch their son throw himself to the ground, tuck in his head, curl up and roll forward like a ball, seemingly without any strain or tire, they would clap with happiness. The applause egged him on. At one year and eleven months, Lenny made his first somersault, Tania had written it down in her photo album, right next to the snapshot showing him lying on the carpet after his first-ever roll with a wine-red head from all his laughter.

'He was so happy,' his mother said to the framed photo on the wall, the cafe quiet in its holiday lighting. She felt the heady desire for another glass. She could have one more shot. She pleasurably leaned her head back, tasted the dark sweetness on her gums and did not have a single bad thought.

Afterwards she was a little ashamed—for not doing anything, for drinking, for her high-spirited looking over and for being at the sea with neither Stephan nor Max.

Soon thereafter the unexpected lightness returned and, with a quick hand, she finished up her work in the guest room, the kitchen, the storeroom and behind the counter. She stuffed the dirty paper towels into a plastic bag and hung the wet rags and cloths over the sink. She straightened out the brushes in the closet and sorted out the palettes and baskets of packaged sweeteners one last time. Tomorrow at noon, she would come back and pick up everything that had to be washed.

For a reason that would only become clear to her later, in a state of complete exhaustion and in the presence of her unexpectedly appearing husband, that evening she hesitated to drag all the things home.

What bothered her were the icy pavements here and there. With her boots, she had to be extremely careful not to trip or slip. She would have liked to be quicker; would have liked to turn in circles a few times; did not want to pay any attention to her steps but to dance with one or two of the dead—just like she had danced with the black ball in Lenny's room after she had promised the inspector a hundred times that she would talk to Stephan and give him the chance to mourn together with her.

Yes, she had said, over and over, yes and yes. Then she had finally closed the door to the flat behind her. Stephan was not there. Tania suspected he was at his lover's, something she supposedly did not know. By the wardrobe she took off her shoes and coat, took the football in both hands, used her elbows to push down the handle to her child's room and went in. She locked the door from inside, laid the ball down on the bed, lit the candle on the windowsill, picked the ball back up and began to turn in a circle, this way then that, the ball pressed to her cheek, in the silence. The piano's melodies echoed inside her. The smell of leather triggered a memory of a football match where Lennard had scored two goals and almost been crushed by his cheering teammates on the pitch. He stood back up and threw his arms into the air. After the final whistle, she snapped a photo of him in his sweaty jersey and out-of-place shorts.

Despite the horrible surface of the pavement, she managed to execute a turn. She did not fall, so she repeated the movement. Continuing not to fall, she kept on going as otherwise Lennard would laugh at her.

Well, she wondered, how could he even know what that meant? Laughing at someone. A few metres later she was not so sure: he had his tricks, she had to admit, he was no longer a child.

Frightened, she stopped; her right foot slid over a patch of ice, she wheeled her right arm through the air, but her other boot found traction on a dry and snowless piece of pavement. Her shoulder hurt and she pressed a hand into her thigh. The icy air going all the way down to her stomach made her feel something she had ignored: hunger. Since that morning—after a piece of bread with butter and a thin slice of gouda—she had not eaten a thing nor even thought of eating.

Everyone told her she looked thin. Her mother thought she had lost a terrible amount of weight and had to start paying attention to her health right away. Everyone said things to her face which were not true and were even mean. According to her husband, she should eat three times a day, drink three litres of water and spend three hours in the fresh air; that was the only way she would gain strength and win back a sense of balance. She stretched out her arms: she was standing there without losing her balance, everyone could see that, instructions were pointless.

Nevertheless, she could hear her stomach growling. She let it; she pulled her coat tighter and pursed her lips. Walking for three hours would be no problem, she already had at least an hour behind her. On top of it, last year she had felt so fat. Naturally, no one had said anything to her about her weight, out of insincere politeness; she had not blamed anyone; she did now. Now all of them—especially her mother—would have to understand that she had no right to stuff herself and act as if a meal was a cosy home. Those days were over, everyone knew it, but she seemed to be the only one who paid any attention.

In front of a bar near Odeonplatz a few men were smoking. Though they were not wearing any jackets, the women smoking with them or simply listening to what they had to say were wrapped up in cashmere coats, wineglasses in hand. Quite the merry crew, Tania Grabbe thought, and would have liked to have a look around inside where, ostensibly, those the world had blessed were making their rounds.

Maybe—once he had been the right age and was interested in getting an exquisitely colourful drink—she would have gone to the bar with Lennard, and he would have explained to her what one drank those days and what one did not by any means; or on a summer day, beyond their dreary everyday duties, they would have taken the time, just the two of them, to go eat outside, at the back of the building, in the shade of the Hofgarten's chestnut tree.

'And that's not so hard to understand,' she said to her mother and the usual tiresome admonishers around her—but they could not hear her, blocked as they were by the sonic barrier of her convictions. Indeed, why should she eat when even Lennay had spurned his favourite dish, Toast Hawaii with ham and cheese and pineapple?

The bread had remained in the oven and turned hard. Had Stephan not thrown it out without her permission, she would have frozen it to save for an emergency. Just in case the inspector with the leather bag rang at the door, accompanied by Lennard, who had just got lost and forgotten what time it was. Then she would defrost everything right away and heat it up and they would all be sitting around the table, Lenny with his parents and even the watchful inspector, and, eating together, they would have a home.

She still did not know where she was going. Her footsteps echoed through the silent street she had turned into unconsciously; she found it unsettling. She was already afraid that someone would begin to follow her. She quickened her pace and reached the square with the monument and forgot her growing fear.

Not having been in that part of the city in a long time, she was touched. With childlike wonder she looked over to the National Theatre's wide stone steps and observed the former city castle's magical-looking Renaissance face bathed in the night-time light.

For a while she was overcome by the idea of another age she could not name, just an incredible sense of awe.

Awkwardly but without the slightest hesitation, she bent down before the bronze king on his throne; she grew dizzy. She turned around with wobbly steps. She felt nauseated; her stomach began to gurgle uncomfortably.

Following a vague intuition, she moved on, on past the, even at that time, brightly lit shop windows whose goods— jewellery, paintings, fashion, exclusive accessories—she saw out of the corners of her eyes. She would have liked to stop.

Yet the voice drove her on.

She could not stop.

Lenny wanted her to come to him and not get distracted.

Dishevelled by all her hurrying, she lost control over her steps.

The man who, as suddenly as a ghost, was bent over her was wearing black clothes, white gloves and a top hat. Tania Grabbe had to think of a circus director, and grinned.

The man said: 'Shall I call an ambulance, madam?'

To the porter's surprise, the woman got up nimbly. She did not remember falling over in front of the hotel. She hastily buttoned her coat and ran an embarrassed hand through her messy hair.

'Are you sure you are all right?' the man in black asked.

'Quite all right,' she said.

'You look a bit pale, do come in, I'll have them bring you something to drink.'

After casting another concerned glance at the upset-looking woman, he opened the glass door. Tania Grabbe looked inside; something confused her, but she was not sure what it was. It was only when the porter continued to hold open the door for her and she walked into the foyer that it suddenly occurred to her. With a strict look, she turned back to the man.

'Isn't there supposed to be a revolving door here?' she asked. 'As is customary for luxury hotels?'

'Renovation a few years ago brought some changes.' He tilted his head. 'Nevertheless, I hope you enjoy your stay with us. Please follow me, I will show you to your place.' A cold breeze brushed her as he passed, and she once again smiled slyly.

She followed the man to a sofa. In the lobby—it was almost two o'clock in the morning—there were just two African-looking men in suits talking and in another corner a man and a woman drinking champagne and kissing.

Voices came from the bar in the next room. A clerk was making a phone call at Reception, his voice as impossible to understand as those of the guests.

Before sitting down, Tania unbuttoned her coat. Taking a good look she realized that neither her wrinkled blouse nor her boots were presentable at all.

'What would you like to drink, madam?'

She did not hesitate. 'A Cynar, please. No ice but with a slice of lemon.'

After a moment of surprise, the black-clothed man said: 'Gladly. My colleague will be happy to serve you.' Once again he tilted his head, then walked to Reception. That surprised her, as she had expected him to give the order to the bar.

The man at Reception had finished his call and was listening to the porter, who apparently had quite a bit to tell him. On his way back to the door, the man in black nodded to Tania once more; she raised a hand with a gesture slowed by shyness and let her arm sink back down.

She was cold. Maybe it would be better to drink a tea than a glass of liquor, she thought. She noticed that the receptionist was once again on the phone.

She was constantly bothered by the question of what happened outside; why she was suddenly lying on the pavement, on top of it, right in front of the famous hotel; and why she had not asked the man in black, he was in fact a witness.

But—and this surprised her the most—she had not been hurt, at least she did not feel hurt. She carefully stretched out her arms, bent forward and then back, moved her upper body to the right and left, touched her legs; her stomach rebelled, but that was nothing new.

She sighed softly and leant into the soft upholstery. Gripped by a shudder of unforeseen relief, she closed her eyes. From the distance she could hear music and the steady sing-song of the voices from the bar. Then the sound of motors coming through the night, car doors closing. A tram ringing its bell.

She put her arm around her son, who was sitting next to her, and inhaled the smell of his freshly washed hair; he was only eleven but already used his own shampoo.

Someone touched her shoulder. She opened her eyes.

Stephan, her husband, was standing in front of her, unshaven, his hair tousled. He looked down at her. She noticed that she was lying across the sofa, with her legs still on the carpet, wrapped in a beige-coloured wool blanket.

That same night, just a few kilometres away from the venerable old Four Seasons hotel in the city centre, Franck and Chief Investigator Elena Holland met up at a newly opened bar on Albrechtstraße in Neuhausen.

Haggard from his tireless, monotonous study of the Lennard files for the hundredth time and from going through the files of halfway similar cases he kept in his special closet, Franck had called her at the station and asked her for, as he promised, one last discussion—without his friend André Block.

He answered her question as to why he did not want her colleague to be present vaguely and, as far as she was concerned, unconvincingly. Ultimately, of course, it did not matter to her as she would tell Block everything anyway.

Franck felt the need to spend an evening with a woman he could talk to about the murder on a professional level and to whom he could put forward—as opposed to trusty Marion—his eternally same evocations and bleak assumptions.

'Over the last few days, we double-checked all the facts one more time, I have no idea how often we have done that in the meantime,' Elena Holland said as they toasted each other with their first glass of wine. 'I know every line by heart. No perpetrator, not even the shadow of a perpetrator.'

'Wrong,' Franck said. 'The shadow is there, even at night.'

That was how their evening began, and it ended the moment Tania Grabbe walked through the lobby a second time, but this time not to the man in black at the door.

'You've got to come back home with me,' Stephan Grabbe said.

'I'm already there,' his wife said.

'What kind of rubbish is that?'

'You're the one talking rubbish. You're the rubbish king of the two of us.'

'They're going to throw us out, get up,' Grabbe said.

'This is a twenty-four-hour hotel and a Four Seasons.'

'You don't know what you're saying any more.'

'You really are deluding yourself something fierce.'

'If the man from the hotel hadn't called, I would have had the police start looking for you.'

'What for?'

'Sorry?'

'Why would you have had the police start looking for me? You know where I am.'

Tania Grabbe had sat up; her husband had taken a seat at the table. He was exhausted, angry. He had just got home when the telephone rang and the man who gave his name and position asked if he was speaking with the Grabbe family; he had got the number from information, a colleague of his had said that he believed *Frau* Grabbe was sitting in the foyer and gave the impression of needing help; his colleague had recognized *Frau* Grabbe from the paper and asked him to inform the family.

Stephan Grabbe did not doubt the truth of the unusual statement whatsoever; he washed his face and hands, drank water out of the tap, changed his trousers and shirt, and got in the car. On the way he made up his mind not to make any fuss. Before getting out, he smelt his palms.

'I don't want to lose you,' he said.

'You've already got another,' she said.

'Nonsense.'

'Don't forget to pick up the dirty rags and tablecloths tomorrow, they're still lying around.'

When she looked at him—directly for the first time since he had appeared like a ghost in front of her—she suddenly remembered why she had not been able to take the things with her that night; they would only have been a burden and would have impeded her on her trip, she needed her hands free.

Everything was preordained, she thought, and reached out for her husband's leg; he was too far away, so she gave up.

'What is that supposed to mean, "I've already got another"?' he asked.

'Have you eaten?'

'Come with me, Tania.'

'No.'

'You're trembling, you're sick, tomorrow I'm going to call Dr Horn.'

'Tomorrow's Sunday, he won't be in.'

'We've got to change something, Tania, our life can't go on like this.'

'It's already changed.'

'This has to do with both of us.'

'No.'

'What?'

'It doesn't have to do with us, we aren't important at all.'

'We have a business, we are responsible, we have a future.'

'You said that already.'

'Stop it. Be reasonable.'

'Am I stupid?'

What he had to say was too much for him. Guests slid past, offering sympathetic looks. If he had spent the evening in that kind of bar, the view of a frustrated married couple at three in the morning would not have been any different. When he arrived, aside from Tania, no one else was in the foyer, and she was not even sitting on the sofa but lying across it in an embarrassing position. The concierge had nodded in her direction with a serious expression.

'I'm stupid, right?'

'Get up, Tania.'

She did not move.

'Let's go.'

'Where?'

'Home.'

'Ah.' She leant back, pressed her knees together. The soft blanket lay across her legs, and she buried her hands inside it. The grumbling in her stomach would not stop.

'If you don't come with me, I'm just going to leave you sitting here.'

'Go on and leave me here, I'm not alone.'

He had to wait for his anger to subside. 'This is what we're going to do. I'm going to get the car, heat it up for you. I'll be right out front. In the meantime, go and give the blanket back and thank them for being so attentive. That clear?'

'Clear.' She liked that he was speaking to her like a child. She looked into his face again.

Her eyes were foreign to him and touching and as if far, far away. He stood up a bit awkwardly, paused. 'So, I'll be waiting for you out front.'

'That's good.'

'Don't stay here.'

'No.'

'Promise?'

'I promise.' She returned his smile.

For a moment that expanded until Grabbe reached the glass door, he felt an irrepressible affection for his wife he thought he had forgotten, for her simple being, for her, even after all the years, surprising and wonderful presence.

He had hardly left her field of vision before she let out another sigh. She carefully folded the cashmere blanket and went to Reception. Her shoulders hurt. Perhaps, she thought, she had taken a few dents when falling over; she would check soon enough.

First, however, she put the blanket down on the counter; then she pulled her wallet out from inside her coat.

'My credit card,' she said. 'I would like a double room, please, for one night, or two, I'll decide later. Or are you full?'

'No,' said the man behind the desk, who still had four more hours to go on his shift. The woman with the feverish eyes and aura of the dead had already been bothering him the whole time. Her falling asleep in the lobby went against house rules; and yet, he had decided not only to put a blanket over her but to protect her from his colleagues as well. He had done so because he had made it through the fourth anniversary of his brother's death and never had any one to talk about it with. In some secret way, he was happy about the woman's decision.

'Welcome, *Frau* Grabbe.' He held her credit card in his hand. 'Is there anything else we can do for you?'

As if not wanting anyone to hear, she leant forward. 'I'd like to have a club sandwich sent to my room, with an extra portion of chips, please.'

'Right away,' said the man, fully aware that Raban, the night chef, would be angry.

Shortly thereafter, Tania silently crossed the lobby one more time—or at least she thought she did—but this time on the way to the lifts. She was standing up straight and did not turn again.

The room was smaller than she had expected. The mirror and marble surfaces shone in the dim light; the bed was snow white, on the pillow there was a piece of chocolate in a red wrapper. She tossed her coat onto the bed, sat down on the edge, took off her boots and rubbed her toes. Then she looked towards the door.

Before they brought the food—with the extra chips for Lennard—she wanted to try something out.

Kneeling on the blue-carpeted floor, she braced herself with both arms and sank her head as far down as she could. She gave herself a push and then put her arms back down.

She would not be winning any prizes now. But considering that she had not practiced in ages, she was quite proud of her roll.

'You never checked him out?' Franck asked again. He thought that maybe he had not heard properly. They had almost finished the third bottle of 13 per cent white wine and each of them had ordered a double Averna after dinner.

'Are you drunk? Why should we have checked him out?' Elena Holland asked with an angry undertone, her voice shifting, which amused Franck. 'There's nothing to smirk about. Listen. We didn't check him out because we didn't need to check him out. The man was dead. Get it? What were we supposed to do with a dead man's name on our list? Why's the water gone again already?' She held up the bottle and looked at it senselessly.

'But he was there,' Franck said. 'He was near the crime scene.'

'I've got to go,' she said and stood up, holding the bottle in her hand. 'Yeah, he was there and then he was dead, run over by a lorry. On top of it . . .' She pointed the bottle at Franck. '. . . it had to do with a colleague, and my cousin's husband at that, and I've already explained this all to you. You and I got to know each other at his funeral. What's wrong with your brain?'

After looking for the waiter in vain—he was nowhere to be seen in the empty restaurant or behind the bar—she put the bottle back on the table and leant on Franck's shoulder. 'Dead lead, my friend.'

'Up till now I hadn't realized his mobile had been logged in at the crime scene on November eighteenth.' Franck imagined that he had not had a drop of alcohol. 'What was he doing there? Does he live there? I've got to know.'

'He lived close by, below Nockherberg. Stop getting your teeth into something again.'

'I want to know everything about him.'

'He's dead, we saw his coffin disappear into the earth.' Elena Holland slapped his shoulder. 'Why were you even at the funeral? You told me, I know, but I've forgotten.'

The fossil, Franck thought.

He was close to jumping up and going to wake the widow from her sleep.

Six hours later he was in front of her door.

CHAPTER EIGHTEEN

On the Way, Fatherless

'My condolences,' Franck said to Melanie Dankwart after introducing himself and mentioning Elena Holland, her cousin, and why he was there unannounced.

The woman in the white jeans and black sweater looked at him out of tired eyes. She was not wearing any makeup, and her dark hair—it seemed a bit too dark to Franck, as if dyed—had been combed carelessly. She held onto the large tea glass with both hands. She seemed frightened, haunted.

'*Frau* Holland told me that your husband was around Spitzingplatz that evening. Do you have any idea what he was doing there?'

'I . . .' Lines appeared on her forehead and her face took on such a rigid, blank look that Franck was afraid she might black out.

'Do you feel all right, *Frau* Dankwart?'

'Yes, yes. Everything's . . . fine, I'm just . . . Where is Spitzingplatz?'

'Shall we go inside and sit down a moment?'

'OK.' She stepped to the side, pressed her back against the wall. 'Please, come in. My apologies, I didn't mean to leave you standing there like some kind of stranger. You're a friend of Elena's, I know that, she told me, please, come in . . .' She stopped; clearly she had forgotten her visitor's name. Franck did not react.

'Thank you,' he said. 'I'll try not to bother you for too long.'

The flat was on the fifth floor of a corner building from the '60s on Mariahilfstraße, its green facade weather-beaten and faded, with non-soundproofed windows and narrow car parks in the back. The bar in front of which Melanie Dankwart's husband was run over by a lorry and received fatal injuries was right around the corner.

'No coffee, really?'

'No.' Ever since getting up shortly before seven, Franck had been painfully tense; he hoped it would not show. He refused the woman's offer to sit on the couch. He stood by the door with his bag and anxious fingers behind his back, impatiently waiting for the woman to sit down in the chair; she looked at him with a frightened expression.

'Your standing there really makes me nervous,' she said.

Before starting with his pre-formulated and repeatedly readjusted, and precise, questions, Franck thought to try and make her feel more trusting, or at least somewhat less confused.

'In any event,' he said in a different tone, 'I was at your husband's funeral, that's where I met your cousin. I sometimes go to colleagues' funerals, I cannot explain to you why exactly, probably out of a form of affiliation and respect. Furthermore, I've been retired for a little while now, so I have the time.'

'But that's . . .' she began before, as so often during the day, being overcome by a wave of sadness and dread. Franck wondered whether he should go and take her hand. 'Thank you for doing so, my husband wasn't in the upper grades of the civil service. But you no doubt know that already. The way he died, it's just so awful . . .'

'Did he call you that evening one more time?' Franck could not think of another digression. His approach seemed rough, and under the circumstances—the tragic death of a police officer had been undeniably explained and the widow was a helpless soul—utterly inappropriate.

Franck, however, was convinced that the dead man had not yet earned his peace.

If Melanie Dankwart gave him answers that he did not trust, or somehow were not enough to lessen his suspicion, he would not put it any other way, of that much Franck was already certain.

Lennard, the child, he thought, had a right to the same pitilessness on the search for his murderer that the murderer had used for the act.

Overcome by a wave of images with the boy's face, Franck went to the table and pulled his shoulder bag over his head. He threw it onto the sofa, grabbed the second chair, sat down in front of the woman and bent closer. 'What happened on that evening, *Frau* Dankwart? Why was your husband at Spitzingplatz? Please do not lie to me.'

Her reaction was surprising. As if she had been expecting some kind of confrontation, she showed no irritation at all. Instead, she placed her hand on his and looked into his eyes with an expression of grief-stricken understanding.

'Do you know, *Herr* Inspector, what I've wanted most over the last few weeks? To be able to lie. To be able to say: yes, my husband dying in the line of duty, his being shot or stabbed by some evil person, was something to be feared of. Just so I could say: I was prepared for that because Heiner had always explained to me, over and over, how dangerous being a patrol officer was. Just so I could say: it's the stress that causes him to go to the pub and have one too many, it's the job that causes him not to sleep and sucks out all his energy. Just so I could say: it's part of my fate as the wife of a police officer.

'I would have liked to be able to say all that. And lie. The truth, however, is that my husband almost never talked about his work, very seldom. I wasn't scared because he wasn't scared. He came home every night, when he got into bed, he fell right asleep, he never said anything about any nightmares. He drank but only when he didn't have to work the following day, or when we were together in the beer garden on Nockherberg or at Flaucher, or when we simply wanted to polish off a bottle of wine or two or three here in our own home. But he never got stone drunk.

'I would have liked to be able to lie, to lie and tell the story so that I didn't break under the strain of all the truth. It didn't work, the truth was stronger. Look at me, I'm completely outside the world. How am I supposed to get back in?

'I stand in front of the mirror but don't see myself. Instead I see a woman who isn't managing to handle life any more. Take a good look.'

She let go of Franck's hand and put both her hands on top of her stomach. 'I'm in the third month. I'm going to have a child, but the child will never meet its father. And its father never learnt about it either—because I didn't have the chance to tell him. When I told him he was going to be a father, he was lying in the forensic pathology institute and could no longer hear. I screamed as loud as I could. The doctor's assistant was worried. Then I was quiet. Everything was quiet. Just like Heiner with his horrible wounds.

'I'm not lying, *Herr* Inspector. Had he called me that evening, I would have told him to come home immediately because I had important news. And there sure was important news later that night, very, very important news. Nothing to lie about there.

'Do you think I know why he went drinking without telling me? He never went drinking when he had to work the next day. Do you think I have something to hide? And what's all this about Spitzingplatz? I'm unfamiliar with it. Who says that Heiner was there? Why would he have been? All the places he knew I know, too. That square doesn't exist, it must be some pipe dream of yours.'

Then nothing mattered any longer. Stephan Grabbe cast one more glance at the entrance of the hotel where no porter awaited any more night-time guests, and drove away, right over Maximilianstraße to turn and step on the gas in the direction of the ring road.

He spent the rest of the evening in front of the TV, dozing off, cursing, yelling at the screen and, in-between, crying.

He dialled the hotel's number two times. Someone answered but he hung up again, tossing the phone onto the couch; twice.

He hated his weakness the most, the way he forgave Tania and her brother, the inseparable ones who would step over corpses if their bond was ever disturbed.

Outside it was light already when Grabbe stumbled into the child's room and began to hit the piano with the hammer he had taken from his toolbox in the storeroom, the bed, the shelves—the handicrafts, books, notebooks, toy cars spreading across the floor. He struck the table and then the instrument again, and then, just as pointlessly as before, the pillow and the leather ball.

Eventually, he smashed the candle on the windowsill into chips of wax; smashed the glass of Lennard's framed photograph which had fallen onto the carpet like the things from the shelves.

Driven by sheer force, he ripped open the closet door; as one stuffed animal after another fell onto the floor, he dropped to his knees and hammered into the lions, leopards, moose, dolphins and bears until out of exhaustion he just continued to beat at the thick, blue carpet next to them.

The piano was covered with deep dents, splinters of wood were sticking out of its body; there were pieces of glass and the debris of battered toys everywhere; mangled, partially broken shelves; torn comic books and books.

Grabbe was wheezing. The hammer slipped out of his sweaty hand.

Then he jumped up.

He stretched out his arm and, using all the strength he could muster, tore down the fishing net from the ceiling, shaking and spinning it through the air; the gulls, starfish, mussels and other assorted souvenirs from a past sunken forever in the depths of a godforsaken sea flew through the room and shattered against the walls.

In the end, Grabbe swung the net like a lasso over his head, threw it against the window and ran out of the room.

Then he went and huddled up on the living-room floor for three hours, shivering with cold and bitterness, begging his son for forgiveness. 'Please, forgive me,' he repeated over and over, counting to reach one thousand.

At some point he fell asleep.

Waking up he had a salty taste on his lips and in his mouth, all the way down his throat.

He did not regret a thing. Not that he had left his wife behind in the hotel (thinking of her made his rage return); not that he had destroyed the child's room (his wife had driven him to it); not that he was huddling on the floor like a coward (he would soon be doing something). It's all over, he thought, even if, in the end, it was not.

He left the flat and sprinted to his car.

On the way, he called his former neighbour and invited him to lunch at one of the respectable restaurants in Bogenhausen. He wanted to talk, Grabbe explained, and to explain the reasons for breaking in and his shameful words. At first the man on the other end of the line said no; Grabbe insisted, he was acting on behalf of his wife as well, who had begged him to a conciliatory talk in Lennard's name. Eventually, Amroth reluctantly agreed.

An hour later, as the old man was driving out of his garage, Grabbe stepped into his path. Seconds later, he was sitting on the backseat holding a knife against the man in the Loden jacket's throat.

'We're going to take a drive to Höllriegelskreuth, Amroth,' Grabbe said in a friendly voice. 'You know the way already.'

At dinner with Chief Inspector Holland, Franck had learnt about details that electrified him immediately and would not let him sleep. He asked himself how his former colleagues, whose crime-solving capabilities he respected, could have been so careless with that kind of information.

He knew that he was acting on nothing more than a hunch; fundamentally, he had no right to confront the widow of Sergeant Heinrich Dankwart, whose mobile had been logged in the night of November eighteenth at the crime scene, with guesswork and a modestly justifiable conviction.

Nevertheless, to him there was no other choice.

He accused the entire special unit—up until now only to himself but the time for clear words was near—of careless, irresponsible behaviour. Under his direction, he said to himself, that kind of sloppiness would never have happened; he would have followed every seemingly hopeless clue, he would have subpoenaed every potential suspect—and even if they were police—for questioning, and for as long as it took for their innocence to be absolutely certain.

(A few days later, Marion Siedler would declare slight doubts about her ex-husband's self-assurance. In her opinion, Franck's unconditional solidarity to his own people determined his view of the work and of his colleagues; and just as he did as a pensioner, he probably would have been sad about the death of a police officer, gone to the funeral and then gone back to the investigations, aware of the fact that the man had only fallen into the search by chance and had nothing to do with the case. Franck would disagree with her.)

After Melanie Dankwart had told him about being pregnant, Franck once again was holding her hand, and she slowly calmed down. She dabbed at her eyes with a tissue. 'I didn't want to offend you,' she said. 'You were just so strict with me.'

Franck leant back, taming his impatience by folding his hands in his lap and looking around as if there were something of interest.

Brown wardrobes, a large flat-screen TV, a tea trolley full of bottles and glasses, photos on a wall featuring a woman and a man in uniform in various situations; Franck did not recognize the faces, yet who else could they be but Melanie and Heinrich Dankwart?

'Your husband,' he began and tried to catch the eyes of the woman who kept getting lost in her thoughts. 'That evening he went to the bar, and you were surprised.'

'Of course I was surprised. He usually only went to the Raven's Head on Saturdays because he had Sundays off.'

The Raven's Head was a Bavarian pub on Ohlmüllerstraße. Following the tragic accidental death of their regular right in front of their door, for a time the pub owners had put a photo outside in the box with the menu.

'He went over there even though he had to work the next day, on Saturday,' Franck said.

'And he had a lot to drink, as the doctor found out. He . . . he . . . he did not see the lorry and the driver didn't see him either. Erich, the pub owner, said Heiner went out of the door and right over the street, he'd brought him to the door, Heiner was indeed . . . he was plastered. And I still don't understand . . .'

She held her hand in front of her mouth and looked away. Franck waited until she could look at him again.

'I'm very sorry,' he said. 'The lorry driver was driving too fast, he was late, half an hour after midnight, hardly any cars on the streets, the driver thought he was all alone. He was on his way to the Autobahn for Salzburg.'

He paused. The woman looked at him out of watery eyes; her mouth was half open, as if she had just received an incomprehensible message.

Franck knew that the colleague responsible had shared all the details with her and *Frau* Dankwart had also wanted to know. He suspected that she was not so much shocked by what he said but by the invisible development in her stomach, over which she had once again folded her hands.

Seconds passed. She sat there and stared at her guest, incapable of saying a word.

'Would you like to drink something?' Franck asked.

She shook her head softly. 'I . . . I haven't offered you any-thing, *Herr* . . . Inspector.'

'Just Franck.'

'Just Franck,' she repeated.

'Among your husband's things that you brought from the forensic pathology institute, there had to be a mobile too. May I see it?'

After a moment, as if relieved, she stood up and, wiping her sweater flat, left the room. Shortly afterwards she came back without making a noise. She held the smartphone in its leather case out to Franck. 'It's always on the little cupboard in the hall,' she said. 'I just turned the sound off, otherwise I haven't touched a thing. If you want it, you can keep it. What am I sup-posed to do with it?'

Franck saw that after Dankwart's death he had received four calls, one two days after the accident from a woman by the name of Irina and three on the night of the accident from a man named Urban.

The widow said she did not know who Irina was—Franck did not believe her—and Urban was a man her husband had worked with in Perlach. Standing in front of Melanie Dankwart, Franck called him from his mobile.

'It unnerved me,' Jens Urban said after Franck had explained why he was calling. 'He called me from the bar, I was already asleep, he left a message. He had to speak with me immediately, some heavy shit had gone down. I still have the message saved . . .'

'The shit had happened, or he had caused it to happen?'

'I can have another listen, but I'm sure he said that it was because of him.'

'He didn't elaborate.'

'No, he was mostly incoherent, then done. Are you investigating the death of the young boy on your own initiative, colleague?'

'Further investigations . . .'

'Let's be straight, mate. What are you accusing my friend Heiner of?'

'At the moment I'm with his widow,' Franck said. 'We're having a chat. Your friend's mobile was logged on in the area of the crime scene the night of the murder, his name was taken off the list because Dankwart had a fatal accident the same night. That's why the investigators were no longer interested in what he was doing close to the crime scene.'

'And you're digging it all back up now. What's that all about?'

'Are you familiar with Spitzingplatz in Obergiesing?'

'The name. Why?'

'That's where the boy was killed. Did Heinrich Dankwart ever mention the place?'

'I can't remember. Is that the square by St-Martin-Straße?'

'Not far from it.'

'Heiner often took that route when he wanted to avoid traffic. St-Martin-Straße and then down Nockherberg. That's how he went home. So, that explains it. I've got a meeting.'

'Could Dankwart have had a reason to make a stop in-between?' Franck's tension had returned; he could feel it from his neck to his legs. He could no longer sit and had to stand. He went to the door, turned around, took another step, stopped, took an audible breath.

'Why would he have stopped anywhere?' Urban asked. 'Don't go scaring our colleagues over in homicide and convincing them of something. Heiner was reliable, a great police officer. Ask his wife, he was a model for everyone after him.'

'I'm not convincing anyone of anything. Answer this one question, please: could there have been a reason for him to have interrupted his trip home? Do you have any idea, Urban?'

The constable called out to a colleague that he would be there in a minute. 'A reason? His bladder was a constant reason.'

'Sorry?'

'His bladder was the size of a little girl's, sometimes he even had to go behind a bush on a deployment. Crazy thing. I told him a hundred times to go see a doctor, but he didn't want to, when we were out he preferred to piss in a cup rather than leave the patrol car. If he stopped anywhere, then that was why.'

'Are you familiar with the Brückenwirt pub in Höllriegels-kreuth?' Franck caught himself holding his breath.

'That's where we all meet up in summer, the whole department. I've got to go.' Urban said goodbye hastily.

Franck stuffed his mobile into his pocket and met the widow's expectant glance.

'He says hello,' he said. 'Where is your husband's car?'

'In the garage. It's been there since his last night.'

'You didn't drive it anywhere?'

'I have my own smaller car, I'm going to really need it once the child's here.'

'May I see his car?'

'Would you like to buy it? I'll make you a good deal.'

A few minutes later, Melanie Dankwart was opening the garage door and unlocking the car with the transponder.

'This is the first time you've been in the garage since your husband's death?' Franck asked.

'I told you already.'

'Truthfully?'

'Don't you believe me? Why not?'

'Where is your car?'

'On the street, I always find a spot. Heiner just bought his BMW a year ago, he put it into the garage every night. I've never driven it, too much technology. What's with the car?'

The wide car barely fit in the garage. Franck looked inside through the side windows. On the passenger-side seat there was a tabloid, the backseat was empty.

Melanie Dankwart was waiting in front of the door. 'Are you looking for something in particular?'

Franck opened the boot.

The car was standing at the edge of the tarred access road to the pub. The driver had been forced to turn off the engine and keep his seatbelt on. The man on the backseat was holding a 15-centimetre-long knife to his throat.

'Say: *I did it*, and you can drive home.'

'It wasn't me,' Siegfried Amroth said.

'You've got to say it, or you're going to die.'

'Please.'

'Please what?' Grabbe tried to remember when he had last used the knife at home and what he had cut with it. He failed.

'I did not kill your son.' Sweat ran down Amroth's face and his neck; he gasped for breath. On the drive from his flat to the southern edge of the city, he had shifted into the wrong gear. At a red light, Grabbe had punched the back of his head. Amroth had almost vomited in pain.

'Stop lying. Say: *I did it, yes, I did it*.'

'No. No.'

The longer he sat in the car breathing in the man's sweat, the more preposterous everything that Grabbe had done the night before and was doing then became to him.

He was holding a knife to the throat of a man he had kidnapped as if intending to stab him. But he had no plan and had never had one. He had gone crazy and would end up in an asylum. His life was ruined, as was his wife's, the woman he had cheated on, lied to and insulted. And with the abduction of his former neighbour, whom he barely knew, he was defiling the thought of his son who had liked Amroth despite his strange habits.

'The police will find the murderer!' Amroth screamed and forcefully rocked his head backwards.

As if all on its own, the tip of the blade sliced into his grey throat. A stream of blood shot across the man on the backseat's arm.

CHAPTER NINETEEN

In Striking Distance of the Sea

II

Sitting in the leather chair thinking about Max and how much she missed him, she had childishly buried her face in her hands, hoping that the world and everyone in it would disappear for ever.

The food she had ordered during the night but left untouched was underneath a shiny silver cover on the table. She felt ashamed. The chips had grown cold; she could have done without the extra portion, what a waste. She felt ashamed for that too, and for not giving the young waiter, who because of her had to make his long way from the kitchen up to the fourth floor with the wobbly tray, a tip; she had only thought of it afterwards.

The employee, at most twenty-five and no doubt still in training, had noticed the chaos: her boots tossed to the ground, the coat thrown over the bed; he had probably even had a few thoughts about the disturbed woman with the rat's nest of hair. She had sent him off with a wispy *thank you* after signing for the food he had held out to her in a leather bill presenter but not a cent of recompense.

There in her chair she was overcome by an incredible sense of guilt. She turned, pressed her face into the leather, curled up into a ball and whimpered like a child; like her son when he took a bad foul on the pitch and had to be carried off.

(Once, watching a match, she had felt like a bad mother because she did not know what to do; she remained sitting on the stands and did not trust herself to *boo* along with the other mothers.)

The thing she was most ashamed of was not being able to leave Lenny alone.

She constantly spoke to him. Overwhelmed him with questions she immediately forgot. Hugged him on the street. Ordered him things to eat even though he was not hungry. She told everyone she ran into that last year that Lenny'd had fifty-seven shots on goal and thirty-three assists, and received an award.

(For a year now, she has wanted to ask Lenny who kept track of such things. Did someone walk along the edge of the pitch every match and count? He probably would have laughed at her.)

Sitting in Room 322, she thought about such things and was ashamed.

Everything that was no longer existed, and she had her part to play. That became clear to her the moment the inspector with the leather bag was out in front of the door to the cafe and the snow turned black, and the sea in the picture across from the beach chair stopped rushing.

All that was left of those wonderful times at the sea was hanging in a dusty net from the ceiling of the boy's room— ignored, rubbish that once, one-thousand-and-one nights ago, had been a wonderful dreamcatcher, keeping watch over a small, helpless child.

'Oh, you, my King of the Goals,' Tania Grabbe said silently, lowering her hands away from her face.

In the room, the lamps' gold-yellow glow expanded as the day coming through the window began to turn grey.

By accident, she almost cast a glance into the attractive mirror by the bed; at the last moment, however, she turned and went to the window.

Pulling the curtain to the side, she looked onto the street with its fashionable, Sunday-like peace. Then she cocked an ear to the room again.

Its peace was dreadful compared to the noise inside her. Her rambling would not stop, Lennard had his hands over his ears, like he always did when he could no longer stand her voice; he would brazenly leave the room and slam the door behind him; he was a cheeky boy, but self-conscious, too, she often thought, certain that her life without him would become meaningless.

Just as she had brought him to the world, he had allowed her to be born a second time; from the first day of his life, she was convinced that it was thanks to him alone that she had achieved a true sense of presence.

And that he was no longer there meant that she too had to go.

She paused a moment longer, her head tilted back.

Then she reached for the window handle, wanting to turn it to the right or left and opening the window wide.

The handle was immovable, the window shut.

She tried eleven times.

Then she tipped forward, and her forehead slammed against the cold glass; all the words inside her ceased abruptly.

She was so frightened that she lost her balance; her hand slipped off the handle and, smacking the back of her head against the bedframe, she hit the floor.

That is how the cleaning woman found her, on her back, eyes towards the ceiling.

When the cleaning woman bent over her, Tania Grabbe whispered: 'Please don't wake my son. In his dreams he's diving.'

CHAPTER TWENTY

The Appointment

Forty minutes after Franck discovered the blue schoolbag in the boot of Heinrich Dankwart's new BMW, André Block, Elena Holland and six other investigators from the special unit met up on Mariahilfstraße. Shortly thereafter, at the same moment as a crane lorry from a towing service, four helpers from forensics covered the car in the garage with white cellophane to prevent evidence from being lost or contaminated on the way to the lab.

The inspectors kept the schoolbag with the conspicuous reflector strips; they had brought along photos of similar bags as well as ones showing Lennard Grabbe wearing his.

After the black football had shown back up, the detectives now had the second object connected to the murdered schoolboy.

A retired investigator had found it, the former head of the homicide division. In the bag, they found notebooks and two books with Lenny's name.

Block needed some time to find the right words. On the trip over, Elena Holland had already prepared herself for the moment they would meet.

'I'd like you to take part in the press conference tomorrow, Jakob,' she said straight away in front of her other colleagues. 'The state prosecutor will give you the floor and you will mention the successful find, not us.'

'Then we will have to say that our colleague, Dankwart, was the perpetrator.' It was hard for Block to say the words, but he was reluctant to just stand there, mute. 'When it comes out that his name had been on one of our lists but that we didn't check out his alibi, they're going to say that we wanted to protect a colleague. No idea how we're going to get out of this one.'

'Let's solve the case first,' Chief Inspector Holland said. 'And we're going to do that, today. Our colleagues over in the lab are on the alert, we'll be receiving the first results of the analysis shortly.'

Two of the men in the protective suits pushed the BMW out into the courtyard where the crane lifted it onto the back of the truck. Franck turned to face the building. Melanie Dankwart was standing on the balcony up on the fifth floor, her arms wrapped around herself, as if petrified by the news. Franck had asked her to go back into her flat and not to call anyone, his colleagues would speak with her later on.

'I don't know a thing,' she had muttered feebly.

When Franck turned away, he saw the tow truck just miss grazing the side of the building by a hair as it turned onto Maria-hilfstraße. On the other side of the street, a woman in a tattered winter coat was poking around in a rubbish bin. Franck had to think of the man at the playground, how he had placed his bags on the bench and gone to do his business in the bushes. Heinrich Dankwart had probably done the exact same thing—and had been interrupted by Lennard.

'He suffered from a so-called girl's bladder,' Franck said and told them about his talk with the sergeant from Pullach. He also told them what he thought about the chance encounter between Dankwart and Lenny.

'Our colleague struck him a blow,' Block said. 'And so hard that the boy didn't have a chance. After that, our colleague put the body into his car and got rid of it in Höllriegelskreuth. But why there?'

'Dankwart knew the area,' Franck said. 'In summer, his department regularly meets up at the Brückenwirt.'

'We've got to notify the parents,' Elena Holland said.

'Not yet.' Now Block had noticed the woman on the balcony too. 'We need to wait for the analysis, the book bag's not enough on its own.'

After a moment of silence that all of them seemed to need, Block went over how the night of the crime unfolded. 'So, he left work, taking his usual route until he noticed traffic—where exactly remains for us to find out. Then he turned, came onto St-Martin-Straße and realized he really needed to go to the toilet. He thinks, *In this kind of crap weather, no one's out on the street, I'll just go on the dark playground.* He stops, gets out, takes a piss. Then what happens?'

'The boy shows up,' Elena Holland said. 'He notices the man, laughs at him.'

'Why does he laugh at him?'

'Or doesn't laugh but . . . He accidentally hits him with the football, he still had it with him, he was kicking it about, he's a striker, he shoots and happens to hit the man, in the dark, and the man goes nuts.'

'We will never be able to prove that,' Block said and turned to Franck. 'Or do you have some kind of convincing theory?'

Franck looked at the schoolbag in front of the garage door, enveloped in see-through plastic wrap. He could not quite understand why Block had not had the bag shipped to the laboratory immediately; he probably needed it for the psychological effect it would have on Melanie Dankwart during questioning.

Franck was convinced the widow had never seen the boy before, just like her husband.

What had caused the crime would forever remain unknown.

With the perpetrator's death, the Lennard Grabbe case was closed.

Shortly after six o'clock that Sunday evening, André Block called. Franck was out around Spitzingplatz again, showing photos of the assumed murderer's car to the two neighbours, Lahner, the car-park security guard, and Ritting, the retired street planner (both witnesses did not completely rule out the possibility that it was indeed the car they had seen; they were, however, unable to identify the man in the photograph).

'The boot's completely full of the boy's traces,' the chief inspector said. 'DNA, blood, fingerprints, the works. Lennard's corpse was in there. We're going to have Dankwart's body exhumed and, hopefully, find a match. In the meantime, all the man's clothes have been sent to the lab. The widow's at wit's end, especially because she's pregnant. Elena's going to help her cousin and stay with her for a while. I don't like the idea. Her parents aren't alive any more, no siblings, the woman's alone. We'll try to keep the press away from her. The state prosecutor, Riemer, says hello, he's going to call you later today. I told him how we got our guy. You still there?'

Franck was standing on the playground in the dim light. Alone. Lights were on in the buildings. Cars were parked at the edge of the street in perfect rows. A lone bird sung despondently in the trees.

Just when Franck was about to answer, the bells of the nearby church began to toll 'Maria, Queen of Peace'. He listened; then he lowered his arm, dropped his mobile into his coat pocket, folded his hands across his stomach and bowed his head.

'Jakob? What's wrong?' Block called out. 'Listen, you don't know the latest, we just arrested the mother's brother, Maximilian Hofmeister. It's like this: he turned himself in for being responsible for the death of . . . of . . . hello? Hello?'

Dressed in his underwear and a T-shirt, Maximilian Hofmeister stumbled through his flat, his mobile ringing. He flipped open the old phone and held it to his left ear with his right hand while opening the refrigerator and grabbing a new bottle of beer. 'Who and why?' he asked.

The voice at the other end sounded garbled. 'We've got to see each other. Right now.'

'Who is this?'

'Stephan. I'm downstairs, on the street, you've got to get down here, it's fucking urgent.'

'Stephan?' Hofmeister laid the mobile down on the wooden cutting board, which was covered in breadcrumbs; he picked up the bottle opener, popped off the crown cap and greedily took a gulp, gagged, spit into the sink and took another gulp. His name rang out of the phone. He banged the bottle down on the countertop.

'Piss off!' he yelled and put the phone back down.

Grabbe yelled too. 'Get down here! I've got a dead person in my car.'

Hofmeister's arm shot forward. With his loose socks, he almost lost his balance on the slippery floor. He reluctantly listened to what his brother-in-law had to tell him; then he shuffled into his bedroom and got dressed. All at once, the day seemed to be a godsend.

With a surprisingly light heart, he left his flat just a little while later.

On the other side of the road, the driver's side door of a parked car was wide open. Grabbe hectically waved him over and cranked up the engine. Hofmeister crossed the street and jumped in; before he had even fastened his seatbelt, Grabbe stepped on the gas.

Despite the air streaming in from the half-open side window, there was a putrid smell. As Grabbe had mentioned a few things on the phone, the state of the car's insides with its blood-stained seats triggered a concentrated kind of curiosity in Hofmeister, as did looking at his brother-in-law whose leather jacket, trousers, shirt and hands were full of dark spots and dried traces of blood.

For at least ten minutes, neither of them spoke a word. On their way through that part of the city where his son had been murdered, Grabbe ignored all speed limits; he took the shortest route to the Autobahn. On the A8, he moved into the left lane and pushed the rattling Opel with its more than 100,000 kilometres south.

They remained silent until Hofmeister pointed to a blue sign. 'Take this exit and go to the car park.'

Grabbe did as he was told. He slowed down, crossed three lanes and stopped in front of a wooden bench. Theirs was the only car there.

It began to rain.

The two men stared through the windscreen as it began to be covered in tiny, equally formed drops.

'I didn't mean to,' Grabbe said. 'The asshole went into the blade himself. Really.'

'What did you want from him?'

'I wanted him to admit it. Admit that he had killed Lenny.'

'And?'

'Nothing. He said it wasn't him.'

'It wasn't.'

'You know that for a fact.'

They were not looking at each other. 'The police let him go,' Hofmeister said. 'And why would he have done something so horrible anyway?'

'Everyone's capable of something like that.'

'That's true.'

'What?'

'If it was him,' Hofmeister said, 'then he can no longer be judged.'

Grabbe felt like he had to get out and urinate, most appropriately in the boot where the body was. It was not as if the car could stink any more. 'What should I do? Tell me.'

Hofmeister had been expecting the question since leaving his flat. After finishing his discussion with Grabbe, he had been overcome by the realization that today, that February Sunday, was his moment and he had to be ready. And he was. He had been from the moment he had gone for a walk with the inspector along the river, the inspector whose presence had transported him into another time, one he had never got over; the only reason he had not decided to speak about Yella was because he believed he had to lie to himself for a little while longer, to experience the legacy of his crime to the full.

At that moment, in an abandoned car park next to the Autobahn, in a stolen car on whose instrument panel he could read the time—2.35 p.m.—Maximilian Hofmeister was overcome by regret and let out such a deep sigh that Grabbe looked at him with an expression of true amazement.

'I'm going to drive you back home,' Hofmeister said. 'Take a bath, drink a beer, lie down on the couch, be nice to my sister and don't think about the old man any more. Wipe him from your mind completely. Will you be able to do that?'

'How many have you put away today?'

'Not enough. Did you hear me?' Hofmeister also turned his head. 'I'm going to drop you off in front of your door, then I'm going to drive through town for a bit before leaving the car somewhere around the cathedral and making my way to the police. I'm going to take the knife with me. Where's the problem?'

'You're going to go and say you killed him?'

'I'm going to repeat myself: is this a problem for you?'

Grabbe shook his head, looked out the side window, rain spit into his eyes. He turned back to Hofmeister. 'Why, Max? What's this all supposed to mean? You crazy? Like your sister who went into a hotel and is never coming back out? Huh?'

Hofmeister did not want to think about his sister at the moment. He intended to call her later, and she would understand. 'You've got to be there for her,' he said. 'She needs you more than ever. You're Lennard's parents, you've got to maintain and protect his memory. You're a team. If you go to jail, Tania will die.' He did not really think so, but he was the only one who knew what it was all about.

'I'm not going to do that,' Grabbe said.

'Of course you will, Stephan. I'm going to be convincing, I promise, the detectives will believe my story. If I'm lucky, I'll be sentenced for manslaughter and not murder, and they'll give me five years. They need a professional hairdresser like me in jail, my career's just getting started.'

'Stop screwing around.' Grabbe ripped open the driver's side door and spit a stream into the rain, then slammed the door shut.

'Let me take over,' Hofmeister said.

Grabbe looked at him. Something in his brother-in-law scared him. Contrary to what he had believed just a few minutes ago, he now thought it entirely possible that Max was serious, that he really wanted to help him and, in a strange way, Tania, and that Max would not allow himself to be dissuaded, for whatever bizarre reasons.

Hofmeister opened the front passenger door.

'Just a second,' Grabbe said. He was trying to find the words, but just felt shabby, like a man without a brain or balls; a feeling that bothered him and—in an even shabbier way— inspired him. 'That'll never work, they'll see through you and then you'll end up in prison anyway. Look at yourself: no dirt, no blood, no traces of the body. It's good of you, but I've got to take care of this myself. Somehow or other I wanted . . . some kind of familial assistance from you . . . or . . . it was insane of me to drag you into this, I didn't know who else to call.'

'You did the right thing, Stephan. You've got to give me your clothes,' Hofmeister said. 'I washed the blood off my skin in the Isar, pure panic, that's the easiest solution. In the Isar canal, of course, where I'd lured him.'

'You're crazy, Max.' He wanted to add that he was quite impressed with his brother-in-law's stubbornness. But Hofmeister, who already had one foot out the door, turned around again. Before Grabbe understood what was happening, Hofmeister grabbed him, patted him softly on the shoulder, then let him go and got out.

A strong wind was blowing. As if it wanted to make the search for clues more difficult, the rain had grown heavier and blew into the car in icy gusts.

With her loose-fitting red dress and freshly dyed, sun-yellow hair that a mess of hair clips just made even more chaotic, Franck liked her particularly well today.

Marion noticed how Franck—secretly, he thought—kept looking her up and down, and she appreciated it.

After getting divorced almost twenty years earlier, she sometimes thought, the love between the two of them had only paused before returning in a new form and given their closeness, which both of them allowed to flow without any expectations, an uncomplicated durability.

Franck poured her some more red wine. Two days had passed since he had found the schoolbag and the murdered boy's uncle by all appearances had killed another man.

In the meantime, the body of the policeman, Dankwart, had been exhumed on the orders of the state prosecutor. The forensic pathologist would be delivering his report within a few hours; the body had hardly been washed off by the time the doctor discovered the presence of fibres in his hair which could clearly be traced back to eleven-year-old Lennard Grabbe.

Together with the numerous isolated traces in the man's car and the message alluding to some kind of disaster left on his colleague's phone, the result of the examinations on Dankwart's corpse led to a bundle of evidence: on the night of November eighteenth, Heinrich Dankwart had come into contact with the boy and, with great probability, had become his murderer.

'Did I understand that right?' Marion asked. 'The mother was still in the hotel when André and Elena confronted her with the news? And her husband wasn't there? And what I still haven't understood: you cancelled your all-important appointment with the mother. Why?'

They had pressured him, but he had stayed by his refusal. Block would not stop asking him whether his decision had to do with the fact that Franck believed under his direction the special unit would have come onto the trace of the perpetrator much sooner. Franck once again said no; looking at Block and Elena Holland, he could see that they doubted his answer. He alone, they said, had the right to share the name of the murderer with Tania Grabbe.

Immediately before meeting with them, Franck had been at the East Cemetery to talk over everything with Lennard.

He did not think there was anything else for him to do.

'Stephan Grabbe,' he said to his ex-wife, 'was picked up at his house earlier. Tania had hurt herself. Apparently, she took a fall in her room. She didn't want to see a doctor, she just wanted to stay there, in the hotel.'

'Thank God she finally knows who killed her boy. But now her brother's got to go to jail. Why did he stab the man? Is the hairdresser really that violent?'

'He's a strange guy,' Franck said. 'The few times I met Hofmeister I always had the feeling that he was carrying around a burden of some sort. I don't know. He maintains that the man's death was an accident. He wanted to threaten him, force him into some kind of confession. But what could Amroth have confessed? Then, Hofmeister says, things got out of hand, the man made an unlucky move and the knife went into his throat.'

'The hairdresser had the knife in his hand,' Marion said. 'So he's clearly guilty.'

'I don't understand him.' Franck stood up, taking the empty beer bottle from the table. 'The way the record looks, he'll go before the court and be sentenced. People will say he wanted to stand by his family, that he acted in a moment of horrible despair.'

'Could be.'

Franck looked as if the confession made him ill. She recognized the expression from the past when suspects would try, as he put it, to play warped games with his feelings and mind.

'The love he felt for his sister drove him to commit a crime,' Marion said. 'And I don't know . . .' She reached for his hand. The boy-like look his face took on whenever he received an unexpected touch had always amused her. 'If you'd been older, you probably would've thought about avenging your sister's death too. And, in a worst-case scenario, acted on it.'

Franck did not respond. He considered that kind of reaction impossible; nevertheless, he had been a detective for too long not to know that every person was capable of any kind of crime.

And what was more: no matter what Tania's brother had done or what had happened to him in the past which, Franck thought, continued to follow him up to today, the fact that Hofmeister had gone off to find and stab a man he knew only as his nephew's football-crazy friend struck him as extremely odd.

But he was not responsible for finding out and would not get involved in the case any further. After everything that had happened—he had declined to appear at the public prosecutor's press conference—he desperately needed time away. The longer he spent away from police affairs, he thought, the more easy-going he would be the next time his colleagues asked him for help.

Then something occurred to him. He put the bottle back on the table, let go of Marion's hand, went into the hall—a bit stooped, his ex-wife thought, almost a bit lazily—and returned with a book which upon closer inspection turned out to be a DVD.

'You could've easily taken the bottle with you,' Marion said.

'I need to move. I'm about to go back. The film's for you.'

'A gift? What's the occasion?'

'February fourteenth,' he said.

'Valentine's Day.' She smiled. 'It didn't occur to me. Sorry, but I don't have anything for you.'

'You're here, aren't you?'

She looked at the cover. 'We haven't seen this film in ages. Antonio and his son Bruno and the bicycle thief. You know this is going to make me cry.'

He pulled a fresh pack of tissues from his pocket. Marion stood up and hugged him.

He thought about the wisp of a woman in the hotel and her brother locked up in jail. About her husband, imploding with helplessness. About their neighbour dying mysteriously. And about the little boy on that rainy night who walked into his murderer's arms, as if they had had an appointment.

Then Jakob Franck stopped thinking. He had a present to inhabit.

CHAPTER TWENTY-ONE

In Heaven

'Are you OK?' Lina asked.

'It's all good.'

'Are you in pain?'

'I'm just staring straight ahead.'

'Me too.'

Seeing as that time did not exist, it did not pass for either of the two.

'What's your name?' Lina asked.

'Lennard. But everyone on my team just calls me Lenny.'

'What position do you play?'

'Striker.'

'I would've guessed you were a goalie.'

'Why?'

'Because you're always off on your own.'

'Strikers are too.'

'You can't be afraid of the other team's goalie.'

'Not a good idea.' His eyes once again turned inward.

'What's wrong?'

'Nothing. What's your name?'

'Lilly. Lina, actually. Tell me what's wrong. Did you have a bad dream?'

'Maybe.'

'What did you dream?'

'It doesn't matter.'

'It does to me.'

'There were three clowns, and they looked at me.'

'That's funny though.'

'It's not funny.'

'Three clowns are super funny.'

'No, they're not.'

'Yes, they are.'

'They're not funny.'

'Were you afraid of them?'

'No. Yeah.'

'But why? Why, Lenny? Why are you afraid of clowns?'

'Because I can't see their faces.'

Lina, close by him, four years older and 26 centimetres taller, pressed her lips to his head and paused. Lennard immediately forgot his dream.

'And you?' he asked. 'Are you afraid of anything?'

Lina said: 'That my brother will become a police officer some day and someone will kill him.'